SALUTIS MEAE

JOCELYNE SOTO

SALUTIS MEAE

JOCELYNE SOTO

Paperback ISBN : 978-1-956430-18-9

I always thought that I would never see past the age of nineteen.

Growing up the way I did, that was normal. It was normal for parents to plan their kids' funerals.

But I was able to get out of that life and create a better one for my family and myself. Even if I was still seen as a lowlife.

Most people saw the tattoos and the clothes and would steer away, most people except *her*. Savannah Campbell. The cheerleader. The rich girl who had no business getting involved with the boy from the bad side of town, but she didn't care. I hated her until I didn't, and in a short period of time she became my everything. Including my salvation.

We were happy.

That is until everything I feared came knocking and brought everything down.

Now I have to ask, if I was able to live past the age of nineteen...

Am I going to live past tonight?

CONTENTS

playlist

R U MINE? - ARTIC MONKEYS
LIKE I WOULD - ZAYN
WRONG - ZAYN
HURTS LIKE HELL - FLEURIE
TODO CAMBIÓ - CAMILA
I'M YOURS - ISABEL LAROSA
STREET - DOJA CAT
LES - CHILDISH GAMBINO
PINK + WHITE - FRANK OCEAN
PRIDE - KENDRICK LAMAR

Check out these song and more on the Salutis Meae official playlist!

To my dad and my nephews.
Los quiero con todo my corazón.

author's note

This book touches upon the subjects of gun violence, gang violence, and death. Some scenes are explained in detail. If that is something that you are not comfortable with, please do not read. Thank you.

THE ROAD IS slick from the rare Los Angeles rain.

I should be more cautious as I make my way through the busy streets. Especially since it seems that people forget how to drive when a little bit of water starts to hit the asphalt.

But I don't, because there's this nagging feeling in me saying that something is wrong.

He didn't show up to class today. I waited and waited for him to walk into the lecture hall, but the door never opened to reveal him.

Yes, we had a fight. Yes, we're angry at each other, but that wouldn't have stopped him from showing up. School is way too important to him and he would have been there regardless, especially on a day with a test.

I should have left the second that I got it through my head that he wasn't going to be there. I should have forgotten all about the test and walked out of there, because I had a gut feeling that something was wrong.

Now, as I drive to his house and him not answering his phone, I feel like I'm right.

Is it him?

Is it his mom?

What if it's Celeste? Or worse yet, Mia?

So many scenarios pop into my head, causing me to push down on the gas pedal some more and take the last exit that I need way above the suggested speed limit.

My knuckles are white as I grip the steering wheel. Nervousness is running through me because I don't know what's going to greet me once I reach my destination.

Car horns sound out as I pass by, but I don't care.

I need to know that everything is okay.

I need to know that *he's* okay.

Making the last turn onto his street, I relax as I drive closer to the house.

Why?

Because not only do I see his bike in the driveway, but I see him getting off it and heading to the front door.

His figure is small given my distance, but I know it's him.

He's here. He's okay from what I can see.

Thank God.

I take my foot off the gas, slowing down, and continue to make my way down the street to him. When I'm a few houses down, I decided to honk my horn at him to tell him that I'm here, and he can't keep ignoring me.

My hand is about to push down on the steering wheel when the sight in front of me makes me.

There's a car at the end of the street that is driving in

my direction faster than they should be in a residential area. Just like I was driving to get here, but whereas I've slowed down, the car doesn't look like it has any plans to even press on the brakes.

Instead of hitting the horn to notify the man that I see more than any ordinary boyfriend, I do it to call attention to the car, but it doesn't do anything.

The car continues to move down the long road lined with houses.

Not wanting to get hit, I pull to the side and keep an eye on the moving vehicle.

Lucas must have heard my horn go off or the car coming down the street because I'm able to see him turn to see what all the commotion is about.

The car keeps driving down the street, coming closer and closer to the house and to me. I think that it's going to crash into the cars that are parked in front of me, but it doesn't. It continues to speed down the street and when it passes the Reyes' house, all the blood that's in my body drains.

Bang.

Bang.

Bang.

Three bangs and a scream is all it takes to change everything.

CHAPTER ONE

LUCAS

AS A KID, I never understood religion.

Never did I understand the need to go to a building that had colored glass windows and pray to a wooden cross. Never did I get why my mom was insistent that I not only be baptized by the Catholic church, but also receive my first communion. I never understood why my mom had a rosary on her bedside table. Or why there were *Jesus Cristos* all over my house.

It never made sense to me, especially since we only went to church on the occasional Sunday, for weddings, or Easter Mass.

I never understood it, that is, until I was thirteen, and I was praying every single day for a month.

That was the first time in my life I understood it. I understood why my mom had her rosary and why she was so instant I believed in a God.

It only took my father going into a coma and dying for me to understand.

All the understanding came on a November Sunday, of all days.

We were getting home from my soccer game, and my mom wanted to decorate the outside of the house for Christmas.

She was going to wait until the following weekend, but my dad insisted that we get it done that day. He wanted to do something that would make my mom happy.

Mom and I were in the back, getting some of the Christmas stuff out of the shed, and Dad was in the front, getting started on hanging the lights.

I was pulling out the blow-up snowman that my mom loved so much when I heard gunshots go off.

Living where we lived in Los Angeles, hearing gunshots, sirens, and helicopters circling the air were normal occurrences.

As long as all of those things weren't anywhere near us, everything was all good. Not hearing them always made things feel a little off.

But that day, the gunshots were a little too close for comfort.

So close that it had me and my mom dropping everything and running to the front of the house.

I don't know what I expected to see when we got there, but it definitely was not the image that played out.

Instead of my dad being on the ladder or possibly running to help whoever might have been struck by the gunshots, he was on the ground.

Blood was everywhere.

For a split second, I thought that he had fallen, and

that was where the blood had come from. But as we ran closer, I saw how wrong that thought was.

The blood was coming from the bullet holes that my dad had in his chest and on the side of his head.

I thought he was dead, but by some miracle, his eyes were still open, and he was breathing heavily.

Seeing all the blood that was gushing out of him had me falling to my knees and my mom letting out screams that sounded like a banshee's cry.

The ambulance arrived about five minutes after the shots rang out, and they rushed him to the hospital.

In the emergency room, doctors told my mom that he wasn't going to survive. The bullets in his chest had pierced his heart. One had hit his spinal cord, and the one in his brain was so far in that it couldn't be touched.

They were surprised that he didn't die as soon as he was shot and that he even made it to the hospital.

My mom didn't like that answer, and she begged them to do anything to save him. She begged the doctors and the hospital until they finally agreed.

That's when Dad was put into a coma and when the praying started. That's when I finally understood why my mom wanted me to believe in a god so badly.

For a whole month, Mom and I didn't leave the hospital. We stayed at my father's side with one of his hands in each of ours and we prayed that they would find a way to save him.

We prayed for a small glimmer of hope. We prayed for a miracle to save the most important man in our lives. We prayed until the doctors said he was brain dead, and there was nothing left to do.

Mom screamed and cried, and I was angry, but eventually we agreed with the doctors and pulled the plug.

Dad died on the first of December.

After the funeral, that's when the police started coming around a lot more to talk to my mom. It wasn't just a random shooting anymore. It was a murder, and they needed all the information that they could get to catch the person that did it.

But we didn't know anything.

My parents had no beef with anyone and never broke the law. Add on the fact that Mom and I didn't see it happen, the police had nothing to go on.

They went to the neighbors and started asking them questions. I thought that was going to go somewhere, that for sure someone had seen something, but they all told the police the same thing.

They didn't know, see, or hear anything.

So the Los Angeles Police Department closed the case.

That's what set something off in me. I now believed in a god that didn't give me what I wanted the most. A god that didn't listen to my prayers to save my father. And because of that, I was also filled with rage.

I was so pissed that my dad was in a box in the ground and that nobody knew the answer as to why he was dead. In my rage, I started looking for answers.

I started looking for the who, the why, and everything in between.

And in my quest to look for who did it, I started getting

involved with people that my mom always told me to stay away from.

Los cholos, she called them. The people that she said were nothing but trouble and were either going to end up in jail or dead.

But they had answers that I needed. They had ways to not only find the person that killed my dad but to make them pay.

And oh, did the bastard pay.

The people I became involved with were able to not only do what the police couldn't and find my father's killer, but they were also able to do to him what he did to my dad.

I had no part in it, but they still told me everything that went down. They said that the guy who killed my father told them that he shot up the wrong house. That he had orders, and he got them wrong.

He may have gotten them wrong, but he still paid for his actions.

And because of that, because of what these people, these men, did for me, I continued to be around them, becoming friends with them.

I was thirteen, and I became one of them.

I became the *cholo* that my mom despised.

Just a kid lost by his father's absence and choosing to be a part of a man's world that I had no business being in. But I didn't care. I was involved and gained respect.

I was so involved with these people that when I realized how bad it was and wanted to step away, it was too late. It had only been a year, but I was already in too deep, knew too many things, had seen too much shit to be able to walk away clean.

For years, five to be exact, I stayed and prayed every morning that I would make it back home that night. I started to wear a cross around my neck and carried my mother's rosary for protection but also to give me peace of mind.

The cross and the holy beads, though, weren't the only things that I wore for protection and peace of mind.

Something that I started to do when I was fifteen. Something that I learn to conceal very well.

Because if you had asked me at the age of fifteen, I would have said that I wasn't going to make it past nineteen years old if I continued on the path I was going. I for sure thought that I was going to end up like my father, and my mom would have to find it in herself to bury me next to him.

My path shifted when, at eighteen, my then girlfriend told me that she was pregnant and that she was going to keep it. Like my mom, she hated who my friends were, so when she told me she was pregnant, she gave me an ultimatum.

Leave my friends or leave her and the baby.

Not knowing what to do with that information, I went to the one person who I knew would help me through anything, even if she didn't agree with my choice of friends. My mom.

She was pissed at first that me and Celeste, my then girlfriend, weren't careful and were going to become parents so young. But then she calmed down and looked me right in the eyes as she spoke her next words.

"Get out, Lucas. Get out, because if you don't, then your child is going to live the same way you and I do. With fear that something bad is going to happen, fear that you won't make it home. Get out while you can, *mijo*, please. If not for me or Celeste, then do it for the baby that will have your blood in their veins. Do not choose those people, choose the baby."

It took me a day or two to get the words my mom told me to finally settle in my head.

She was right.

If I didn't get out, my child would either be living in fear that something was going to happen to me all the time, while I lived in fear that something was going to happen to them, or they weren't going to know me at all.

So I made the decision to walk away.

It wasn't easy.

These people, this life, were a part of me. They were a part of who I was as a person and in a way, defined me.

They defined the way I dressed, what I tattooed on my body, the people I associated with. Everything I was, was because of their influence and I didn't know how to be anything else.

But I needed to be.

I went to talk to the guy in charge, or at least the one who called the shots that someone else might have passed on.

Hector Jimenez is a scary as fuck dude. I've been terrified of him since I was thirteen and went to him for help. He has kids, so he would understand why I wanted out.

And for the most part he did but getting out of the life we lived wasn't an easy feat. Something I learned a long time ago.

I'd been in too long. I knew too much. I'd seen things that could get other people in trouble and those people knew things about me. Thankfully I've never been arrested, but others have, and I knew information that cops would kill for.

So, leaving was going to take some work.

And the first line of business, take a beating that served as a warning of what could happen if I ever talked. A beating that left me with more than a few scars on my back, a broken arm and ribs, and nearly losing the ability to walk.

But it was with beating and heady warning that I was able to walk. As long as I didn't go looking for trouble, they wouldn't come looking for me.

For the first time in six years, I was free.

But everyone knows that, no matter what you believe, you are never really free from that life. Because of what happened with my dad and my need to take down the fucker that did it, I chose a life that would forever have me looking over my shoulder.

At least for the time being, as long as I stayed out of trouble, I could concentrate on raising my kid without much fear.

And that's what I've been doing for the last year and a half.

I left gang life three months before my daughter, Mia was born.

Now, my life consists of working at a garage as a mechanic, taking care of my daughter when I have her, making sure my mom is also taken care of, and my new venture. School.

I always liked school. It always came easy to me, and whenever I was asked what my favorite subject was, I would answer with math. As I got older, school still came easy, but the life I was living took top priority.

Effort was still put in, and I was still able to get a high school diploma, but I acted as if I didn't give two shits about it. That wasn't the case, though. Somewhere deep inside, I did care.

It wasn't enough to leave that life behind and extend my education, though.

But now I have my daughter, and she *is* enough, so I applied to a few colleges and by some miracle, I got into one of the top schools in the state.

The University of Southern California.

Before the streets took over everything that made me *me*, I always dreamed of opening up my own mechanic shop with my dad at my side. Working together every day and being able to live life as happily as we could be. That dream died when he did.

But now that Mia is in my life, that dream is back, and I'm going to try to do everything in my power to make it happen.

I need to give my daughter a better life, and this is the way to do it.

Which is why I'm currently pulling on a black long sleeve and getting ready for my first day of college.

Never did I think that was going to happen.

I also thought I was going to be dead at this age, so I guess going to college is something.

CHAPTER TWO

LUCAS

ONCE THE SHIRT IS ON, I adjust it so that the sleeves are covering the majority of the tattoos on my arms and that the neckline is just above my collarbones.

When it comes to my tattoos, I don't usually put in the effort to cover them up.

Nothing bad is on my body. Nothing that tells people I once had, or still have, I guess, gang affiliations, but I have enough of them that tend to put people off and make assumptions. Given that it's the first day at a rich kids' school, covering up is ideal. But there's nothing I can do about the neck and finger tattoos. Hopefully those don't garner too much attention.

Once I'm happy with the shirt placement, and my jeans are sitting in the right spot, I give myself one last look in the mirror.

I look somewhat normal, somewhat like a college kid. Take away some of my experiences, the dark shit, and I would fit right in.

The alarm that I set for myself starts to ring out, telling me that it's time to go.

Even though the campus is only fifteen miles from my house, I have to leave at least an hour early. With Los Angeles having traffic at all times, it's a pain in the ass getting to places.

Grabbing all the things I need for the day, including my hat, I leave the room and head out to the kitchen where I find my mom getting ready for her own day.

"Did you buy new clothes?" she asks, eyeing me suspiciously as she pours her coffee into her travel mug.

I give her a nod. "I did. Thought it would be a good change."

After leaving my old life behind, I never really changed the way I dressed, not even when Mia was born.

Up until a few months ago, I was still wearing the clothes that were associated with the streets, clothes that were still way too big for my body. Since I'm starting a new chapter in my life, I thought it would be fitting to start dressing differently. Wear something that won't have people judging me for how low my jeans sit.

"*Ya era tiempo*." It was time, she says, giving me a small smile.

If it were up to my mom, I would have gotten rid of those clothes a long time ago.

"Yeah, well, I'll probably be home before you. iIss there anything you want to eat for dinner? Celeste has Mia until Friday."

A lot of college students my age, the ripe age of twenty-two, wouldn't be living with their mom. They would be living in dorms or have their own place. They also wouldn't be helping their parents with the bills in return for them helping out with their grandchild when needed. But everyone's situation is different, and this one is mine.

"Don't worry, *mijo*. I'm pulling a double today, so I won't be home until after midnight. You just worry about dinner for yourself. I'll grab something on my way home."

My mom is the hardest working woman that I know.

Ever since my dad died, she has tried everything to provide for the two of us. It helped somewhat that my dad's life insurance paid for the house, but there were still bills to pay. Mom took on two jobs when she had to, and the second that I was legally able, I found a place that would take on a kid like me as their employee.

Now we're stable even with the added expenses that come with Mia and my schooling, but that doesn't stop Mom from picking up a double shift at the nursing home where she works at to bring in more money.

She's another reason I decided to go back to school. If I am able to get my degree and open my own shop, then maybe I will be able to make enough money for the three of us, and she can quit. Maybe then she won't look like she's aging more and more every passing day.

I give her a nod. "I'll still go to the store and get stuff. Send me a list of anything you want."

"Thank you, *mijo*," she says, coming over and leaning up to place a kiss against my cheek. "You should get going. I don't want you to be late for your first day."

I give her a tight smile. Uneasiness about the day starting to settle. "I'll see you when you get home."

After giving her a kiss on the cheek, I start making my way out of the house, Mom following behind.

It's as I'm about to get into my car that my mom calls out to me.

"I'm proud of you, Lucas. Really proud. This will be a good thing for you. You'll see." My mom gives me another smile before throwing a wave in my direction and heading back into the house.

The whole way to campus, and as I pull into one of the parking structures, I think about my mom's words.

She has always told me that she was proud of me. Especially as a kid, those words were always coming in my direction. But as I got older and got into a few questionable things, those words started coming less and less. The last time that I heard them was when Mia was born, and the time before that was at my high school graduation.

Hearing those words now is messing with my head more than it needs to. I think a part of me needed to hear them so that I knew I was making the right choice by going back to school. Making the right decision by leaving who I once was behind.

And that's where my head is at as I walk to my first class, and it stays there until I enter the building.

It's when I'm walking through the classroom door and into the auditorium-style room that the thought that I made the right decision starts to fade. It's not because I'm nervous about class or even the fact that I'm new. The feeling goes away the second I pull the door open, and I hear a group of fuckwads talk.

Normally I tune out obnoxious bastards, but right now,

all I can concentrate on is them and their words. Especially when their words start being about me.

Fifteen seconds. It took fifteen seconds to have people start talking about me. Fucking fantastic.

"I guess the school would let anyone in."

"Do you see those tattoos on his neck? Do you think he got them in juvie?"

"Juvie? More like a state prison."

My teeth grind as I make my way to an open seat a few rows down.

If I was still in high school, I would be confronting the fuckers and beating the shit out of them. Now though, as much as I want to beat them to the ground, I won't. I know better.

Well, at least somewhat.

Without a doubt, these fuckers are going to try and make this place a living hell. They are going to try their hardest to make me feel as if I don't belong here.

Not if I have anything to do with it.

The second I finally take my seat, I turn my hat over and take a good look at the loudmouths.

There are five of them. Three guys and two girls, and from the looks of things, I can tell right away that they are rich boys and girls who get everything handed to them by Daddy.

They are everything that I'm not, and I hate them already, and the way that they are looking at me doesn't help either.

All of them are looking at me with disgust, all of them except one.

The blonde.

The blonde who's sitting next to the guy who looks like he was thrown up by a frat house. Her blue eyes are piercing, an icy blue that is calling my attention even from this distance. She isn't looking at me with disgust like her friends are. No, she's looking at me in a different light.

She's looking at me with indifference, like I'm below her. Like she's the rich princess and I'm the servant. Like I mean nothing to her.

Well, she means nothing to me. She is an absolute nobody who I don't give two shits about. Yet, we are still looking at each other like that wasn't the case.

Wanting to get a rise out of her and her friends, I throw a kiss in her direction, and the second I do, you would think I initiated a war by the way her friends' faces change. They go from being disgusted to being pissed.

That's okay though, they want to spew hate in my direction, I can spew it back in theirs.

These rich pricks and pretty blondes want to make me regret my decision in coming here, then so be it.

They want to hate me, I can hate them too.

CHAPTER THREE

SAVANNAH

IF I HAD MY WAY, I wouldn't be here right now. I wouldn't be at a school that only accepted me because of my father's name and money.

If I had my way, I wouldn't be studying a subject I hated, or even within touching distance of a douchebag who has cheated on me with half my teammates.

My way would have been away from my father's influence, away from this soul sucking school and away from the bastard who calls himself my boyfriend. My way would be at a school that's hundreds of miles away, studying something that I actually want to learn about and love. Yet, here I am.

When people look at me, they see someone who they think gets whatever she wants often. They see a pretty blonde girl with blue eyes, who happens to be a dancer for a prestigious school, and they think that every little thing is handed to her. That she just has to wiggle a finger, and whatever she wants is handed over.

That's far from the truth.

Yes, I may have blonde hair, wear the dance uniform for a well-respected college, and carry my father's last name, but who I am and who I'm perceived to be are two very different people.

Nobody, not even my inner circle, knows who I really am, and at the ripe old age of twenty, I don't feel the need to show them. The only person who knew who I really am, who I am at my core, was my mom but she died three years ago.

So now, I'm sitting with people I don't care for and who don't even like me, at a school that I despise, and wearing a persona that I wish I could burn, all in a class that I don't even want to be in.

If I could ram a pencil into my eye socket just to be able to get out of this place, I would.

"Is there a reason why you're not smiling right now?" Jason, the cheating bastard who continues to label himself as my boyfriend, says from where he sits next to me in this auditorium-style classroom.

Hearing his voice makes me want to puke.

Jason Wright is what people would describe as the epitome of frat boy. The rich boy who wasn't good enough to make the school football team but had enough money to become a fraternity president. A title that I'm sure will devastate him to lose once he graduates. He's a douchebag who uses his name and his parents' money to get anything he wants. Including me.

This boy, and yes, I mean boy, because Jason never wants to grow up, is very into his image. So when he needed a girlfriend, of course, he went to look for one on the dance team.

Somehow, I caught his eye.

When he first approached me, it was during my first year here at USC, and I didn't know what I know now. If I had, if I had even a small inclination of who this man was, I would have said no the second he asked me out. But I was naïve, and an older guy was paying attention to me so I was captivated by him.

Turns out, he only approached me because he knew who I was and who my father was. He thought that by making me his girlfriend every single door would open for him.

How do I know this?

Because he told me when I caught him with another girl in his bed on our one-year anniversary. For one year I let the bastard brainwash me and make me believe that he loved me and would do anything for me.

I walked away, but then I got a call from my dad.

Turns out during our whole relationship, Jason had struck up a friendship with my father. I have no idea how, since I only introduced them once, and they hardly talked to each other. So the second I broke up with him, he called my father to make me come back.

I cannot explain the amount of anger that flowed through my body, and it wasn't because I caught my boyfriend cheating.

Jason knew I would do anything my father told me to do, so he made me stay with him by going around me.

The hatred that I had for him grew to the point that

now, every time he's within a few feet of me, I want to punch his face in. Or puke.

We have a deal, Jason and I. I act like the devoted girlfriend in public, but there is nothing going on behind closed doors. He can also keep fucking anyone he wants, just as long as he keeps it quiet.

People think that I don't know that Jason is walking all over me, that I'm a naïve little girl, but all of that is far from the truth. I could set them right, but I honestly don't care enough about the type of person they think I am.

I turn to my "boyfriend" and give him the sweetest smile I have.

"Is this better?" I say, fighting the urge to roll my eyes.

"I mean, you still have a resting bitch face, but I guess that's fine for right now."

The eye roll I was holding back finally escapes. This man has a lovely way with words.

"Maybe if I wasn't sitting next to you against my own will, the bitch face would disappear, yet here I am. Sitting next to a cheating douchebag who went to my father so I wouldn't break up with him," I whisper yell at him through my smile.

Jason's face changes instantly going from annoyed to downright pissed. He's not mad that I brought up the fact that we're not together, no he's mad that I brought it up in a classroom where anyone could hear.

Like I said, to this man, image is everything.

"Maybe if you would have let me fuck you, I wouldn't have cheated, and we wouldn't be in this shit of a mess," Jason growls back at me, one of his hands coming up to my neck. To someone looking at us, they would see it as a tender move, but that's far from the truth. The grip he has on my neck is one he's used before when he's tried to show me who has the control in this relationship.

I was able to have control over one thing though, and that is not sleeping with him.

From the very beginning, I told Jason that I wanted to wait and not jump straight into anything sexual. He told me that he was completely fine with waiting until I was ready, and I loved him for that. I just didn't know that him being fine with it meant he was going to look somewhere else for sex. That tells you how naïve I was in that aspect of our relationship.

Now he uses it as an excuse every chance he gets. Like it's my fault, and it's one hundred percent not.

"Like that would have made a difference," I throw back at him, getting out of his hold.

"Now we would never know, would we?" This time his hand lands on my thigh, his fingers digging into my skin.

I hate having his hands on me.

"If you two keep staring at each other like that, the whole room is going to burst up in flames. It's so damn hot." A male voice sounds out from next to Jason.

I don't need to turn to know that the person that spoke those words just so happens to be Jason's best friend Justin. Yet another man-child with a god complex just because he's a frat boy with a J name. J names make me want to puke.

"Fuck off, Justin," I say, turning away from Jason with a flip of my hair.

"God, you're such a damn bitch," Jason mutters as he turns to look over at his best friend.

"Break up with me, and me being a bitch to you and your friends won't be a problem anymore," I state just low enough for him to hear.

"You look too pretty on my arm for that to happen," he states right before leaning in and placing a kiss on my cheek.

Justin, the other frat boy bastard who is sitting next to him and a girl that I think is Justin's flavor of the week, all let out an *aww* at the kiss. And when I shove Jason away, they laugh.

I ignore all of them and start getting ready for this class to start.

The class I don't even want to be in.

Like my school, my father also chose my major. Business.

In all honesty, I wouldn't have minded him choosing the major for me. Business is a good thing to study. But of course, like everything that my father does, choosing my major had an ulterior motive behind it.

He has high hopes that one day, I will finally come to my senses and want to work at his company. He thinks that by studying business, I will follow in his footsteps.

My dad, Reed Campbell, is a high-level executive at an accounting company here in Los Angeles. A company that caters to the rich and famous and all their financial needs.

But I want no part of it. Not a single thing. But when you are financially dependent on someone, you have no other choice. Add in the fact that I do everything that my father tells me to do, I am stuck.

No matter how much I would rather be studying something like art history, or anything art related.

So now I'm part of a major that holds my interest as much as a bag of shit. The same major that Jason and his stupid frat boy bros happen to also be a part of.

Yay fucking me.

It's only the first day of spring semester in my second year at the school, and this course already seems like it's going to be a long one.

Even though I will hate every second of this class, I will still try at it. Which is why, even on the first day of class, I'm pulling out my notebook to take notes on the syllabus.

I may be a dancer and may not be getting the education that I want, but I have always given school my all.

Jason and his stupid-ass friends continue to laugh and joke around, making me want to punch them more as I watch as the room starts to fill up with students.

Even though this may be a class I don't want to be in, I can definitely appreciate seeing a few eager faces around the room. They're excited about this. I may not be, but they are, so good for them.

I continue to watch the room fill but also listening to what Jason and his stupid buddies are saying.

It's as I'm listening to their stupid frat boy conversation I notice that something catches their attention, so I'm guessing that someone just walked into the room.

The only type of people who catch their weasels eyes

are those they feel threatened by or women who may pay attention to them. Turning slightly, I catch a glimpse of who has walked in, and instantly I know it's the former in this scenario.

A guy with a black long-sleeve shirt on and a baseball hat covering most of his face has walked into the room, and when he turns, I can see why the morons next to me might feel threatened.

He has broad shoulders that stretch out his long-sleeve shirt perfectly. He has height to him, may even have a good body under the clothes. And even though most of his face and body are covered, I can tell he has a natural tan that will most definitely glow in the sun. On top of all that, the number of tattoos that are on display on his hands and neck, are making this man look like a badass who shouldn't be messed with.

This guy is the complete opposite of Jason and his stupid frat buddies, and he's making everyone notice.

Including me. Color me intrigued. Very intrigued. And I haven't even heard him speak or seen his face. This is the first time that I have ever seen this guy in my life, and just looking at how he holds himself has captured my attention.

That could be a very good thing or a very bad one. Because he definitely looks like someone I should not be associated with.

"Look at this fucker," Jason lets out followed by a snort that sound more like a snarl.

"Dude looks like a gangbanger," Justin throws out, but it sounds more like he is admiring the guy than insulting him.

"I guess the school would let anyone in," Jason says, and I'm sure if I were to look over at him, his mouth would be all twisted with disgust.

But I don't turn. I keep my eyes on the tattooed student as he walks down a few steps.

"Do you see those tattoos on his neck? Do you think he got them in juvie?"

"Juvie? More like a state prison," Greg, the other frat boy asshole, spits out.

Jason and his friends continue to talk shit about our new classmate as he finally walks into a row and takes a seat.

My eyes don't move away from this person, no matter how hard I try, not even when he turns around, moving his hat so that we can see his face, and looks over at the douchebags talking about him.

He meets every one of our gazes until his gaze lands on me. The second his eyes meet mine, it's as if I lose sight of everything but him.

I'm no longer hearing what Jason and his friends are saying. I'm no longer paying attention to what is going around in the room. All of my concentration is solely on this stranger.

As I look at him, a chill runs down my spine.

I'm not usually affected by people. I've met some pretty amazing individuals in life, both pretty on the inside and out, but they never cause chills.

If a chill runs through me, it usually means that I'm cold or scared of something. But right now, the chill has nothing to do with either of those things and everything to do with the set of brown eyes that are staring back at me.

The chill is one that has me at the edge of my seat and my back going straight. It's in anticipation, but what exactly am I anticipating, I have no idea. It may be that the set of eyes are making it feel like they are staring into my soul. Like they are seeing right through me and can see who I really am and automatically know that everything about how I present myself is a lie.

Brown eyes have always been my weakness, and right at this moment, it's as if the owner of them knows it and is holding it against me.

As much as I want to look away, I don't.

I keep my eyes on him, trying to keep my facial expression as collected as possible so that he won't notice that his gaze is affecting me more than it should.

He keeps his eyes on me too, but while my face is controlled, his is not. This complete stranger is looking at me like he could eat me alive, and at this moment, I think I would let him.

It takes me a second to realize what this guy is doing. He's looking at me like he wants to eat me alive, not because he is captivated by me like I am by him. No, he's looking at me that way because he is lumping me together with Jason and his friends and their words. They are the bad guys, and because I'm sitting with them, so am I.

I want to silently tell this stranger with my eyes that their words and who they are, have no reflection on me, but I can't.

My image, how I portray myself to be, doesn't allow me.

So, when the stranger with eyes of chocolate blows in a kiss in my direction, a kiss that stirs a reaction out of Jason, I know I just made an enemy.

I'm used to having enemies, so having one more shouldn't be a big deal. Yet for some reason, becoming enemies with a set of eyes that can see right through me feels like it will be the end of me.

And maybe it will.

CHAPTER FOUR

LUCAS

AFTER I BLEW a kiss in the blonde's direction and turned around, I felt five pairs of eyes trying to sear their stare into my skull.

As the professor was going on about what to expect from the course, I looked over at my new friends on occasion. Every time my eyes diverted in that direction; I was met with murderous stares. It took everything in me not to let out a booming laugh at how they were looking at me.

I've dealt with some of the toughest men that the streets of Los Angeles has to offer, seen shit that no teenager has a right to see. The fact that the preppy douchebags think that I will be shitting my pants by the way they look at me is fucking hilarious.

The stares became even deadlier when I turned to look at them during the last ten minutes of class and a snort almost came out.

Once class was dismissed, I was going to drop it. I was going to stop trying to piss off the pretty boys and girls and just go about my business. I have school to concentrate on. I don't have time to deal with rich kids who get shit handed to them.

That was the plan, but of course with these preppy little shits, things don't go as I had planned.

I walk out of the classroom, holding the door for a girl who looks fresh out of high school, giving her a small smile in the process, and start making my way out of the building.

It's as I step out of the building, ready to head to my next class, that the preppies start to approach me. I catch a glimpse of them from the corner of my eye, and I can help but roll my eyes at the whole thing.

As I watch them step closer to me, for a split second, I'm taken back to a time when I was fourteen. It was my first year of high school and I was getting cornered by someone who would be considered a rival. It's only for a second but then I remember who I am dealing with, and my mind comes back to the present.

Where I am being approached by three assholes wearing Abercrombie.

"Can I help you with something?" I voice when they are about five feet away from me. My eyes narrow in the process and assess them as they come closer.

One of the guys, the one that thinks he is the ruler or something, looks me up and down like I'm a pile of shit was dropped in front of him.

If anyone is a pile of shit in this scenario, it's him, not me.

The other two guys look more like they're resisting the

urge to ask me for an autograph or something. One guy even looks like he is trying hard not to drool. He looks like he would be a cool dude to hang out with if he wasn't friends with the preppy *pendejo*.

My eyes then travel to the two girls. The brunette is looking down at her phone, not caring about what is currently happening. She's in her own world.

The blonde though, her eyes haven't left me since I stepped outside.

She's acting like she doesn't care about what is going on between me and her friends. Her face still shows the same indifference that it showed in the classroom, but her body and her eyes are telling me a different story.

Her body, one of a dancer, is angled in my direction, as if to hear every little thing that I say. And her eyes, fuck, her eyes are brighter than they were inside. The way her eyes are looking at me makes me think that, if I were a weaker man, they would have me on my knees.

She's hot, beautiful, especially with that "don't mess with me" kind of vibe she has to her that makes a guy's dick twitch. But given her choice of friends, I would steer clear of her.

Actually, there's no *would* about it. I *will* steer clear of her.

Steering clear though, doesn't mean I won't mess with the pretty princess. She may have shitty friends, but she still has my attention for some weird reason.

"Just wanted to introduce ourselves, since it looks like you might be new around here," Captain Preppy says, sizing me up in the process, before extending a hand to me. "I'm Jason, the Sigma Alpha president."

A douchebag name, for a douchebag guy with a stupid-ass title, go figure.

I ignore his outstretched hand. "Great," I say before turning around and walking away.

Two steps I'm able to walk before Jason, the preppy king is back in my line of sight.

"So you get my name but I don't get yours?" Jason spits out a smile on his face telling me that he'd rather spit on me than be friendly.

Maybe he should, so he can see what happens.

"Why would I tell you my name? It's not like you will give two shits about using it," I spit back at him.

This guy apparently has never had someone talk back to him, because my one comment has him going rigid.

Dude even narrows his eyes at me like I'm going to cower by the way he looks at me.

I couldn't give two shits about pissing him off.

"I'm just trying to be friendly here, buddy. You know, since you threw a kiss at my girl. I gotta know who I'm telling to stay away from my property."

If I didn't hate the dude already, I definitely would now. Not only is he a preppy asshole who probably bought that frat president title, but he's also an asshole who treats women like shit.

Of course, the blonde is his girlfriend.

I look over at the girl in question and give her a good look. She still has a look of indifference on her face but from the way her hands are balled up into fists, she's irritated. Maybe she's irritated because it looks like her boyfriend wants to fight me and she doesn't want to deal with it. Maybe she's irritated because Jason here is talking about her like she's a piece of land who doesn't mean anything. Maybe she doesn't even want to be his.

From the way her blue eyes are burning and the veins in her arms are popping, I'm going to take a wild guess that it's the latter two in this scenario.

I would be pissed too. I'm all for being possessive over your girl, hell, I may have punched a guy or two for flirting with my daughter's mother when we were together, but there's a difference between me and Jason. I don't treat women like they're dogs.

I take a step toward Jason. "Look, *buddy*. I really don't want to be friendly, especially with a preppy boy like you. You may think you own the place, but you really don't. The only reason that you're in the position you're in at this school is because of your daddy's money." I close the distance between the two of us. I get all up in Jason's face, loving the fact that I have a good four inches on this *güey*. "As for the kiss, I can blow a kiss to whoever I want, and if that's *your girl,* then I will continue. Since it looks like *your girl* needs a real man to show her attention, because she sure as hell isn't getting anything from you."

Hands land on my chest, and I get shoved back. The shove isn't enough to land me on the concrete floor but it is enough to serve its purpose.

Jason just declared war.

"Is that all you got, pretty boy?" I say through a laugh

before composing myself and coming toe to toe with him. "You don't want to mess with me."

"Why?" Jason asks through his teeth. "You going to shank me or something?"

There it is. That little comment right there tells me everything about Jason and what he thinks about him.

To him I'm a thug, nothing else, and he's going to use every chance he gets to remind me.

Right now, he's trying to provoke me and if I'm not careful, this fool is going to make me do something I don't want to do.

So, I deflect.

I give him a shrug. "You're the one who suggested it, not me."

Jason stares me down, trying to intimidate me.

He's silent for a few long seconds before he finally spits something out. "You think you're so tough. You ain't shit. This school is going to eat you up and spit you back out. By the end of this semester, you will be on your knees, begging teachers to pass you."

What the fuck is this guy on?

He sounds like some poorly-written sitcom villain.

"Is that a promise?" I say, a smirk on my face.

Jason Boy didn't like that, because his face gets all red, and I think he's going to punch me when he shoves past me like we're in middle school.

All of this is starting to feel like middle school shit. Aren't we all supposed to be grown adults here?

I let out a chuckle as I watch Jason walk back to his friends like his ass was on fire.

"C'mon, Savannah," he says, grabbing the blonde by her elbow and dragging her along as he walks away.

Savannah.

A pretty name for a pretty girl.

I watch Savannah as Jason drags her behind him. Her blue eyes burn with anger, and I think if she could, she would kick him in the balls for touching her.

If I had to guess, this girl hates her boyfriend as much as I do.

"Bye, Savannah," I yell out, causing everything around me to go still.

Both the girl in question and her lovely boyfriend turn to look at me. Her with wide eyes that may have a tinge of excitement in them, and him with eyes so narrowed you would think he was trying to see through me.

Their eyes stay on me as I walk over to them and lean in to tell something to the blonde that she can only hear.

"When you finally decide to leave the prick, *Corazón*, come find me. I'll show what a real man is like."

It's as I pull back that Savannah's expression of indifference finally disappears. Her face looks as if she's scared, but her eyes tell me that she's intrigued by what I just told her.

She doesn't say anything, and neither does her prick of a boyfriend, which is surprising, to say the least. So I blow her one more kiss and turn around to head to my next class.

I shouldn't play these childish games, but these rich pricks should know I'm not one to be messed with.

CHAPTER FIVE

SAVANNAH

"WHEN YOU FINALLY DECIDE TO LEAVE THE *prick, Corazón, come find me. I'll show what a real man is like.*"

Those words shouldn't be replaying in my head, yet they are. And they have been since I heard them almost three weeks ago.

I hear them when I'm alone in my dorm. I hear them as I walk around campus, and I most definitely hear them as I sit in my business class, as I watch the speaker of the words instead of the professor.

I hear them all the damn time, and I'm starting to think that something is severely wrong with me.

Even more so because I keep looking for the guy that said them.

The very guy who I don't even know what his name is. He knows my name. How come I don't know his?

Bye, Savannah.

Urgh, that's what I'm talking about. At random times

throughout the day, the way his words sounded in my ear, the way my name flowed off his tongue, the way he called me *Corazón*, all come rushing in.

And it does things to me. Things that should definitely not be happening, like tingles and butterflies in my stomach type things.

The butterflies become prominent too when I think about the way the word *Corazón* came out of his mouth.

I know enough Spanish to know that the word means heart. Why he called me that is beyond me, but my guess is to get a rise of both me and Jason.

Which worked.

After the confrontation three weeks ago, and I felt his breath against my ear, and he walked away, Jason dug his pudgy fingers deeper into my arm and dragged me away.

For a good twenty minutes, all I heard was that he was going to destroy the fucker for disrespecting him and trying to go after what's his.

I let him ramble on until I finally got tired of him and his voice and dislodged myself from his grip and went to my dorm.

He yelled out to me as I walked away, but I ignored him. I wasn't his. Not his girlfriend and not his damn property. He wanted to show jealousy in front of others, he can go right ahead, but I wanted no part of it. I could end this stupid "relationship" in a second if my dad wasn't holding me back.

Given the person that Jason is, I thought that he was going to drop it, that he was going to forget about our new classmate. I thought wrong.

For the three weeks since the confrontation, Jason has not stopped talking about him. Talking about how he is going to make the guy suffer and regret ever applying to this school. Every time he sees the guy, Jason gets pissed, even if the guy doesn't even look in his direction.

He may not look in Jason's direction, but he does look in mine.

That he does. Every chance he gets, the nameless classmate throws me a wink or another kiss.

I should hate it, but I think a big part of me likes it. I like getting attention from someone who isn't Jason, especially from someone who doesn't think of me as a naïve little girl who turns a blind eye wo her boyfriend's cheating.

I think that's what is getting to Jason the most. The guy hitting on me and me not doing anything to stop him.

Maybe Jason isn't the only one with the problem when it comes to this guy, because I just spent the last ten minutes thinking about him.

And again, I don't even know his name!

I seriously need to get my head checked.

Trying my hardest to put my nameless classmate out of my head, I walk into the campus coffee shop.

I need caffeine not only to get by for the rest of the day, but to also clear my head.

This coffee place is one of my favorites. While the on-campus Starbucks is always jammed packed with people, this one isn't. It has more of a homey feel to it.

Especially with the cinnamon buns that are made in-house.

There is nobody standing in line, so I go directly to the counter to place my order.

"Can I have a lavender latte, please? And if you have any cinnamon buns, I will take one of those too," I tell the guy at the register, who gives me a nod.

"Anything else?"

I shake my head, giving him my name for the order before handing him a twenty. When he gives me my change, I put the larger bill in the tip jar and the small ones back in my purse.

Some people need money more than I do.

"Aww look at that, the bitchy ice queen can be sweet and have a heart after all," a voice says from behind me.

I don't need to turn to know who spoke those words.

His voice has been stuck in my head for three weeks. There is a deepness to the way he speaks, but also an elegance and a carefree feel to it. If this guy had the ability to sing, without a doubt it would be beautiful.

Turning, I meet the brown eyes that have been stuck in my head since I first saw them.

They are still as intense as they were that first day, but now given the small distance between us, I'm getting a good look at all the shades of brown swimming in his irises.

As I stare into his eyes, he stares into mine and again, I'm left feeling like he can see right through me.

I take a step back, breaking whatever trace he has over me.

"What are you doing here?" I ask, my voice having a small shake to it. I don't know why, but I'm not scared of the guy.

Am I?

Of course not.

"Getting coffee. What do you think I'm doing here? Robbing the place?" He gives me a smirk as if to challenge him.

"N-no," I stutter out. Why is this guy affecting me so much? I clear my throat and add more to my answer. "I just didn't peg you as a coffee guy."

That smirk of his deepens. "Oh yeah? What type of guy did you peg me as then?"

He comes closer to me, flipping his baseball hat backward in the process. That's when I get a real good look at my nameless classmate.

His face is sharp in all the right places. His nose, his jawline, his cheekbones. He gives off fashion model vibes, which I'm sure is far from who he really is. His hair is dark, and a little bit longer than it was on the first day of class. It's starting to peek out from the rim of his hat.

After studying his face, my eyes move down to his neck. More specifically to the tattoo that he has on the side of his neck. From far away, the tattoo looks like a few simple lines, but up close, I see it's a masterpiece filled with detail. It's a rosary with such intricate detail that you wouldn't think it possible for the size. It's absolutely beautiful. It suits him.

Why I even decided to think that is beyond me, I don't even know the guy.

I clear my throat again and answer his question. "Not one that spends time in a coffee shop, that's all."

He looks at me, his eyes burning into mine. "Really?"

"Yup, really."

"Your assumption wouldn't have anything to do with the tattoo on my neck that you just spent a solid minute analyzing? Or even the ones on my hands?" he says, bringing one of those said hands into view.

I shake my head a little too quickly. "Of course not. People with neck tattoos drink coffee every day."

Am I rambling?

I think I am. I never ramble, and it's absolutely insane that I'm doing it now.

Nameless classmate notices. "Do I scare you, *Corazón?*"

He steps closer to me, his mouth mere inches from mine. The position feels way too intimate to be happening in the middle of a coffee shop, and he's not even touching me.

I swallow. "No, of course not. Why would you?"

Finally he backs away, putting space between us, giving me a shrug. "I don't know how pretty white girl brains work, so I thought I would ask. Can I order my coffee now?"

Looking around him, I see that a line has started to form behind us. Feeling a little bit embarrassed, I step to the side and let him step up to the counter.

For some reason, I don't find the need to move from my position and just stand there and watch my classmate.

As he gives the employee his order, a large Americano, I replay the words he just said to me.

He called me a pretty white girl.

Does he really think that I would be afraid of him because I'm white and he's Hispanic?

I'm so in my head with that very question that I nearly miss him telling the employee a name for his order.

"Lucas," he says, pulling out his wallet and handing his card over.

The nameless guy who has captivated my thoughts for three weeks finally has a name to the face.

Lucas. It suits him, but knowing his name doesn't diminish all the ideas running amuck in my head.

"Thanks," Lucas says to the coffee shop employee when he says his drink will be at the end of the counter.

Still standing in the same place as before, I watch as he goes from one side of the counter to the other to wait for his drink.

I watch him until my own name is called, and I finally have to move.

Digging my teeth into my bottom lip, I walk over to the other end of the counter and grab my drink and cinnamon roll that the barista placed down and give a silent thank you.

With my things in hand, I should walk out of the coffee shop and be on my way, and forget about the fact that I ran into the nameless classmate, found out his name, and whatever words might have come out of his mouth.

That's what I should do, but of course, just like with everything else that comes with this guy, I don't.

I walk over to where Lucas stands and stare him down until he looks up from his phone.

"Can I help you with something, *Corazón?*" he asks, not moving his attention away from his phone screen.

"What did you mean when you said about not knowing how pretty white girl brains work?" I ask, my voice trying to portray some of the anger I feel, but I keep it controlled as best I can.

Finally Lucas looks up, giving me another shrug. "Exactly what I said."

"Well let me show you how wrong you are. I'm not scared of you, and even if I was, it wouldn't be because of your skin tone. Your skin could be purple, red, green, or orange, and I still wouldn't be scared of you. I don't judge a person by the color of their skin, that's not who I am, not now, not ever. If I were to judge someone it would be because of who they are as a person and their actions against others. Never because of who they are ethnically or racially. Is that understood?"

It feels like the whole place just went absolutely quiet and that all eyes are on the two of us. They might be, but I'm not turning to see if I'm right. I'm not standing down until Lucas gets it through his thick-ass head that I'm not who he thinks I am.

After a minute of his brown eyes staring into my soul, he finally nods.

"Understood."

"Good," I say, digging my heels into the linoleum floor, and start making my way out of the coffee shop.

I'm not even five feet away from him when I hear his voice again.

"You should really rethink who your boyfriend is

then," he says, the sounds of the coffee shop starting up again.

I stop, frustrated, and turn back to look at him.

In the two seconds since I turned around, his coffee was handed to him because he has it in his hand, bringing it up to his mouth to take a sip.

"What is that supposed to mean?" I ask, trying not to roll my eyes.

"You may not be someone who judges someone by the color of their skin, but from the looks of things, your boyfriend does."

He's... not wrong.

Jason Wright is very much that person. It's the thing I hate about him the most.

"You don't know that," I say. I wish I could light myself on fire for even defending Jason.

Lucas lets out a chuckle and walks closer to me. "I'm not blind, *Corazón*. He's hated me since the second his eyes landed on me. Is it because he thinks of me as a threat? Maybe, but I'm going to take a wild guess that it goes deeper than that. You know, since they will let just about *anyone* into this school."

I don't say anything because he's right on all accounts. Every last one of them.

"Maybe you should look for a better boyfriend," Lucas says, before taking a sip of his coffee and giving me a nod. "See you later, *Corazón*."

He gives me a smirk before walking past me and out of the shop.

Without thinking about it, I follow behind me.

"Stop calling me that," I yell out to him as soon as the coffee shop door is closed behind me.

Lucas stops in his tracks and turns to face me, a smirk more prominent on his face.

"Stop calling you what?"

"Stop calling me *Corazón*. My name is Savannah."

This is foolish, I know it is, yet here I am trying to stand my ground on something as stupid as a nickname.

Lucas lets out a laugh that has the butterflies in my stomach waking up and fluttering.

He comes over to me, leaving about a foot of distance between us.

Being this close to him, I'm able to smell his cologne. Or aftershave, whatever it might be. It smells like freshness and leather and vanilla, and just like his name, it fits him so well.

In the coffee shop, I wasn't able to smell it but now that we're outside, it's overpowering every one of my senses.

A hand comes up to my peripheral vision, taking my concentration from how the guy in front of me smells.

Lucas's hand is reaching up and moving a strand of hair behind my ear.

"Don't worry, *Corazón*. I know what your name is."

His thumb glides against his cheek for a second, and then it's gone, and then so is Lucas.

It takes me a second to find my bearings.

This guy is doing something to me, and that something is settling in deep.

Very, very deep.

CHAPTER SIX

LUCAS

THE DOORBELL RINGS through the house, taking my concentration away from the jumbled-up words on my laptop screen.

I'm supposed to be fine-tuning a marketing plan for a make-believe business for my classes. The plan was to finish up today and have the rest of the week free, but I've spent the last hour staring at my screen, waiting for something to come to me, and nothing does.

Now, with the doorbell ringing, the assignment is going to have to wait until tonight.

Getting up from my place at the dining room table, I close my laptop and walk over to open the front door.

The second I open it, a smile spreads across my face.

"*Papi!*" my two-year-old daughter yells out from her place in her mother's arms.

"Mia Mia," I say, extending my arms so that my little girl can come over to me.

Celeste, Mia's mom and my ex-girlfriend, hands her over, and the second that my little girl is in my arms, her little face lands into the crook of my neck.

I haven't seen her since Celeste picked her up on Sunday, and the more I don't see her, the more I miss her.

With my daughter in my arms, I step to the side to let Celeste in and close the door behind her.

Mia and I follow her as she walks to the living room and puts down Mia's bag of clothes and toys. Our daughter may only be two, but the girl needs to travel with at least thirty toys everywhere she goes.

"Did you have a good time with mommy, Mia?" I ask her, as I sit us on the couch and shift her on my lap.

She gives me a nod. "Yeah."

"*Y te portaste bien?*" 'Did you behave', I ask. This is a little routine that both Celeste and I do whenever we drop her off.

Mia gives me another nod, this time giving me a bright smile that my mom tells me is just like mine.

"*Si.*"

I place a kiss on her cheek, and then put her down on the floor so that she can go play.

Mia runs off and leaves me with Celeste, and from the look on her face, she wants to tell me something.

"You two have a good week?" I ask my ex, letting my elbows fall to my knees.

"Of course. Took her to the park, went to watch a movie. My dad was even able to come over and spend some time with her," she says, taking a seat on the other end of the couch.

"That's good. How is he?"

"He's good. Has a lot more gray hair than he used to. Says he wants to come by more often."

Celeste has lived on her own since she was eighteen. Like me, she made friends with the wrong people as a teenager, friends that included me, and it was something her parents didn't approve of.

She was kicked out and went to live with an aunt. That arrangement didn't last long though, so she came to live with me and my mom for a little bit before she found a place that worked for her. She could have stayed here with me and my mom, but Celeste has always said she never wants someone to take care of her, she can do it on her own.

When she got pregnant with Mia, she tried to get support from her parents, but because I was the baby's father, and we were still together at the time, they shut her out yet again.

Her dad barely started coming around in the last year and a half, but tensions are still high with her mom.

"I'm glad that he's putting in the effort," I tell her sincerely. I want her to have that same parental support system that I do.

"Yeah, me too," Celeste says, giving me a small smile before taking a pause and starting up again. "Thank you for switching days with me."

Celeste and I don't have a court order that dictates how much time either of us spends with Mia. Once a month, we come together and come up with a plan that has us splitting time equally. It's what works for us, and sometimes changes need to be made.

She was more than helpful when I started going to school, so when she has something come up, I'm more than willing to help.

I get to spend more time with my daughter and have a happy baby mama.

"Of course. She's my daughter too, and you know I'm always happy to help. You've helped me out more than once."

"Yeah, but it can be a lot with school and then your hours at the shop, and I know your mom is working night shifts."

I snort. "I can handle all of that and still take care of Mia."

"Are you sure? I can ask my manager to push my start a week later or something," she says, biting her bottom lip like she's really considering it.

The thing about Celeste, she doesn't want to be taken care of, but she wants to take care of anyone else.

She's starting a new job this week that she's excited for, so if taking some of the stress that comes with Mia helps her this week, then I will take it.

"Celeste, I will be fine," I say to her.

"If you say so," she grumbles. "Anyway, how's school going? Are you liking it?" she asks.

This is the first time Celeste and I have really sat down and talked in a few weeks. So she hasn't had a chance to ask me about school. Lately, all our conversations have been strictly about Mia.

Right now, it's good to have a friend to talk to.

"School is school. Definitely a lot harder than high school ever was. I like it though, some of the professors are dope and definitely are passionate about what they are teaching."

It's only been a little over six weeks since the beginning of the semester, almost halfway to the end, and I can honestly say I made the right decision going back to school.

"That's great. Have you made any friends?"

I resist the urge to roll my eyes.

"I'm there to go to school, not make friends," I grumble at her.

"Let me guess, you've gotten on people's bad side."

I hate that this woman knows me so damn well.

It's been weeks since I was in the coffee shop with Savannah. Weeks since I was so close to her that I was able to smell her perfume.

Since then, things between us have been ice cold. I antagonize her every chance I get by flirting with her and calling her *Corazón*. A part of me thinks that she likes it, but another part of me thinks I should stop.

But she antagonizes me as well, what with how she throws dirty looks in my direction and the snide comments that have started to come out of her mouth every time she sees me. I find it fun, and it's even more fun when her boyfriend is around. The dude wants to punch me, but he doesn't have the balls to do it.

I wouldn't call that being on someone's bad side.

"No, just a few rich pricks who think they own the place."

"It is a rich school in the middle of South Central. What did you expect?"

"Definitely not a pompous ass frat boy and his pretty blonde girlfriend," I grumbled under my breath, but apparently it wasn't low enough for Celeste not to hear.

"I'm sorry, did you say pretty blonde?" Celeste asks.

I shake my head. "Nope."

"I think you did. Is someone's girlfriend getting under your skin?" Celeste teases, using the baby voices she uses on Mia on me.

"Nope. I have no idea what you're talking about," I say to her, cursing myself for letting anything slip.

"Yeah, you do. What's her name? She must really be something if you mentioning her has your face going red."

Would it be too much if I kicked my daughter's mother out of my house?

Thankfully, Mia comes into the room and takes all the attention. She hands me one of her baby dolls that looks like it was electrocuted.

From the looks of things, she was trying to brush the doll's hair when the small plastic hair comb got stuck in its hair.

I try to pull it out as gently as possible to not cause more damage to the doll. Unfortunately, I'm not able to do that without sacrificing a few plastic pieces of hair.

I hand the doll back to Mia, and the second she has it in her hands, she runs over to show her mom.

"Oh wow, your *papi* did a good job."

Celeste and I play with our daughter for a good half

hour, my ex dropping the subject of the pretty blonde, until her phone rings, and Celeste announces that she has to get going.

As she gets up from the floor, I remember how she looked like she wanted to tell me something when she first got here.

"Did you want to tell me something?" I ask, as Mia and I walk her to the car.

When she reaches the driver's side door, she lets out a sigh.

"Remember that guy I told you about a few months ago?" she asks, giving me a sad smile.

Celeste and I may not have worked as a couple, but we do work as co-parents and as friends, and because of that, she tends to be more open about the people she sees. Mostly because of Mia, but also because, like me, she doesn't have a whole lot of friends she can talk to about relationships.

"The dude who thought he was a big shot because he delivered to Beverly Hills?" I ask.

I never met the dude, but from what Celeste told me about the guy, he was something else.

She lets out a sigh. "Yes, that one."

"What about him?"

She looks down at the keys in her hand. "We broke up."

"Okay."

"You don't want to know why?" she asks, like it's mind blowing that I don't want every single detail.

"Not really. I told you he sounded like a jackoff when you told me about him. Maybe now you can go looking for a guy who's actually worth your time."

She better not be thinking about us getting back together. Nothing good will come from that. Ever. The only thing that did was Mia.

"Well, you were right, I guess. He was a jackass. I'm so happy I never brought him around Mia."

"Yeah," I say, because what else do I say? She has a shit taste in men, I should be a prime example of that.

"You're a great friend, Lucas. I'm so happy I have you to talk to about my relationship woes." Celeste deadpans, looking at me with no amusement whatsoever in her eyes.

"That's what ex-boyfriends turned baby daddies are for," I say with a shrug.

"You suck, you know that?" she says, a smile playing on her lips.

"Yeah, you've told me a time or two. Don't you have somewhere else to be or something?"

"Yeah." Celeste rolls her eyes before looking over at our daughter in my arms. "You be good for *Papi* and *Abuelita*, okay Mia?"

Mia nods at her mom and throws her a wave.

"I'll check in during the week," she throws in my direction.

Now I'm the one nodding. "Call whenever you want."

Mia and I throw her another wave before we turn and head back into the house.

We make it halfway up the driveway when Celeste is calling out my name.

"She's never going to leave," I whisper to Mia before turning around, raising an eyebrow in her direction.

"If you're going to go after a girl, make sure she doesn't have a man already. You don't want it to come back and bite you in the ass."

I swear, she better not mention anything about the two of us getting back together.

"I'm not going after anyone, and nothing is going to come back and bite me in the ass," I yell back to her.

"Ass," Mia repeats causing me to let out a sigh.

Great.

"You should take care of that before she starts to repeat something else," Celeste yells out before getting into the car, finally.

Mia and I walk back into the house, and as I watch Mia play with her toys and I open my laptop, I think about what Celeste said.

Not about her being single again, but about not going after someone with a man.

I'm not going after Savannah. No way in fucking hell.

She's the type of person I hate. She's all about money and image and probably only cares about materialistic things, the big expensive things. The complete opposite of who I am. She's the pretty girl with the money, and I'm the boy from the wrong side of the tracks who has to help provide for his mom and kid.

Sure, I saw a sweet side of her at the coffee shop and she told me she wasn't judgmental against people, but a small moment doesn't make a person.

Savannah, whatever her last name is, is definitely not a person I want to get into bed with.

Maybe if I see something different, that will change…

Even then, though, it will be a big *if*.

Especially if Jason the douchebag is in the picture.

CHAPTER SEVEN

SAVANNAH

AS SOON AS I get into my car and turn it on, the tire pressure light turns on.

Great.

Getting out of the car, I walk around but see all the tires are perfectly fine, which means one of them probably has a screw or something stuck in it.

As if my day wasn't bad enough, now I have to find a place that is open on a Sunday so that they can fix it. No way am I going to drive with a screw in a tire and have it explode on the freeway.

I guess I have to find a place before heading to my dad's house.

Pulling out my phone, I do a quick Google search and find that there's only one place that is open on Sundays within a ten-mile radius.

Deciding that the open shop will be my best bet, I tap on the address and let my phone guide me there.

When I get to the garage, it looks like it's about to

close since all the bay doors are halfway shut. Hopefully someone is still here who can help me, otherwise I will be leaving my car and taking an Uber to my dad's.

I pull up to one of the bays, and when I get out of the car and hear music, I let out a sigh of relief.

The front door is locked, so I go through one of the bay doors, hoping to find someone.

My search doesn't last very long because as soon as I step into the garage, an older gentleman comes out of what looks like an office to greet me.

"Can I help you?" the man asks in broken English with a smile on his face.

I give him a smile back. "I was wondering if you had time to look at my tires. I think one of them might have a screw in them."

The older gentleman, whose name tag says 'Flaco', gives me a nod. "*Si, señorita*. Let me open up one of the bay doors and have someone take a look at the tires for you."

"*Muchas gracias*," I tell him in the best Spanish I can muster.

He gives me a nod.

"*¡Reyes, llantas!*" he yells out into the garage, with what I'm going to say is the Spanish word for tires, to get the person who is going to look at the tires for me.

Flaco instructs me to bring the car over to the second bay as he heads over to raise the door.

I do as I'm told, and once the car is all situated, I get out of the car with a smile.

The second I go over to the bay door though, my smile drops when I see who Flaco called over to help me out.

Lucas.

What the hell? He works here?

I'm not the only one who stops in their tracks. Lucas does too. He looks me up and down like he too can't believe that I'm here.

Finally, his stare lands back on my face, and he gives me an eye roll.

"Of course you're a damn cheerleader," he snorts, before coming over and inspecting my car.

I look down at my practice shirt uniform because I completely forgot I was wearing it. "Trojan Dance" is proudly displayed across my chest.

We had early morning practice because of the disaster that happened yesterday during the basketball game.

Our school came out on top for basketball, beating out Stanford, but our dance team messed up more than once during our halftime performance. So, our lovely coach thought it would be appropriate to have practice on a Sunday to rectify our mistakes. Today's practice makes me so happy that the season is almost over. Then I won't have to think about dance until the summer.

I was going to change before heading to my dad's, but the whole tire sensor thing made me forget.

"I will have you know, I'm not a cheerleader. I'm a Song Girl," I say as I follow behind him.

Lucas stops his inspection of the car and looks at me like I have three heads. "What the fuck is a Song Girl?"

"A dancer. You know the official dance team for the

school. We're the ones who perform with the marching band."

The more I explain, the more he continues to look at me as if I'm crazy.

"Do you wear a skirt as a uniform and have pompoms?"

"Well, yeah."

"Do you dance during a football or basketball game?"

"Yes."

"Then you're a cheerleader," he says, crouching down to be at eye level with the driver's side tire.

He's technically right, but Song Girls are definitely a lot more than cheerleaders, more so in a traditional manner, but I will give them all the credit. I sure as hell will never be able to do the things that they do. There's a reason they should be included in the Olympics.

I know when to accept defeat.

"Okay, fine, I'm a cheerleader. What does it matter to you?"

Lucas gives me a shrug as he moves onto the next tire. "It doesn't. It just explains a lot."

"What does that even mean?"

I watch as Lucas runs a hand along the back passenger tire.

"It means that I was right about you being a hoity-toity little princess who gets everything handed to her and can be a bitch on top of everything else."

Hoity-toity.

Is he fucking serious? I am nothing like that. Yes, I portray myself as cold and act like nothing can affect me, just like he described, but that's just a fucking front. So many things affect me. He doesn't know who the fuck I am, so he doesn't get to judge.

"Not all cheerleaders are like that," I say through my teeth.

Again, he gives me a shrug. "The ones I've met are."

"Just because you met someone like that doesn't mean you can lump everyone together. I can tell you right now that you're completely wrong about who you think I am."

Why do I care so much about how this guy perceives me? He is a nobody to me. I shouldn't be defending myself and who I am to a complete stranger. I shouldn't care that he thinks I'm a hoity-toity bitch. After this semester, I probably will never see him again.

So why, why do I care what he thinks of me?

Lucas stands up and comes over to where I'm standing, meeting my stare head on. "So tell me. Tell me who you really are, *Corazón*. Tell me how wrong I am. Better yet, show me."

I go completely silent. I don't owe this man anything. Not even my true self. He's put me together with other people who may look like me but do not have the same thought process as me. He doesn't deserve to know who I am at my core.

But why is revealing who I really am on the tip of my tongue? Why do I want to answer him and tell him everything about myself?

So many questions I need answers to but have no way to find said answers.

I stay quiet for way so long that Lucas takes my silence as defeat.

"Thought so," he says before letting out a sigh, nodding toward the car. "Look, you have two different tires with screws in them. I can take them out and repair them. It will take a few minutes."

I have to take a second to get my head on straight and drop the previous conversation. "I don't need new tires?"

I'm already in hot water with my dad about something that happened earlier in the week, which is why I'm heading over there today. I don't need an added bill of a thousand dollars added to it.

Lucas shakes his head. "These should be good for another thirty thousand miles. Do you live on campus?"

I look at him suspiciously. "Yeah, why?"

"I'm not going to stalk you or anything," he says with an eye roll. "Just trying to get an idea of how much more the tires can run."

"Oh. I usually just drive it when I have to go off campus or go to visit my dad. Living close to the center of campus helps with that."

Lucas gives me a nod like a light bulb lit up in his brain.

"That would explain the screws. There's construction going on by one of the parking structures around there."

Now that I think about it, I do remember driving past some safety cones and over metal plates. I guess I have to find another place to park my car until construction ends. No way do I want to end up here again.

I let out a sigh. "So can you fix it?"

"Give me twenty minutes, and you will be good to go." Lucas gives me a small smile before heading back into the garage.

He comes back a few minutes later and after giving him my keys, the car is up on the lift with Lucas getting right to work.

Since the front office is closed, I hang out by the bay door, watching as my tires get fixed.

As Lucas works on my front tire, I realize that, for a few minutes there, we were having a conversation like actual human beings. It may have been really short, but it was enough for me to notice.

I wonder if he noticed he was being nice to me.

Lucas was right on the money when he said the job would only take twenty minutes, because no more than twenty minutes later, he's done, and my car is back on the ground.

"How much do I owe you?" I ask as Lucas gets out of the car and hands me back the keys.

He looks at me like he is trying to figure out if he should charge me an extreme amount or the actual price.

"Thirty."

I wait for him to tell me the rest of the amount, because no way it's only thirty. He has to be under charging me or something. I've had tire rotations more expensive than that.

But he doesn't say anything else.

So I grab my wallet from my car and take out a hundred and hand it to him.

"Let me get you your change." Lucas nods, turning to head back into the garage.

"No, it's okay, you can keep it," I say to his retreating back.

If he is undercharging me, the leftover money will help cover it and he can keep whatever is left.

"That's a seventy-dollar tip." He says each word as if I'm stupid and can't do math on my own.

"I know. And like I said, you can keep it." I give him a smile, but it's one that is definitely not being returned.

"I'll get you your change," Lucas says again, this time in a much harder tone.

My mouth falls open as he walks inside the garage, and it takes a second to find myself again and run after him.

"Wait, why? I don't want my change.," I say, grabbing him by the arm to stop him.

The second my skin meets his, it's as if fire burns all through my body, but I don't pull it away.

"Yeah, and I don't want your charity. So, you can have your money." Lucas turns to face me. His eyes are burning with anger.

"It's not charity. You did a job for me, you helped me out. I'm thanking you for it. There's nothing wrong with that."

"Maybe not to you, but I don't need monetary thanks from a girl like you."

There are those words again.

A girl like you.

This guy will never see me as anything more than a rich girl with blonde hair. No matter what I tell him otherwise.

"What the fuck is wrong with you? Do you seriously

hate me so much that you can't accept an act of kindness and gratitude? That you have to keep lumping me into a stereotype?"

Lucas crossed his arms across his chest, and I try my hardest not to notice how good his upper arms look at the action. "If the shoe fits."

I'm done.

I give up trying to show this guy I can be a decent human.

"Fuck you," I say through my teeth before turning and heading back to the car. "Keep the money. I don't want it. Give it to Flaco. He'd probably be more grateful about it than you ever will."

I walk out of the garage and get into my car without a backward glance in Lucas's direction.

The only glimpse I catch from him is as I pull away.

"Asshole."

CHAPTER EIGHT

LUCAS

MY EYES FEEL heavy as I look at my laptop, and no amount of coffee is helping the cause. It's four in the afternoon, and the only thing that my eyes want in this moment is my pillow.

I got about an hour of sleep last night and if the texts I'm getting from my mom are any indication, tonight is going to be the same way.

Mia is with me this week, a new system that me and Celeste came up with a few weeks ago after she started her new job. I have Mia one week, and then we switch, and she has Mia the next. We switch every Sunday afternoon, and so far, everything has worked out. We even enrolled her in a daycare center so she can interact with kids during the weekdays while we are at work and at school.

It's a good system, and it has been running smoothly, but this week we hit a little snag.

Mia caught a small cold at day care in the last day or two and has not been a happy little girl.

She had a fever all day yesterday, and last night she didn't end up falling asleep until about three in the morning. As for me, I stayed awake to make sure that her little chest was still moving up and down and reapplying vapor rub under her nose and chest every so often. I last checked the clock around five, and I must have fallen asleep soon after because next thing I knew, it was after six when Mia stirred awake.

It gutted me seeing her sick. I swear, every time she looked at me, her little eyes were begging me to take the sickness away.

I was able to call out from the garage yesterday and spend the day with her, Mia going from my arms to her bed, and I was going to miss school today, but with finals coming up, I couldn't.

Thankfully, my mom had the day off and she was able to stay with her. I've checked on Mia throughout the day, my mom telling me that she bathed her in lemon, a Mexican remedy, and gave her medicine, but that isn't enough to stop me from rethinking not staying home.

The last message from my mom doesn't help get rid of that feeling. According to my mom, Mia is slightly better than she was yesterday, but she still has a fever and doesn't want to eat.

It will definitely be another long night.

I should be home with my baby girl, but instead I'm trying to stay awake as I sit in the library working on a damn group project.

If you go into college thinking that you've escaped the hell that is group projects of high school, you are mistaken.

Group projects in college are very much a thing and very frequent. I've only been at this school for a semester, and I've already had to do four.

Thankfully, this is the last one until fall semester starts.

"Lucas, awesome job on all the promotional graphics you did. They are perfect and look like they took you a while," my classmate, whose name is Arabella and named herself the leader of the group, tells me.

I throw her a nod as a thank you.

Those suckers did take me a while, but because they were for a subject that I'm passionate about, I was happy to do it.

This group project is for the same class that had me creating a marketing plan a few weeks back.

It was supposed to be for a fake business, something that will never see the light of day. But I didn't see it that way. I saw it as an opportunity to build up a dream that hopefully one day becomes a reality.

The dream of one day opening up a shop with my dad. Yes, the dream is already fractured with my dad being gone, but I can still make the dream come true in some way.

When it came to the group project, each group was supposed to pick one fake business and build it up. Do everything that we need to get the business off the ground in this make-believe world.

Surprisingly, my group chose my make-believe business to build up.

I was shocked but at the same time excited, so I poured

everything I had into it. No matter how much I hate group projects.

"Alright, I think we have everything ready for the presentation and to submit the paper. I definitely think that \ our business plan and the graphics will put us on top. We just need someone to go over the paper one more time for proofreading and we can submit it."

I'm definitely not going to volunteer to read a thirty-page paper. I don't have time for that shit.

"I'll do it," one of the other girls in the group volunteers.

Arabella gives her a smile. "Awesome, then I think we are done. We have the presentation down, so all we need to do is give it and this class is over with."

One step closer to finishing up my first semester at USC.

A few of the group members say a "thank god" right before all of us start collecting our stuff so we can head out of here.

"Want to grab a bite to eat at the dining hall?" the other guy in the group Kaiden, asks.

During my short time here, I've become somewhat friendly with some people, Kaiden being one of them.

We've gotten a bite to eat or a drink after class before. I would classify him as almost a friend, so him asking now isn't out of the ordinary.

Unfortunately, today, I have to turn down his invitation.

"Sorry, man, my kid is sick, and I have to get home," I say as I sling my backpack over my shoulder.

Kaiden's eyes go wide. "You have a kid?"

I give him a nod. "I do. A little girl."

"How old are you?" he asks, looking at me like he is trying to analyze me to find out my age.

"Twenty-two," I answer him, and when his mouth drops, I can't help but laugh a little.

"Damn. How did I not know that?" he asks as we make our way out of the library.

"That I was twenty-two, or that I had a kid?" I ask with a chuckle.

"Both, I guess. Like, I knew you were older than your normal first-year student, but I didn't think you were way beyond your age too."

"I mean, I wouldn't say I'm beyond my age. I just had a kid young, no big deal," I say.

We fall silent as we make our way to the first floor of the library.

As soon as we step onto the first floor, I start to think that maybe I should stop at the pharmacy on the way home. Maybe I can get a humidifier that I can put next to Mia's bed tonight. That way she could get a little more sleep.

My mind is so busy making a list of all the things that I should get, that I don't realize that I'm about to walk into someone until it's a little too late.

"Motherfucker. You should really look where the fuck you're going." The voice rings in my ear, and instantly I'm pissed.

Taking a step back, the douche canoe Jason is standing

in front of me, looking annoyed as hell, as if I planned to run into him.

Trust me, I would never voluntarily run into this dude. I've spent enough time on this campus to know just how much of a scumbag he really is.

"Maybe you should be the one looking," I throw back, trying to keep myself centered. I don't need any of Jason's shit today.

"Watch who you're talking to," Jason growls, sounding like a chihuahua.

I can't help but to roll my eyes at this fucker. "You may be the president of a frat, but you're not the president of this fucking country, or even me for that matter. So you can fuck off. Better yet, walk away before I punch your face in."

I've been tempted to do it since I first met the bastard. Maybe now may be my chance to do it. Who knows if I will see this fucker after finals end and a new semester starts.

"You wouldn't dare threaten me. If you do, your time here is done."

I let out a snort, stepping into Jason's space. "Try me, fucker. Try me and see what happens."

My blood is boiling. I've had it with my frat boy president. If he wants to mess with me, I'm not going to hesitate anymore.

Jason looks pissed beyond belief as we stare each other down. He looks like he's ready to pull back and swing at me, and if he does, I will be ready.

The stare down continues and for a solid minute, there

is nothing else going on around us. It's just me and this fucker who is about to buy a new nose if he doesn't back down.

For a solid minute, I think that I will be going to the pharmacy for more than cold medicine for Mia, but that thought goes away when Jason the twat surprises me and takes a step back.

He looks up at me, probably wishing for the four inches of height that separates us so he can spit right in my face, and snarls.

Disgusted.

He's disgusted with me.

What else is new?

"Let's go," he barks out and it takes me a second to put together that he's not talking to me, but to someone else.

I finally look away from the dickwad's face and realize that there is a girl standing a few feet behind him.

A brunette who is very much not his girlfriend.

The brunette takes a few steps closer to Jason before he grabs her arm and stomps away with her stumbling behind.

This whole semester I've only seen him dig his slimy fingers into Savannah. Did they break up? I swear I saw him give her a kiss in our class together a few days ago. Maybe I imagined it.

Or maybe I'm thinking way too much about him being with another girl. Why the fuck do I care if they broke up and he's with someone else?

"I hate that guy so much," Kaiden says from next to me as I watch Jason and the girl walk away.

I completely forgot that he was with me.

"That makes two of us," I grumble, trying to clear my head.

"Yeah, well you don't have to deal with him as a fraternity president. Dude is a sleazeball and a half. Did you know he cheats on his girlfriend?" Kaiden asks as we walk out of the library and to the parking lot.

I shake my head.

I had my suspicions, especially now after seeing him with the brunette, but it wasn't my place.

"Savannah can be a bitch, don't get me wrong." Why do I have this internal desire to punch Kaiden in the face for calling Savannah a bitch? "But she doesn't deserve that shit. That girl can do a whole lot better than Jason. She just doesn't see it."

Or maybe she does and is just turning a blind eye to everything.

There's definitely been a time or two when I've seen them together, and Savannah is either shoving Jason away or looks like she wants to murder him.

Maybe she can't stand him and is only with him because it's convenient for her.

He's a fraternity president, if her position on the Song Girls doesn't give her status, maybe that will.

And yes, I looked up what a Song Girl was. I now know more about the dance group that I care to admit.

"Maybe she needs someone to show her," I say under my breath.

What the fuck am I even saying right now?

"Maybe," Kaiden muses, having heard what I just said.

He quickly changes the subject though. "Oh, hey, if you're free next weekend, there's an end-of-the-semester celebration over at the Sigma Alpha house. You should totally stop by."

Definitely not. No way am I going to step foot into a frat house, let alone one that has Jason as their fucking president.

I don't tell Kaiden that though. I have to have at least one friend on this campus after the semester ends.

"I'll think about it," I offer.

"Awesome," he says, giving me a bright smile. "Anyway, I'll let you go. No need for you to be late getting to your little girl."

We say our goodbye, and I walk to my car.

After my trip to the pharmacy, I spend the rest of my day with my daughter, crossing my fingers I don't catch her cold. But taking care of my daughter isn't the only thing that is occupying my time.

Whenever I have a second for myself, my mind wanders to a certain blonde and her cheating boyfriend.

I keep telling myself that I don't care. That I couldn't care less about the girl. But she ends up so deep in my thoughts that I dream about her.

A dream I don't want to wake up from.

Maybe I do care and a whole lot more than I should.

CHAPTER NINE

SAVANNAH

MY PHONE CONTINUES to vibrate in my hand as I walk to the elevator.

It's been going off for the past half hour, and the more it vibrates, the more I roll my eyes and ignore it.

I don't even have to look at the screen to know who is trying to get in touch with me. Who is calling to give me excuses for their actions.

It's Jason.

For the last three days, he's been trying to get ahold of me or see me, but I haven't answered my phone or opened my door.

I'm acting like a sulking teenager, I know that. I'm in my twenties now, I should be learning on how to hold myself better. But when you get bombarded by text messages and DMs from random people around campus telling you that they saw your "boyfriend" making out with another girl, you would reach your limit too.

I couldn't care less about Jason and his side piece.

We're not together, and we made a deal that he can screw anyone he wants. But part of that deal was that he use fucking discretion and not drag my name through the mud.

Now he's been trying to not only apologize but tell me that people are lying.

They're not, and I don't give a shit about his apology.

Before this semester started, there were rumors flying everywhere about the girls who Jason was with. I would always turn a blind eye to those rumors and act as if they didn't affect me and, at the time, they didn't.

Now though, now, it's different.

I don't know when it happened, but I came to the realization that I no longer want to be perceived as the naïve rich girl who lets her boyfriend walk all over her. The girl who is blind to everything going on around her.

That's not who I am, and I was only harming myself for letting people think of me in that light.

So, I'm done.

I'm done with Jason and his stupid antics, and I'm ending things between us for good. No more pretending.

He can go to my father if he wants, but I'm putting myself first. Jason Wright does not warrant an ounce of my life.

I honestly shouldn't have let him dictate me for as long as I did, and that's all on me.

I haven't officially "ended" things with Jason, but I will. There's a party this weekend at the Sigma Alpha house, one where I have to act like the perfect girlfriend. I will do my duties, but after that it's over.

For now, though, I'm going to concentrate on taking

care of myself, and the first thing in accomplishing that is enjoying myself today.

My father may have chosen my major and the classes that I'm supposed to take, but he didn't choose all of them.

This semester, I was able to sneak in an art history course as an elective. Going to that class two times a week has been highlight for me. Every time I walked into the room, I had a smile on my face.

It was my happy place.

Today, though, is the last day of that happy place. Our final was done last week, and as a treat, our professor decided it would be fun to take a small field trip to the Getty Center. I can't even express how much excitement swam through my body when he made the announcement.

The smile on my face grows as I get into the elevator that leaves the parking garage and goes up to where the tram is to take visitor to the main entrance to get to the Center is proof that excitement.

As a little girl, I loved coming here. It was always me and my mom, and we would spend hours here. We would go to the garden and then walk through each exhibit like it was our first time.

I have distinct memories of her here, and how she would stop at a painting, not one in particular, and tell me a story of what she thought the painting meant. Her stories always included princesses and dragons.

She made this place special.

When she died, I came here every chance I had for a year, all so that I could feel her close to me.

I came until it became an obsession, and I realized that

I needed to stop. So after that, I only come here on her birthday.

It may not be her birthday today, but I'm still making it special. Maybe I'll even see if they have little music boxes available in the gift shop.

The elevator arrives at the tram station, and my smile grows even more as I get in line for it to take me up the hill to the museum.

As far as a field trip goes, this isn't your typical one. There is no meeting with the other students from the class. No meeting with the professor. The only thing for today was to come, by ourselves or with a classmate, and email the professor a picture of us being at an exhibit. Once the picture is in, we would get extra credit points.

For someone who loves art, this is the easiest assignment to ever have.

A few minutes after arriving on the tram platform, I'm in the small train being taken up to the museum on the hill.

I decided to come a little later in the day. That way there are fewer people around, and I get to see the sun as it sets over the Santa Monica Bay.

The second the tram arrives at the entrance of the museum, and I step out of the cart, I take a deep breath. Closing my eyes, I let all the memories of being here with my mom rush in.

For a few glorious seconds, I can hear her voice, her laugh and see her eyes. For a few seconds, she is here with me.

I take in everything that my mind conjures up for a few

minutes before I finally open my eyes and make my way to the entrance.

Even though I know some of the exhibits by heart, I still grab a map as I walk in. There could be something new that I don't know about.

I also know the grounds like they are the back of my hand, but that doesn't stop me from taking in every aspect of them as if it were the first time.

Never will I get over how beautiful this place is.

My first stop is the gardens. I have this distinct memory of me and my mom coming here once for my birthday. She had a box with her, and when we sat down on one of the many benches the gardens have to offer, she opened it and reveal a cupcake.

A simple cupcake with pink frosting. She pulled out a candle and lit it as she sang "Happy Birthday" in a soft voice.

That memory stays with me as I walk through and becomes more prominent as I find the very bench.

I don't know how long I sit there, reliving my memories and people watching, but it's enough for my heart to sing and to be thankful to my professor for giving us this field trip.

I really needed it.

Eventually, I stand up from the bench and make my way through and into the first exhibit.

One of the things that I love about the Getty is the way the place itself is structured.

There are separate buildings with three floors and each floor has a new exhibit that captivates you. And the best part is all the buildings are interconnected. No need to even step foot outside.

I walk through the first three exhibits and make my way into the Early Renaissance exhibit.

The second that I step into the main room of the exhibit, the paintings aren't what take my attention.

No, my attention goes directly to the figure that is standing right in front of one of the paintings.

A male figure that looks to be writing something in a notebook.

One who I've spent the last couple of weeks avoiding.

Lucas.

Ever since the garage, I've said next to nothing to the guy. I have stayed out of his way, and he's stayed out of mine.

It's worked out these last couple of weeks, and I thought that I was done seeing him since the final for our shared class was yesterday, but here he is.

In my damn safe space.

He hasn't seen me yet, so I can walk away, go about my way, and act like I never saw him here.

It's a simple act.

So why am I not doing it? Why am I standing here like an idiot and not walking away?

And why the actual hell does it feel like butterflies are flying in my stomach right now just from looking at him?

Just by being near him.

Nope. Not going to look for the answer to that question.

Walk away, Savannah. Just walk away, go about your

day, and forget that you ever saw Lucas Reyes here. It's that simple.

Well, it would be that simple if Lucas Reyes hadn't looked up from what he was writing in his notebook, turned, and is now looking right at me.

I should really act faster.

My mind must be completely clouded by where I am because I actually send a small wave in his direction.

He ignores the wave and just stares at me. Silence surrounds us.

"What are you doing here?" Lucas breaks the silence, his voice low, and not in the tone that I'm used. The majority of the time, when this man speaks to me, he sounds annoyed, but for some reason, I'm not getting that today.

I could be snotty about the way I answer his question, but I don't feel like putting on that persona right now. So I rein in the cold-hearted bitch.

"Art history assignment," I tell him. "What about you?"

Lucas's eyebrows furrow a bit at my question. Me being nice to him, especially after our last conversation, definitely is throwing him off.

It takes him a few seconds to respond, but eventually he does.

"Um, it's a free museum, and I needed some inspiration for a project," he says, holding up his notebook.

A small smile can't help but spread across my lips. I want to ask him what the project is, but I don't. "That's nice. I'll be on my merry way then. Leave you to find your inspiration."

I give him another smile, take a step back and slowly start making my way around the small room.

As I move from one painting to the next, I feel as though Lucas's eyes are on me. He's probably as surprised as I am by the fact, we were able to say a few sentences to each other without biting each other's heads off.

I want to turn and meet his gaze, but I don't. I just continue on to every painting as if it's the first time that I'm seeing them.

Eventually, I make my way out of the room and head on to the next.

For the next half hour or so, I walk through the whole exhibit, taking in every little detail of each painting, ceramic piece, and sculpture, making up stories about each and every one of them as I go along.

On occasion, I run into Lucas again. But I just send a smile in his direction and continue on. I do take notice of the fact that he is drawing in his notebook instead of writing. I try to catch a glimpse of it every time I pass him by, but I can never get a clear picture.

From what I can see, Lucas is talented. Maybe if he didn't hate me as much as he does, I would ask him to see it.

Eventually, I lose sight of Lucas, even getting a little disappointed when I walk into a new room, and don't find him there.

I push that feeling down and continue on to the next building.

A painting of a woman holding a small child captures my attention as soon as I step into the room. I walk over to it, and as soon as I step in front of it, a story comes to my mind.

Closing my eyes, I picture my mom standing next to me, with a big smile on her face and taking in every single one of my words.

I tell her a story of the way I think the mom is holding the child because she is trying to protect them. Protect them from the world around them. From the people. I tell her how all the mother wants to do is give her child the best life that she can, and when the child grows up, they will be extremely grateful for her.

"I never would have looked at that painting that way," a male voice says from right next to me.

After letting out a small yelp and jumping a little, I open my eyes to find Lucas standing right next to me.

Where did he come from?

I resist the urge to reach out and slap his arm for scarring him.

"Looked at it how?" I ask, trying to bring my heart rate down a bit.

I gaze up at him, his brown eyes on the painting. From this angle, I can see all the sharp lines that his face has to offer, and I like every single one of them.

Damn. I really need to rein myself in before I end up jumping this guy.

"How you were describing it. How you said the woman was protecting her child and how the child would have been grateful."

Great.

I was talking to my mom out loud, and Lucas heard me.

"You weren't supposed to hear that," I whisper, feeling embarrassed by the fact that he caught me talking to a ghost.

Lucas doesn't take his eyes off the painting as he gives me a shrug. "Maybe not, but it was nice. It sounded like you were telling someone a story."

He finally turns in my direction, his brown eyes almost glowing in the museum light. They almost take my breath away.

Almost.

"Maybe I was," I mumble, turning back to face the painting. Staring into his eyes is too much.

"Who?"

My lips tremble a bit at his question.

Lucas must notice it because he clears his throat before he speaks again. "What story do you have for this one?"

I look up, and I see him walking away and pointing toward a painting that is three paintings down.

My eyes meet his questionably. "What?" I ask through a shaky breath.

"Tell me the story that this painting says," he says, nodding toward the piece of art.

"Why?"

He gives me another shrug. "Because I want to hear it."

CHAPTER TEN

LUCAS

IS THIS A MISTAKE? Possibly. More so since this is the same girl who told me to go fuck myself when I wouldn't take a tip from her.

That was weeks ago, and in those weeks, my interactions with Savannah have been limited. Even though they may have been limited, I've still thought about her. She's especially been on my mind more and more ever since my interaction with her douchebag boyfriend last week.

I came to the Center to not only get some inspiration like I told her, but to also clear my head a bit.

It's been swimming in thoughts and dreams about her, and I felt like I needed a reset.

Work hadn't helped and neither had spending time with Mia. So I came here, to a place I thought I would be safe from anything that had to do with her. Plus, I really did need to look at some art in person for a car I'm working on.

Horrible mistake.

When I saw her, I thought that my mind was playing tricks on me, but sure enough, it was her.

Something about her was off though. The Savannah who was standing in front of me, giving me a few small smiles and a wave, was definitely not the one I was used to.

She was being nice. To me. For a second, I thought that she had been abducted by aliens or something.

I lost her for a bit after that, then I found her whispering a story to a painting with her eyes closed.

Walking away would have been the sane thing to do, but instead, I stood there and listened to every single word.

It was as if she was talking to someone.

The way that she told the story captivated me, so when I saw her lips tremble, I suggested more of it.

I should have dropped it.

I should have never said anything, because I have no right to spend any time with this woman.

Yet here I am, following her through the exhibits like a sad little puppy, listening to what she has to say about every piece of art that we see.

"Look at it. Like really look at it and tell me what you see," Savannah orders as we look at a painting that looks like a green spray can exploded.

"Green. Lots and lots of green," I say, which earns me a slap against the arm.

Apparently, we are past the whole hating me thing and into the slapping phase.

"There's more to it than just green," she says, with an eye roll.

"Sure, there's also specks of brown in it." Another slap.

"You need to look at it a little deeper," she grumbles, but I can see a smile playing at her mouth. I don't think I've seen her smile this much in all the months I've known her.

"I would rather you just tell me what you see. I like it better that way," I say, my words sounding as if they have a flirty tone behind them. Hopefully she didn't catch on to it.

"You're serious?" she asks, raising a perfectly shaped eyebrow at me.

I give her a nod.

The smile on her lips grows a little more, and she turns back to look at the painting.

Her shoulder brushes up against my arm, and I feel the urge to lift it so I can wrap it around her and bring her body closer to mine.

Her very sweet, delectable body.

Fuck. I really shouldn't be thinking about her this way.

"Okay, I see the painter being lost. All the greens are leaves, right? So, I think that when it was painted, the artist felt suffocated, like he needed to escape. The fact that the painting is filled with leaves could mean that he went somewhere with a lot of trees to get away. The number of leaves, though, could represent suffocation. Like he was under the weight and was feeling pressure."

I watch her as she speaks, and I can't help but want to kick myself in the ass for thinking that this girl wasn't capable of showing emotions other than indifference. That she wasn't capable of being anything other than a bitch.

I wholeheartedly admit that I got this woman all wrong.

Looking over the description of the painting, I see nothing described as she said. Yet, I like her words better.

"Interesting," I say, not taking my eyes off her.

"Right? Definitely makes the piece a lot more intriguing."

I want to add that she is the one who makes it more intriguing, not her story, but I don't. I keep those words on the back of my tongue.

"Yeah, you're right. It does," I tell her, giving her a smile.

Her eyes travel from my eyes, down to my mouth and I watch as she watches me with such intensity that her tongue pops out a little before she looks away.

Savannah, the bitchy Song Girl, wouldn't be affected by me the same way I'm affected by her, would she?

No way in hell. I must be imagining things.

Clearing my throat, I break both of our trances.

The blush that creeps up Savannah's cheeks is cute and has my thumb twitching with the need to reach out to see how deep it can get.

"What exhibit should we see next?" she asks, looking a bit flustered.

A chuckle escapes me, and I lean down and speak, my lips only an inch or two away from her ear. "Well, unless you want to go back to the very beginning, I think our story adventure is over."

Savannah lets out a little gasp, and I don't know if it's from my closeness to her or because our little adventure has come to an end.

My body wants it to be the former.

When I pull back, I see that her blush has gotten deeper as she takes in our surroundings.

It takes her a quick second to realize that we are at the last of the exhibits.

"Darn, how is it already over?" she asks, sounding a bit disappointed.

"That's what happens when you are having a good time, I guess."

And it was a good time. I can't believe I just admitted to myself that I had a good time with the cheerleader who hates my guts.

How did that happen?

I'm blaming it on the museum.

"I guess so," Savannah says, a small hint of sadness I think on her face. "Should we get out of here?"

Our time together is done, and as much as I tell myself that I dislike this girl, I want to spend more time with her.

In the last few hours, I saw a side of her that I wasn't privy to before and I liked it. I liked it so fucking much.

I give her a nod. "Sure."

She throws another smile in my direction, and we make it out of the last exhibit.

The second that we step foot outside, I'm a little surprised at how close we are to the sun setting.

"Oh, the sun is about to set," Savannah lets out, walking to the other side of the courtyard that overlooks part of the garden.

I can just leave right now, but for some reason, I follow behind her.

"This is one of the reasons I came today, to see the

sunset. It was one of my favorite things when I was little and came with my mom," she tells me.

I don't think she meant to give me that little snippet about herself, but I'm not going to say anything.

After spending a few hours with this person, I'm starting to really like seeing the way her smile lights up her whole face.

As we watch the sunset, Savannah pulls out her phone to take a few pictures, and after a minute or two, her bright smile dims.

The same thing happened when we were inside, and I asked her who she was telling her story to.

"Is that who you were telling the story to earlier? Your mom?" I ask.

Savannah doesn't look at me, but I see her shoulders go a little rigid at my question. By that reaction alone, I know the answer to my question.

I hit a nerve and a big one at that.

Surprisingly though, even though my question was hella personal, she still answers it after a long minute.

A long sigh leaves her body. "Yeah," she says, her voice so small. "She died three years ago. This was one of her favorite places to visit. Every time I come here, I tell her stories just like she would tell me. All so I could feel like she is here with me." She looks up at me, tears forming in her eyes. When one escapes, she wipes it away quickly and lets out a nervous laugh. "Sorry, it's stupid. I know."

Never did I think that I would have something in common with this girl, yet here I am.

"It's not stupid. I came here for the same reason," I tell

her, trying my hardest to not reach over and help her wipe away the tears.

"You wanted to feel closer to your mom too?" she says, a sad smile on her lips.

I shake my head. "My dad, and not really telling him stories, but to help me with this project I'm working on for work."

"I'm sorry," she says, reaching out and placing a hand against my arm.

She's touched me once before and that was at the garage. Then her touch felt as if it was searing into my skin. Right now, not only is it searing into my skin, but it's tattooing itself in every muscle under it.

I shrug, her hand dropping in the process. "I'm sorry about your mom."

Her blue eyes dim a bit before she shakes her head and gives me another smile. "The project for work, is that why you were drawing earlier?"

And here I thought she didn't pay attention to anything outside of herself.

"Yeah, I'm painting a hood at the garage, and the owner wanted something that stood out, so I came here for some ideas."

The blue in her irises brighten up a bit more. "Can I see?"

Now I'm the one whose shoulders are going rigid. I've only shown three people my drawing. My mom, Flaco, and Celeste. No one else sees the things I draw outside of the finished product.

But for some reason, I want to show Savannah. Especially now that I know she likes art and can give good advice about it.

Letting out a sigh, I swing over my backpack and take out the sketchbook I put away before I approached her earlier.

After flipping to the right page, I hand the book over to her and watch her intently as she looks over my sketches.

"They're a little rough."

It's nothing big, just a few line sketches with some small details. I needed to jot down some quick ideas, and later I will cross reference them with the pictures I took on my phone.

"Wow, these are really good, Lucas."

I think that's the first time she has called me by my name, and my body is having a weird reaction to it. It likes it too much. My dick likes it too much.

Yeah, this whole thing was a huge mistake.

"Thanks," I say as she hands me back the book.

"Is that something you do a lot, paint hoods?" she asks.

We are getting oddly personal right now. Add that to spending time together, and the fact that we have yet to bite each other's head off, it's throwing me off.

This isn't who we are to each other.

"I've only done a few of them. Hopefully, as more time goes by, I'm able to do more of them. It's cool."

That seems like enough information. No need to tell her that my dream is to open up a shop one day that specializes in restoring cars and doing paint jobs.

"That's awesome. Hopefully, I get to see the finished product." Again, she gives me a smile as she speaks.

So many smiles are getting thrown in my direction tonight. This is definitely not going to help with my dreams about her.

"Sure," I say, not making any promises about showing her. Tonight might be a fluke, and we could go back to hating each other tomorrow. Or, we might never see each other again, which might be a good thing, I don't know.

We finish up watching the sunset, and then we start heading down to where the tram is.

Before we make it there though, Savannah decides to divert to the gift shop, and there I go again, following behind her like a damn puppy.

Something must be seriously wrong with me if I'm willingly following this girl around.

It's not like I can be with her.

We are nothing alike, aside from the fact that we both have a dead parent and have an appreciation for art. Add on the fact that she has a boyfriend, a cheating one at that, but still a boyfriend, to the list. And I have Mia, Savannah and I will never work. No matter how much my body reacts to her, how beautiful I think she is, we are too different. Way too different.

I put all thoughts of the two of us being together out of my head and try to actually look around the little store that the museum has to offer.

I end up finding a book for Mia, and when I'm paying, Savannah stands to the side, waiting for me. From the looks of things, she didn't find anything, and she looks sad about it.

See, the girl is materialistic. She probably has to leave

any store she walks into with something.

"Do you guys have any more music boxes?" she asks after the employee hands me my purchase.

The lady gives her a shake of her head. "No, I'm sorry. We ran out earlier, and we're not slated to get another shipment until the end of the month."

Savannah's face goes back to the sad expression she wore when she was talking about her mom earlier. She quickly puts a smile on her face though.

"Oh, okay. Thank you."

Her reaction stays with me as we walk out of the store and the museum all together and head to the tram.

Given what she told me, the music boxes probably have something to do with her mom. From the looks of it, she probably gets one every time she comes here or something.

I don't ask her though. We just get on the tram, sit next to each other, and head down to the parking garage.

We don't say a word to each other the whole time. The only time words are spoken is when I ask her in the elevator what floor she parked on. We're parked on the same floor.

Once in the garage, I don't know what to do.

Do I walk her to her car?

Do I just head to my bike and not say a word?

Do we say goodbye? What the fuck do we do?

The both of us must be thinking the same thing, because we stand in the almost empty parking garage not moving or saying a word.

Eventually Savannah breaks the silence.

"Thank you for not hating me today and listening to all my stories," she says, her voice small and not as powerful as I'm used to hearing it.

A part of me wants to tell her that, after today I don't hate her, or that I don't hate her as much, but I can't find the words.

I also want to tell her to leave her dick of a boyfriend, but that's not my place.

"Thank you for not hating me either and making today interesting," I say, deciding that complimenting her would work best.

"Look at us being friendly with each other. Maybe that can happen more often."

I roll my eyes at her suggestion not, because I don't want it to happen but because she has an idea of me that I have to uphold.

"Maybe."

She gives another smile, but this time it reaches her eyes. "Bye, Lucas."

There's my name again on her lips, and my dick can't help but twitch at how breathy it sounds.

"See you later, Savannah."

A small gasp leaves her mouth as I say her name. I think she was expecting me to call her *Corazón*. I wanted to, but her name is what came out.

I give her one last wave and make my way to my bike without a backward glance in her direction.

The second I'm on my bike, I speed out of the parking lot. If I stayed any longer, I might have done something stupid.

Like kiss Savannah.

CHAPTER ELEVEN

SAVANNAH

THE SECOND I step into my dorm and close the door behind me, I let my mind do what I didn't let it do in the car.

Think about Lucas.

From the second that I saw him in the museum to when he sped away on his motorcycle, my mind was filled with thoughts of the man.

Thoughts of how good he was at listening when I talked about my mom. Thoughts of how I appreciated him for letting me tell him the stories that the art said to me and didn't judge me for it. How we both have experienced the same pain that comes with losing a parent. Thoughts about how good of an artist he was and how happy I was when he showed me a part of himself that I know he was hesitant to show. How I saw him see my disappointment in not finding the music box and how he forced himself not to ask me about it.

Lucas Reyes made me see a different side of him today.

A caring side. A side that didn't judge for every little thing that I did or said. A side that I liked very, *very* much and wanted to see more of.

My mind was so enveloped in everything Lucas, I made myself think of something other than him as I made my way home. If I thought about him, I for sure would have over analyzed everything that happened the last couple of hours.

The closeness between us at times. The way he looked at me as I described an art piece. The way he smiled and the way his eyes glowed at times. The way he said my name.

I made myself not think about those things in the car, but now that I'm in my dorm, I'm giving myself free rein.

Thank God I don't have a roommate, because me having to explain why I'm obsessing over someone who not only hates me, but is not my-supposed boyfriend is a little embarrassing.

Maybe even thinking about the man in my room is dangerous.

I throw myself on my bed and take out my phone from my sweater pocket and look at the pictures I took today. That won't have me thinking about Lucas.

Starting with the picture I took for the assignment. I had set up my phone on the floor and put on the timer to take a full body picture with a few art pieces in the back. The phone was in a corner, and I had set up the camera so that it was zoomed out, and it was able to capture most of the room.

It's a cute picture and my smile is bright. It's worth of

not only sending it to my professor for extra credit points but also to posting it on social media.

The thing that is stopping me from posting it, though, is the individual in the back. I'm the only person in the room, but from the angle of the camera, you can see into the next room, straight into the neighboring exhibit. An exhibit that Lucas happened to be in while I took the picture.

His sketchbook is in his hand and he is looking over his shoulder, right at me. It must have been just a quick action because I see that he has a small smile on his face when I zoom in.

He was probably smiling at something he was drawing and then turned, and my camera captured the action.

I zoom out and look at the other pictures.

Most of them are pictures of the art pieces that I really liked and of the sunset. There are only two other pictures besides the first one that have Lucas in them.

One is of a piece in the second to last exhibit that was also taken with a wide angle, and I was able to get Lucas as he faced it. And the other, I didn't realize I had even taken it.

The last picture is of the parking garage. I must have opened my camera accidentally and took a picture of Lucas speeding off on his bike.

I stare at the picture a lot longer than I should.

From what I've seen, Lucas drives a four-door to school, so seeing him on a bike threw me off a bit. I won't lie though, there is something hot about seeing Lucas riding a bike like that. No, not hot. Sexy.

There is definitely something sexy about it.

I guess I will add that to the list of things that make me attracted to this guy.

And I am attracted to Lucas, and after seeing him today and spending time with him and talking to him, that attraction has gone through the roof.

Before today, that attraction was just superficial, solely based on his looks. Lucas is a very beautiful man, and that voice of his melts me every time, but what I was experiencing from him as a person was not something I liked.

Today I saw a different person. One I wish I could see more of.

But I highly doubt he would ever see me in the same light I see him. He probably will always see me as a spoiled girl who only cares about herself and has a shitty boyfriend.

Speaking of which... he must have put a mind-reading device in my head or something, because as soon as I think about Jason, my phone starts ringing with a call from him.

I didn't have the patience to deal with him earlier today, and I sure as hell don't have the patience to deal with him now.

Ignoring the call, I go back to looking at the pictures from today, specifically the three that have Lucas in them.

They might be my favorites.

One day with the guy, and I'm already developing feelings for him. That's definitely not good, but I don't care.

At least not tonight.

Tonight, I'm going to let my mind think every thought that it can that has Lucas in it.

I'm going to let my mind think about the way his voice sounds.

Of what it feels like to have his eyes on me.

Of what it might feel like for him to touch me.

My hand has been on him a few times, and it has been electrifying. The second my skin meets his, it's like this electrical current is traveling through me and lighting up every nerve that my body has.

I can't help but wonder if it would feel that way if he were the one to touch me and with purpose.

Would it be the same? Would it be more?

He's a mechanic, he works with cars and tools. Would his hands feel rough against my skin? Would he be gentle with me?

How would it feel if he kissed me? If his full lips met mine? Would I see stars and want more?

Or if he was kissing me and his mouth started to travel down my body and he didn't stop until his mouth settled between my thighs, what would that feel like?

It would probably feel like the best feeling in the world.

So many fantasies and scenarios are running wild in my head right now, all thanks to Lucas, that I can't help but to start touching myself.

I start at my chest and then move down, and when my fingers meet the apex of my thighs, I find myself wet. Soaking wet for a man who hates me and who I'm supposed to hate back.

I don't hate him. Not tonight at least.

Reaching into my nightstand, I bring out my favorite

vibrator and let myself experience multiple orgasms at the thought of Lucas Reyes.

It will never happen in real life. Might as well let my mind run wild with everything, I want him to do to my body.

Brand every inch of it and mark me as his. All the while, I scream out his name and beg for more.

CHAPTER TWELVE

LUCAS

THE SECOND I take off my helmet, I regret my decision to tell Kaiden I was going to come tonight.

I'm not even inside the house yet, and I already hate this party.

The music is way too fucking loud, it looks like it jammed packed with people, and I swear I already smell puke all over the place. I already want to leave.

But, I told Kaiden earlier this week that I would stop by for a few. I'll go in, find him, and then get out. I don't have to be here more than necessary, especially since Jason is the president. If he were to see me, without a doubt, all hell would break loose.

So, the quicker I'm out of here the better.

Locking my helmet to my bike, I make my way to the main entrance.

If someone would have told me that there would be a line to get into this party, I would have thought that they were crazy. But there is, and on top of there being a line, there's a freaking list.

I give the guy, who looks like he just turned eighteen, my name, and he waves me in. I guess Kaiden put me on the list because it sure as hell wasn't his president.

It makes me wonder, though, if Jason checked the list before handing it to the door guy and knows that I'm coming or if Kaiden was able to add me without him noticing it.

Since Jason and his posse of frat bros aren't standing by the door waiting for me, I'm going to guess that Kaiden snuck me in.

As I walk deeper into the house, I'm taken back to my teen years and the parties that my friends would throw. They were exactly like this, except with a lot more beer and a different type of music.

This was my scene for a bit but now that I rarely see those people and became a dad, it's definitely not my scene now.

Before grabbing a drink, I shoot off a text to Kaiden letting him know that I'm here.

As I get a drink, I come to learn that Jason and his posse are the only severe douchebags, because everyone I've encountered so far has been friendly enough. Even had a guy compliment me on the tattoo on my neck.

I'm swapping tattoo stories with another guy when Kaiden comes into the room, a huge smile on his face.

"Lucas! I'm glad you can make it, dude," he says, as we give each other a clap on the back.

"Yeah. I figure it wouldn't hurt to come hang out for a bit."

"That's my man," Kaiden says.

The three of us spend a few more minutes standing around by the drinks just shooting the shit. Eventually, we make our way outside where we aren't being suffocated by people looking to get a drink in their hands.

"I'm surprised that Jason let you put my name on the list." I muse to Kaiden after taking a drink of my second beer.

Kaiden rolls his eyes at my statement, his cheeks getting a little red from what I can see in the night sky.

"I might have snuck you in after he approved the list. Paid the door guy fifty bucks." He grabs at his neck, looking a little embarrassed.

I let out a bark of a laugh. "I want to see his face when he sees me. He might finally snap and try to hit me."

"Jason hates you?" Arden, the guy who I struck up a conversation with in the kitchen, asks.

I give him a nod. "Has from day one. Doesn't like me calling him out on his shit."

"Fuck. But hey, I'm glad someone called him out. The guy is in serious need of a reality check. He thinks the world revolves around him."

I guess Jason gets on everyone's nerves.

"I have no idea how you guys deal with him day in and day out. I'd be stabbing a fork into my eyes every time I heard him speak."

"Trust me, I've thought about it," Arden says.

The more I talk to these two guys, the more I'm liking

them. I was definitely wrong in clumping together all these frat guys. It only takes one bad seed to make you hate all the others.

That's exactly what I did with Savannah, and I hate myself for it. Especially after spending a few hours with her at the museum. In those few hours, I saw her bring down a mask that she wears so well, and I like her for it.

It makes me wonder if the person she is in everyday life is just a front to hide who she really is.

That's what's on my mind as I look around the yard to see if maybe I can find her in the crowd of people.

Her boyfriend is here, so maybe she is too.

Do I plan on approaching her? No, but I feel the need to have eyes on her for some reason.

Kaiden, Arden, and I continue our conversation about everything and anything, and when I'm about to suggest a third beer, I hear a voice right behind me that makes my blood boil.

Jason.

"What the actual fuck is he doing here? This is an invitation-only party, and he wasn't invited."

Turning, I'm met with Jason's bitty eyes and a scowl that would only scare a bunny rabbit. Dude looks high out of his mind on top of everything else.

"I *was* invited," I say to him, just to piss him off some more.

"By who?" he growls out his question, looking at the two guys behind me.

"Who knows? I just got a random text and was told that my name was on the list. Maybe you missed it. For all

I know, you sent the text." No way am I going to throw Kaiden under the bus.

"Bullshit." He takes a step closer to me, but in the process, he stumbles a bit, confirming that he's high. Once he stabilizes himself, he steps into my space.

My hands form into fists, and I stare the fucker down.

I won't throw the first punch, but I won't hesitate in throwing the second.

"If I were you, I would take a step back," I say through gritted teeth.

"What are you going to do? Hit me? I'll have your ass in jail by the morning. I'm sure you're used to it."

Tensions are running high, and people are taking notice, because soon we are surrounded by more people on top of Kaiden and Arden. There are people telling Jason to back down, while others are encouraging him.

"You don't know what you're talking about," I growl.

"I know exactly what I'm talking about. You already look the part. It's where you belong. Especially since you're trying to go after my girl."

You send a kiss to a girl one time in front of her boyfriend, and he goes batshit crazy.

He doesn't give a shit about her, but he probably sees how affected she is by me, and because he sees me as below him, as the gang banger with a reputation, he is going to do anything to bring me down.

He can try, but he won't succeed.

"Maybe your girl would rather be with someone else who's not you. Someone who would treat her with some decency." Do I mean that person could be me? No, but the way Jason's face shifts, he sees it that way.

My statement was my declaration of war for Savannah.

If he wants to fight for her, let's have at it. It's not like we'll end up together. But I rather see her alone than with fucker.

"I treat her with fucking decency," he says through his teeth.

"Sure you do. From what I hear, you cheat on her every chance you get. Take the brunette, for example. I bet she was more than happy to be your side piece."

A fist slams against my jaw before I even finish my sentence.

I stumble back and reach up to touch where the fist landed. No blood, but fuck, it hurt. It looks like Jason boy here, has some power behind him.

For thirty seconds—I know because I counted—I try to keep myself controlled, to keep myself from beating the ever-living shit out of this bastard.

It doesn't work though. Once the thirty seconds are up, I'm not controlled in the way I want to be, and I start swinging.

My fist lands against Jason's nose, and another lands against his jaw. Jason lands one right in the center of my face. I get one more hit in before I'm pulled away from him by Kaiden and Arden.

Jason looks like he wants to strangle me, and maybe he would have if his buddies weren't holding him back.

"You motherfucker. How dare you come into my fucking house and disrespect me. Do you have any idea who I am? I can fucking end you!" Jason yells out as he thrashes against his friends, ready for the next round.

I could end this guy right here and now, but given that he already threatened me with jail, and I wouldn't put it past him. It's better to get out of here while I still can. While I still have a clean record.

I untangle myself from Arden's and Kaiden's hold and walk straight over to Jason. His friends jump back a little bit as I get closer to him, but I couldn't care less about them.

"You may be a rich fucker, but I have friends in high places who couldn't give two shits about a guy like you. Do what you want but know your stupid-ass threats don't mean anything to me." I pull back my arm and land one last punch right into his stomach.

Jason doubles over, and I walk away. I'll apologize to my friends later, but right now I need to leave before shit gets more out of hand.

I make my way through the yard and then through the house. I'm almost to the front door when someone steps into my line of sight.

For a second, I think that it is Jason or one of his buddies looking for more trouble but when my eyes focus in the darkness of the room, I see I'm wrong.

It's not Jason and his buddies, but Savannah.

That might be worse.

"What are you doing here?" she asks, a smile playing at her lips. Her tone tells me that she is happy that I'm here. Definitely a change from before, when that same question came out with a bite to it.

"I was invited. Now I'm leaving," I say, side stepping her and heading toward the door.

But, of course, she is quick and a second later she's back to being in front of me.

"Wait, why?" I hear the hurt in her tone.

She thinks I'm leaving because of her.

"Because if I stay any longer, you may have to plan your boyfriend's funeral."

Even with music playing all around us, I can still hear a small gasp leave her.

I think she's going to drop it, that she's going to let me go, when takes out her phone and turns on her flashlight, shining it on my face.

My eyes can't help but close at the brightness.

"You're bleeding," she states, stepping closer to me.

"Yeah, thanks to your boyfriend," I say, trying to walk around her, but she keeps getting in the way. "Savannah, move."

"No. Tell me why you're bleeding."

"I told you, it's thanks to your boyfriend. Now move." I don't mean to raise my voice at her, but she doesn't even flinch.

Savannah shakes her head and steps even closer to me, taking my hand in hers.

Before I can even ask what the hell she is even doing, she is trying to drag me in a different direction.

"C'mon."

"Savannah, I fucking swear I don't want to deal with your shit right now."

I could easily take my hand out of hers. I could easily

stop us from walking any further and get out of here, but I don't. I just continue to follow her until we reach a bathroom, and she pulls me in, closing the door behind me.

The light gets flipped on, and my eyes take a second to adjust.

I'm still blinking through the brightness of the room when I feel a gentle, soft hand against my cheek.

The action makes me flinch, not because she's touching me but because of the pain, but it still causes her to drop her hand.

"It's swollen," she says, looking at me with concern in her eyes.

"That's what happens when you get punched in the face," I state, my voice a bit cold.

"Why did Jason punch you?" she asks, and doesn't it go over my head that she's in here with me and not out in the yard with her man.

I could lie. I could lie and tell her that it was just a misunderstanding, that I got in his way or something. I can even tell her that he didn't like the fact that I was here. That would be the truth.

That's what I could do, what should come out of my mouth, but I don't give a shit anymore.

Her boyfriend is a scum, and she deserves to know. What she does with the information is on her, not me.

"Because I called him out on how he treated you. How you need someone who will treat you with some decency and respect," I say, watching her as she listens to my words.

Her eyes go a wide, but she quickly controls her expression.

"He treats me just fine," she throws back.

From the look on her face, she is trying her hardest to make me believe her words, but from what I can see, she has a hard time believing them too.

Hearing those words pisses me off.

"Are you seriously blind to all the shit that he does behind your back? Do you seriously not know that he cheats on you with any girl who gives him attention? That the fucker is walking all over you?"

With every one of my words, she backs up until she is resting against the vanity. Her bottom lip is between her teeth, and her eyes are looking anywhere but me.

She knows. She knows that Jason is a cheating bastard, and she's still with him. I can see it written all over her face.

"All of that isn't news to you, isn't it? You know that your preppy boyfriend is fucking every girl on this campus. You know, and you're turning a blind eye to it. Why the fuck don't you just leave him?"

My voice is getting higher the more questions I ask. I can feel anger starting to form in my body. I thought this girl was smarter than this. I thought that, given the persona that she puts out, that she wouldn't stand for this shit. Guess I was wrong.

"It's complicated," she yells back, her face getting red.

"Fuck complicated, Savannah. That fucker is walking all over you, and you're letting it happen. What? Did he promise you a pretty ring and all the money in the world to not kick him to the curb?"

"No," she says lower now. My eyes watch as she

crosses her arms along her chest, her perfect tits on full display through the neckline of her shirt.

My hand twitches to reach out and touch her smooth skin.

"Then why the fuck are you still with him? You can have any guy in the world and you're with that fucker? That makes no sense," I say through gritted teeth.

"Why do you care? Maybe I want to be. Maybe I want to be with him. You don't even like me. Why the fuck do you care what happens in my relationship?"

All of those are good questions, and I don't have an answer to them.

All I know is what my body is telling me.

So I show her.

I show her why I care.

CHAPTER THIRTEEN

SAVANNAH

THERE IS a fire in his eyes that I have never seen before. In all the weeks that we have spent in the same classroom and during our limited interaction, I have never seen him look at me this way.

Like I hold the air that his body needs, and like his life depends on me.

That's the look I got a glimpse of before he closes the distance between us, and Lucas presses his lips against mine.

For a long second, I didn't know what to do. I didn't know what was happening, and I lost all my bearings. But I quickly recovered, and now I'm opening my mouth for him and letting him in.

Given our history, and all the shit that we've said to each other and all the hate we throw in each other's direction, I should push him away. He has no right to kiss me.

Yet, I can't find it in myself to stop. I can't find it in myself to push him away.

Lucas's hands are in my hair and on my body, his lips are against mine, and his tongue is dancing along with mine.

This image is the same one that I have been playing on repeat in my head ever since the museum. I've played with myself to this image, and now I'm experiencing it in real life, and I don't want it to stop.

I don't even care that this is happening in a bathroom inside of a frat house.

Lucas pulls at my hair, leaning my head back so when he detaches his lips from mine, he has enough room to travel down the column of my neck.

"I shouldn't care. I don't *want* to care. But I fucking do," he says, right before he sticks out his tongue and flattens it against my pulse point. "He doesn't deserve you."

I'm a panting mess, but I'm still able to respond. "And you do?"

He doesn't need to give me an answer. I know just from the museum alone that Lucas Reyes would be a hell of a better boyfriend than Jason ever was.

Lucas pulls his face back from its place against my neck and looks down at me once again with that look of hunger.

"*Corazón*, I'm a delinquent from the wrong side of the tracks. I will never be deserving of you."

I want to tell him that he's wrong, but I keep my words to myself.

Wanting to feel Lucas's mouth on me again, I thread my fingers through his hair and bring his face back down to mine.

This man knows what he's doing with his mouth, tongue, and hands and is, most definitely, the complete opposite of Jason.

In all the time that Jason and I were together, he had never once kissed me the way that Lucas is kissing me now. With Jason, it was just a pastime. With Lucas, it's everything.

I feel Lucas's hands travel down my body until they are at my waist, lifting me up and depositing me on the counter of the vanity.

He steps into the space between my thighs, and I bring him close enough that there is barely an inch of space between us.

We kiss for who knows how long, and as I feel his fingers digging into my bare thighs, I wish that he would lift my skirt just a tiny bit and make me feel his fingers somewhere else.

As if he reads my mind, Lucas slides one of his hands up my thigh little by little. Enough to caress my skin but not enough to get where I want him to.

I've never wanted a man to touch my pussy as badly as I do now.

Eventually though, I get my wish. I just needed to be patient.

As we continue to kiss, I feel my skirt go up higher, until I feel his knuckles glide against my most sensitive area.

I'm wet, and I know he feels it.

"Tell me, *Corazón*. Has the bastard ever gotten you this excited? Or does your pussy only get this wet for me?" He takes my bottom lip between his teeth, and I can't help but let out a whimper. "Answer the question, Savannah. Does your boyfriend make you as excited as I do?"

I don't even have to think about it. The answer is no. Jason never made me feel like this, never made me excited for anything sexual with him. I thought that it was just a phase, that when we got deeper into our relationship, I would, but it never happened.

Now, one kiss from Lucas and I want to feel so much more than what I'm feeling right now.

"No," I answer truthfully through a pant, as Lucas's mouth travels back to my neck and then down to my chest, his knuckles still stroking me through my panties.

"I bet the fucker has never touched you right. Or even been on his knees for you."

I shake my head, even though he's not looking up. "No, he hasn't."

"That should be reason enough to walk away, *Corazón.*" My head is spinning to make a scene of his words. Even more so when I feel him slide my panties to the side, and he slides a finger along the fold of my pussy.

Oh my god, other than myself and my toys, nobody has ever touched me there before. Not even Jason.

And the fact that it's Lucas doing it, it's making me a little crazy.

"You need a man who will worship you, not a boy who fucks around."

Is that man going to be him? If I leave Jason for good, will Lucas be the man that will worship me?

Everything in me wants him to answer yes.

If my body is this responsive to him with a few simple touches and kisses, imagine what would happen with more.

I'm about to ask him, when there's a bang on the door, causing me to jump and pull away from Lucas.

"It's busy," Lucas yells toward the door.

We wait for the person on the other side to say something, and when they don't, we assume that they decided to look for another bathroom.

The second that the bang sounded through the room; it was as if an ice bucket was poured on me.

I just made out with Lucas. I had his hand on me all the while I was in a house where my supposed boyfriend is.

Jason and I may not be together, but I still have an image to uphold. If I walk out of here with Lucas, and someone sees us, they are going to think that I'm just like Jason. A cheater.

"You're closing off," Lucas voices, taking me out of my mental spiral.

"What?" I ask, jumping off the vanity and fixing my skirt in the process.

"As soon as the knock sounded, you started to close off. Your body was alive a minute ago, and now it's dim."

He picks up on everything, doesn't he?

I let out a sigh. "We shouldn't have done that, and it can't happen again." No matter how much I want it to.

Lucas looks at me for a long minute, not saying a single word, scrutinizing me.

Eventually, he just nods and takes a step away toward the door.

When he has a hand on the doorknob, I stop him. "Lucas. I'm sorry," I whisper.

What am I sorry for exactly? I don't know but I felt the need to apologize.

"I'm not the one who you need to apologize to," he says, his face stoic when he turns back to face me.

"What do you mean?" Is he seriously suggesting I apologize to Jason for kissing someone else while we're not together? Never. He's never apologized to me.

"I mean that you should apologize to yourself. For staying with that fucker. He's a piece of shit and everyone knows it. Except you, apparently. But hey, what do I know? I can be a piece of shit too. Maybe that's your type or something."

Maybe it is.

"You should leave. Nobody can see us together," I say to him, not meeting his stare.

"Yeah, because god forbid you get seen with a guy like me," he states.

I finally look up and met his gaze. "I didn't mean it that way, and you know it," I growl at him.

"Do I, though?" he asks, and at this point, he is just being an ass.

Gone is the man who was making my body sing like no one else has and telling me that he cares. Gone is the guy I spent hours with at the museum or the guy who helped me with my tires.

In his place is the guy who has hated me from the first second he saw me.

I don't want to be anywhere near that person.

"You can leave now," I say to him through my teeth.

"Gladly. If the fucker destroys the light in you even more, don't come running to me. I will just tell you, 'I told you so' and that you should have walked a long time ago." He gives me one final look before he opens the door and starts to head out. "Have fun with your asshole boyfriend, Savannah."

"We can never work," I throw out right before he closes the door behind him.

Lucas stops, the halfway closed door blocking my view of him. "I'm not asking you for a relationship, Savannah. Hell, I'm not even asking you for one night. I'm asking you to put yourself first and throw the asshole who is cheating on you out of your life. Besides, with my past, I probably wouldn't be good for you either."

And with that, the door closes, and he's gone.

And I'm left in a bathroom, wanting to cry at what my life has turned into.

CHAPTER FOURTEEN

SAVANNAH

I STAYED in the bathroom a whole lot longer than I needed to.

Mostly to collect myself so nobody would accuse me of being with a guy in here, but also to get my head on straight about everything that happened with Lucas.

For the first time in my life, a guy made me feel alive, and I told him to leave because I put my toxic situationship first.

I could have told Lucas what was going on between me and Jason. He could have left the bathroom knowing that Jason and I weren't together. But he already thinks of me as a girl who is letting someone walk all over her. What would he think if he knew the actual truth?

At this point, I don't want to know.

So, after about twenty minutes, I left the bathroom and went back to the party.

I went back to the group of girls who I was with when I saw Lucas. The game girls who don't a shit about me and only hang out with me because of who my boyfriend is and the uniform I wear. They didn't even notice that I was gone. To them, I hardly matter.

I bet I hardly matter to anyone in this house.

Not even to my so-called boyfriend.

About twenty minutes or so after I left the bathroom, the guys came back into the house. They had left to smoke some weed outside about an hour ago, which might have been when Jason and Lucas had their run-in.

Now they're back, and I can't help but to look at each of their faces and see if they have any bruising.

Lucas had said that Jason had punched him but didn't say if anyone else was involved.

From the looks of things, everyone is un-scratched. Everyone except Jason, of course.

The second he comes into the room, my eyes go directly to the bag of ice he's holding against his face. More specifically, his nose. The room may be dark, but some light is shining, and it's enough for me to see blood on his shirt.

Without a doubt, Lucas had the upper hand.

Jason looks around the room, and when he meets my stare, he waves me over.

With a sigh, I leave the group of girls and head over to him.

The second I'm within a two-foot radius of him, he reaches out and grabs me by the arm, dragging my body as close to his as possible.

He drops the bag of eyes and gives me a murderous glare.

"Did you invite him?" he ask, through his teeth.

From where I'm standing, I can see how dilated his eyes are.

I try to get out of his hold, but it's no use, his fingers are digging so deep into my skin that the pain is holding me in place.

"Did I invite who? And what the hell happened to your face?" I have to play dumb. He can't know that I know, or that Lucas was the one that told me.

"Don't play fucking dumb with me. Did you invite the fucker who you've been flirting with all semester into my house?"

Flirting with?

He thinks I've been flirting with Lucas all semester?

Lucas and I have been at each other's throats all damn semester. Besides him calling me *Corazón* and throwing a kiss or two in my direction, there hasn't been any flirting.

Is Jason fucking delusional?

I know he hates the guy and saw him as a threat, but I didn't think it was this bad.

Besides, nothing has happened between me and Lucas until this week. Even then, I don't owe anything to Jason. We're not together.

I reach over and try to pry Jason's hand off me. "One, I wouldn't invite anyone to this party. The people who would come hate me, and the people who might actually like me don't want to be at a party you're hosting. Two, I haven't been flirting with anyone. You have. Why the hell would you care who I do and don't flirt with?"

His fingers dig deeper into my arm. Without a doubt he is going to leave a mark.

"Shut up," he says through his teeth.

"Why? It's the truth," I spit back.

I'm being a brat at this point. I know why he wants me to shut up. He has an image to uphold. He may be sleeping with every girl who comes his way and acts like a big man on campus for it, but he still wants people to see him in a certain light. He wants people to see him as the best boyfriend in the world.

Newsflash, he can't have it both ways.

"You don't know what you're talking about."

"You're serious? I'm not fucking blind, Jason, or stupid, for that matter. I know all the shit you do."

Why is he acting like me knowing all of this is new to him?

"And why do I do the shit I do, huh? Because you wouldn't give me what I fucking wanted. I gave you your precious time of waiting and when I got impatient, I looked somewhere else. Maybe now, if you put out, things will be different," Jason spits out, his face getting red, finally letting down the shield of the perfect boyfriend.

"Maybe, if you would accept our break up for what it is, instead of going to my father to force me to stay with you, you wouldn't have to do your shit in secret."

I try to shove him off me again, but he isn't budging.

"Where's the fun in that?" he snarls. From the corner of my eye, I see that we've captured the attention of a few people. Maybe if they see who this guy really is, Jason will finally stop.

"We're over. Jason. Fucking accept it, and let me go," I say, meaning it both in the figurative and literal sense.

"You're mine, Savannah." Jason brings his face inches away from mine. His breath reeks of alcohol. "Your father said so. Why else do you think he forced you to stay with me? You're mine, no matter how much whining you do. Nothing is going to change. You have a problem with my cheating, then do something about it." His other hand lands between my thighs and he cups me to the point of pain. "I've told you before, Savannah. If you let me fuck you, the cheating stops, but you won't listen. You need to open your damn legs, and we can be the perfect couple that you know we can be."

The feeling of his hand on my most sensitive area makes me want to puke. Having his hands on me makes me feel disgusting and nothing like how I felt when Lucas touched me.

As I stare up at Jason, I realize that Lucas was right. Jason is a scumbag, and I need to leave him. I need to end whatever is going on with us, or he will destroy me beyond repair. Take my light away, as Lucas stated.

I already hate myself for the person I've become while being with him this long. How much hate is going to be running through me if I let him get away with this for longer?

I don't want to find out.

"No," I say with as much conviction as I can muster. "I don't belong to you. I don't belong to anyone. You can go to fucking hell, because I'm done with you, with this, with everything. I'm fucking done."

With all the strength that I have, I'm able to get my arm out of Jason's death grip and shove him back. He wasn't expecting it, so he stumbles back, his whole body falling to the floor.

The music around us stops, and the lights turn on. Everyone at this party just witnessed what happened, probably heard our words, but I don't give a shit anymore.

They can think whatever the hell they want. I'm done with this fucked up shit show.

"You walk away from me, Savannah, and you're done with. Nobody will want anything to do with you!" Jason yells at me as I turn and walk away.

"I don't fucking care. You can go fuck yourself," I yell back, not turning to give him a second glance.

As I walk out of the house, I feel powerful. I feel as if I'm someone who I'm proud of.

Someone who my mom would be proud of.

———

ME PUSHING Jason to the floor and walking out on him has made it to social media, specifically TikTok and Instagram. There are videos and pictures of the whole thing all over my feeds, and I can't seem to escape them. New angles pop up every so often.

People are talking, and some of the things that they are saying are surprising, to say the least.

Some people are standing behind me and are saying how proud they are of me for walking away from such a toxic asshole.

Others are calling me a bitch for breaking up with Jason. I guess those people are blind to the bastard that Jason is too.

After seeing so many posts, my head started to hurt. To add to the headache, Jason has been texting nonstop since I left the frat house last night.

I've read them, every single one, and after each one, I couldn't stop thinking how stupid I was to even get into a relationship with this guy in the first place.

He's a narcissistic asshole who sees nothing wrong with his actions. In his mind, he can do no wrong and, in this scenario, I'm the bad guy.

Yes, I have my flaws. Yes, I'm a damn bitch, but I'm not at his level.

Either way, people are right to have hate toward me. Lucas has every right to hate me, because I associated myself with someone as controlling and egotistical as Jason. And for so long.

I really need to reevaluate myself, something that I should have done when I first called it off with Jason. Maybe then, I would have had more of a sense of the person I really am and the person that I want to be.

But instead, I spent nearly a year stewing in my hatred and dislike for a person and became someone who I don't even recognize.

Weirdly enough, the only time I've gotten some sort of recognition as to who I really am, was when I was with someone who hated everything that I portrayed.

I was only really myself when Lucas was around.

At the museum, in the bathroom.

Why only Lucas?

It may be because, for the first time in a while, someone came into my life who didn't know me, who didn't know my father's name and wanted something in return because of it.

Lucas called it as he saw it, though. He saw the rich girl who hasn't worked a day in her life at this elite school and slapped a label on me. He saw me for who I was portraying to the world and judged me for it.

No matter how hard I tried to tell him I wasn't that person, he still judged me.

But even through the judgment, he still cared.

That's the mind-boggling part. We both have hatred towards each other, and yet he still cared. He said so himself.

He cared enough to tell me to leave Jason because he knew Jason was just using me. He knew that, if I continued with Jason, I would never forgive myself for it.

I'm asking you to put yourself first.

Not a relationship with him. Not a one-night stand, but to put myself first.

Out of everything that Lucas has said to me, those are the words that I need to listen to.

Leaving Jason once and for all was the first step in that.

But what's the second and the one after that?

I probably wouldn't be good for you either.

What if he is?

I won't know if I don't ask, right?

CHAPTER FIFTEEN

LUCAS

MY MIND IS A JUMBLED-UP MESS. It has been since I left the party last night.

I can't seem to take my mind off a certain blonde with a mouth so sweet that it has me craving more.

Savannah's mouth isn't the only thing that has been taking up every single one of my thoughts. I've also been thinking about how her heat felt against my hand. My thoughts haven't been all sexual, though.

I've also been thinking about the relationship between her and the fuckwad.

Look, I'm not one to talk when it comes to being in a bad relationship. The one between Celeste and me was not healthy for either of us, no matter how many times or how hard we tried. We may be good co-parents and friends, but we didn't work in a relationship.

Celeste and I realized that and there were no hard feelings. Both of us were good to walk away and move on with no thoughts of reconciliation.

I made sure of that last one a few weeks ago, because neither of us are mentally nor emotionally capable of going through that again. Thank God Celeste agreed.

That's the difference between the two relationships. Celeste and I didn't hold each other back when walking away, but from the looks of things, Jason holds back Savannah. In everything.

The line I was drawing skips a bit, and I let out a frustrated sigh. This is what I was talking about, my mind is a mess and even drawing isn't helping.

It's Sunday, and even though the garage closes at two, I told Flaco that I was going to stay behind to put in some work on the hood I needed to finish. Since I have Mia this week, it might be the only time I will be able to stay late.

I'm trying to get the work done, but every time I think I have my concentration on point, I think about Savannah and the douchebag and get thrown off.

Grabbing a clean shop towel, I wipe away the line I just drew and start it over.

I'm currently working on customizing the hood of a '66 Impala. I've been working on it all month but because I had finals, the semester was about to end and Mia to take care of, I'm not at the stage I want to be at with it.

When I planned things out, as I got to this point, I should have been around ninety percent done, but with the way life played out, I'm not.

Thankfully, the guy who contracted us to do the job for him isn't picking it up until the beginning of June, so I have time.

I look over at my sketchbook to double check my

design, and when I'm happy with the placement of things, I continue to mark up the hood.

When I was a kid, I would draw on any surface my mom would let me draw on. Drawing is to me what reading is to others. It calms me, lets me forget about everything going on in life. For a few years though, I abandoned it and did other things to calm me.

It wasn't until I was sixteen that I picked up a pencil again to draw something. Weirdly enough, it was here at the garage, and when Flaco saw that I could draw, he started teaching me about car restoration and customization.

He taught me so much, that by my twentieth birthday, I was making a few extra bucks painting hoods.

I haven't done a whole lot, since hood paintings aren't as popular as they were in the nineties, but I've done enough to get my name out there and get clients every now and then.

Hopefully, with a few more years under my belt, I will be able to build a car from the ground up.

For now, though, I'm happy doing what I'm doing.

I take another look at my references and sketch out the next part, the design finally coming along.

For the next hour or so, I get lost in my work. Solely thinking about the design and getting it right, and not thinking about a certain blonde.

Though she does try to creep up into my thoughts every so often. I just push those thoughts down and go back to working.

I'm so enthralled in the movement of my marker, I

don't realize how late it has gotten until I look up and see that it's almost dark outside.

Looking over at the clock over the door, I see that it's almost time for Celeste to drop off Mia.

I guess it's time to close up shop.

I'm in the middle of putting away my things and shutting off the radio when I hear a car pull up to one of the bay doors.

There are times where we get a customer this time of day, hoping that we are open so they can get a quick oil change or put air in their tires. Ninety-nine percent of the time, it doesn't work in their favor.

Given that I have to head home to get my kid, tonight won't work in their favor either.

I head outside, and I'm about to tell the person that we are closed when the words die in my mouth.

Someone did, in fact, pull into the bay, but it's not a customer. It's Savannah.

My mind had to conjure her up somehow as punishment for going an hour or so without thinking about her.

I take a second to look at her.

Her hair is down and in waves cascading down her back. She's wearing a school sweatshirt that looks to be about four times too big that happens to land at her mid-thigh. Even though she is dressed down, it still looks like she put some effort into her appearance.

She looks gorgeous.

"We're closed," I say to her, my voice sounding a bit harsh.

"I know," she says as she fidgets with her hands.

"Then what are you doing here, Savannah?" I ask, crossing my arms across my chest.

Given what happened last night, I can guess.

"I was passing by and saw that the shop light was on and so I stopped to see if anyone was still here. If you were still here," she says, in almost a whisper. Like a little kid who's about to get in trouble.

"Why?"

"Because I needed help with my tires?" she speaks. There's still enough light out for me to see that a small blush creeps up her face.

She's lying, but I'll go along with her game. "What's wrong with them?" I ask, raising an eyebrow at her.

That blush of hers gets slightly deeper. "Um, they need air, I think."

I close my eyes and let out a sigh in the process. "What are you really doing here, Savannah?"

She continues to look at me, not saying a word, and fidgeting with her hands.

Eventually she sighs and breaks the silence. "I was hoping that maybe we could talk."

"Talk," I state.

She gives me a nod.

"We talked quite a lot last night, don't you think?" I say to her.

Well, we argued back and forth, and in between, we had a make out session that has embedded itself in my mind.

If I think hard enough, I can still feel her heat against my knuckles.

"We did, but I wanted to come by and get my 'I told you so' and apologize." Savannah bows her head, and her voice lowers.

Get my 'I told you so'.

What I told her before I left the bathroom comes running back to my mind. I was annoyed at the whole situation, annoyed that she was letting some asshole walk all over her and she wasn't doing anything about it. When I told her that she deserved a whole lot more, I wasn't lying. She deserves everything and not what Jason was giving her.

I thought that if we were ever to have this conversation, it would be way later in the future, not the day after.

"Apologize for what?" I ask, ignoring the 'I told you so' for now.

"For a lot of things," she says, taking a step closer to me. "For kicking you out of the bathroom. For closing off. For treating you like crap when all you were trying to do is help me open my eyes to something that was right in front of me. For treating you like crap in general."

I look at her, really look at her, and all I see is sincerity in her face and in her eyes. She means every word. She sees herself as the bad guy in this scenario, and she shouldn't. Both of us are at fault, not just her.

"I treated you like crap too. You know that right? I said things to you that I shouldn't have and judged even though you kept telling me I was wrong."

She gives me a nod. "I do know that, but I still want to say I'm sorry."

More than one time, I accused her of judging me for

the way I looked, insinuated that she was racist, and she's the one apologizing. That's messed up.

"Since my mom died, I've been a little cold. Well, more than a little cold. So when everything happened with Jason, I just closed off and became a total bitch. Hoity-toity like you said. It took me a while to realize that that personality wasn't who I am or who I want to be. So I'm here to apologize for being a bitch and to tell you that I finally left Jason. It wasn't without a fight, but he and I are officially over." She gives me a small smile and looks nothing like the girl that gave me a look of indifference the first day of the semester.

She was pretty then, but she is beautiful now.

"I'm sorry too," I tell her, my arms falling to my side, feeling a bit defeated.

She gives a smile and takes another step closer.

"What did you mean by you left Jason, but it wasn't without a fight?"

Her eyes cast down as if she is debating telling me the truth or not.

"Things got a little heated after you left. He grabbed me in... places. Leaving marks on my arm. Said a few things. After a bit, I was able to shove him away and leave."

Places.

He grabbed her in *places*. I don't need a degree to know what those places are.

I feel the urge to kill the bastard even more.

I look down at my feet, taking a few deep breaths, trying to control myself from going ballistic. "Are you okay?"

When she doesn't answer, I look up at her. Her bottom lip is back to being between her teeth. From where I'm standing, she looks like she is going to cry.

Finally, after a minute, she gives me a nod.

She may be okay physically, but I don't know if she's okay emotionally or mentally.

As much as I want to ask, I don't. She may have opened up about a few things, but I don't think we are there for things that go deeper.

"If Jason tries anything else, let me know. I wouldn't mind punching the fucker a few more times," I offer instead. I don't know why, it's not like we're friends or anything.

"You don't have to do that." Another smile in my direction.

"I know, but maybe I want to."

Savannah comes closer to me, and all I can do is stuff my hands into my pockets so that I don't reach out for her and have a repeat of last night.

"Look, I know I said that the kiss from shouldn't have happened and that it can't happen again, but—"

She stops talking when another car drives up and parks right next to her car.

I'm so busy trying to piece together what she was about to say that I don't realize who just pulled up until Celeste gets out of the car.

Taking my gaze off Savannah, I look over at my ex.

"What are you doing here? I thought I was meeting you at the house."

Celeste looks at me, then looks over at Savannah before turning back to me and raising an eyebrow at me.

Before she can answer my question, something bangs against her back window.

Mia has seen me and is getting impatient that she's not getting out of the car fast enough.

Leaving my proximity to Savannah, I head over to Celeste's car and take out Mia.

The second that she's in my arms I give a kiss on her cheek.

I hear a gasp from a few feet away.

Looking up, I see Savannah staring at me, Mia, and Celeste, with her mouth slightly open.

Bet she wasn't expecting this when she decided to come here today.

CHAPTER SIXTEEN

SAVANNAH

OH MY GOD, he has a *family?*

I look at Lucas and then at the little girl in his arms and then at the girl standing a few feet away.

The little girl looks like Lucas but also looks like the woman. I don't even have to ask to know that she's their daughter.

Holy crap, he has a *daughter.*

When the car pulled up, I didn't think anything of it. I just thought it was a customer, looking for some help with their car.

But then the driver got out, and instantly I knew that she was here for Lucas.

She didn't have to say anything for me to know. It was all in the way she looked over at us as she got out of the car. Or should I say how she looked at me?

I didn't have to ask, I knew right away that this woman, this gorgeous woman, was something to Lucas. Now I know that she's the mother of his child.

The woman, who can't be more than a few years older than me, must see the surprised look I have on my face because she comes over to me with a hand extended.

"I didn't mean to take you guys by surprise," she says, giving me a smile. "I'm Celeste."

Even her name is pretty.

It takes me a second to recover and shake her outstretched hand. "Savannah," I say, a sheepish smile on my face.

Oh my god, I just introduced myself to the girlfriend of the guy who had his tongue in my mouth last night. And who almost finger banged me! What the fuck?

Lucas was going on about Jason being a cheater, yet he's just like him.

I can't believe that I fell for the act and was going to ask him out on a date. I really am stupid and naïve.

God, why the hell do I keep going after guys who are a bunch of assholes?

"You're the pretty blonde," she voices, taking me out of my thought process.

"I'm sorry, what?" I ask her. She knows about me?

"What are you doing here, Celeste?" Lucas interrupts, not letting Celeste answer my question.

My head is swimming with all the possible things that Lucas might have told his girlfriend. I'm going to definitely need more to go off of than just the fact that he called me a pretty blonde.

Did he say it as a compliment? A joke?

I need to know, because if it is the latter, I need to walk away before I waste my time.

He has a girlfriend, there won't be any time wasted.

True. He and Jason may be cheaters, but I sure as hell am not. I felt bad for kissing last night for fuck's sake.

"I texted you. When you didn't answer, I thought I would drive by to see if you were still here before I headed to the house."

Lucas lets out a sigh, coming to stand next to Celeste. "My phone died a while ago. I haven't checked it since I plugged it in."

Celeste starts saying something to him, but I'm not paying attention to them. My eyes are on the little girl in Lucas's arms, on her little head that is covered in light brown curls cradled into his neck. Her brown eyes, the same ones that her father has, look right at me. Looking into her eyes reminds me so much of the first day of the semester when Lucas looked at me with the same intensity. Like they could see right into my soul.

The little girl is gorgeous, the perfect mixture of her parents.

She watches me as I watch her.

After a long minute, she shifts the stuffed mermaid she has in her hands, and she gives me a wave and a toothy smile. I give her a small wave and smile back.

Somehow, I'm brought back to reality and look up to find both Lucas and Celeste staring at me while I interact with their daughter.

As if things weren't awkward enough.

"Um, I should go," I say, taking a step back.

I need to get out of here before things get heated. I won't be the reason that breaks up this little girl's family.

"Oh no, stay. I was just dropping off Mia and heading out," Celeste offers.

Mia. A pretty name for a pretty girl.

"No, it's fine. I already got what I came for. I don't want to be in the way," I say to her, giving her a tight smile before turning to Lucas. "Thanks, for the air."

I give the three of them a small smile and speed walk back to my car. When I turn to get into the car, I see Lucas hand Mia over to her mom and start making his way over to me.

"Savannah," he says, his voice filling the distance.

"Nope," I say shaking my head at him. "It's cool, it's fine. Forget that I even came here and even said anything. Have a good night with your family."

I open the car door and get it. Right before I shut it, I hear him say my name once more.

"Savannah, just listen to me," he says, but I close the door right before he can say anything else.

As I put the car in reverse, Celeste, and Mia both send a wave in my direction. Not even thinking how I feel about the whole thing, I send one back.

I don't even turn to look at Lucas as I drive away.

God, I have horrible taste in men.

———

LUCAS

I watch Savannah's car drive away, and for some reason, I feel something pinging into my chest.

The one time I want to actually talk to her and explain shit, she drives away.

Once the car disappears around the corner, I let out a sigh and walk back to Celeste and Mia.

"Oh, look Mia, *Papi* looks all sad," Celeste teases, a smile playing at her lips.

Mia lets out a small little giggle as if she knows what Celeste is saying to her.

"I think that *Papi* likes Savannah," she whispers to the little girl, throwing a smile in my direction. I throw an eye roll back.

"You don't know what you're talking about," I say as I take my daughter back.

"Sure, I do. I saw the way you were looking at her when I pulled up. If I hadn't interrupted you, she would have been your dinner."

I could argue with her but knowing us, we will be bickering back and forth for hours, and I will come out losing and admitting things I'm not sure I'm ready to admit.

Because Celeste is right, I might have been looking at Savannah in that way. But I'm coughing it up to my mouth being on her the night before. Definitely not because I want to be with her.

Definitely not because of that.

"She thinks we're together. You know that, right?"

I let out a sigh. "I know."

"You should fix that," she throws out, giving me a knowing look. I can't with this right now, so I change the subject.

"You never answered my question. I thought I was

meeting you at the house," I throw out.

Thankfully it works and Celeste answers.

"We were, but the girl I'm going out with asked if we can meet up a little earlier since she has to go into work early tomorrow. I figured that you would be okay with it," she says, giving me a shrug.

From the very beginning of this whole co-parenting thing, Celeste and I have been open about our dating life. Especially since it involves Mia.

Yeah, I wasn't so invested in that guy she was seeing a few months ago, but I do want her to be happy. If me taking my daughter for a few extra hours helps that, then I will gladly take it.

"A girl, huh?" I ask, putting Mia on the ground and letting her run around a bit.

Celeste came out as bisexual when she was seventeen. First to me, and then to her parents. When she got kicked out, that was one of the things that her parents used against her on top of everything else.

The way I saw it, the fact that her parents didn't accept her hurt Celeste more than she will ever say. She hides it well, but I've known her long enough to know the truth.

She knows she will always have my acceptance. Hopefully this girl she's seeing turns out to be a good thing for her.

"Yeah, I met her about three weeks ago, nothing serious. Just getting to know each other and seeing where it goes," she says, giving me a sly smile.

"Well then, you should get going. You don't want to be late." I state, waving toward her car.

"You just want me to go, so I don't ask you any questions about Savannah." Her eyes narrow at me, as if that's what I'm doing.

It might be.

"I want you to go because you're annoying, and I want to spend time with my daughter."

"Just admit it. You like her." She stabs a finger into my chest and since she has acrylics on that shit hurts.

"I'm not admitting shit," I say, taking my eyes off her and looking down at Mia, who decided it was a good idea to lay down on the dirty floor and play with her mermaid.

I guess I'm doing laundry tonight.

"Fine. Have it your way, *pero te voy a dar un mes,*." Celeste says, walking over to Mia and giving her a kiss goodbye.

"Giving me a month for what?" I say, following behind her as she walks back to her car.

"One month, and you will be calling Savannah your girlfriend," she says, a smug look on her face.

"Yeah, right. That's not going to happen. She left here practically running, remember?"

"I bet you a month's worth of dance practice that it will."

Last week when I was dropping off Mia, I was told that she had been signed up for dance class starting next week. The second the words left Celeste's mouth, I made a face.

Dance meant not only taking Mia to multiple practices a week but also interacting with other parents. It's the parents part that makes me cringe. I have a strong dislike for parents.

But if Celeste is offering a month of not interacting with parents and them thinking their kid is perfect, then I will take it.

"Fine."

"Great. Now you grab Mia and head home and think of a way to tell Savannah that we aren't together and how you feel about her. While you do that, I'm going to go on my date. Have fun!" Celeste waves, gets in her car, and drives away.

After Celeste leaves, I grab Mia and finish closing up the shop and within fifteen minutes, we are on our way home.

As I drive home, I think about Savannah. Think about what she was about to say right before Celeste showed up. How her face looked when she saw her and Mia.

I saw the way she looked at me right before she got into her car. She thought that I was just like Jason, a cheating bastard.

Maybe Celeste is right, and I should fix it.

I spend the rest of the ride home thinking of ways to fix it, and I can only come up with one thing.

Pulling Mia out of her car seat, I ask her a question. "You want to go to the Getty Center tomorrow?"

The little girl doesn't know what I'm asking, but that doesn't stop her saying yes.

I guess I figured out a way to fix things with Savannah.

Now I just have to figure out how to win the bet with Celeste. No way am I going to spend a whole month at dance practice.

Those parents will eat me alive.

CHAPTER SEVENTEEN

SAVANNAH

THE SEMESTER IS OFFICIALLY OVER, and all I can think about is how I'm going to spend my summer doing absolutely nothing.

This past semester, no, this past school year, has been so damn stressful. What with classes, being a Song Girl, and then everything with Jason and then Lucas coming into the picture. A girl can only take so much.

After today, I'm free from thinking about anything until August. Two and a half months of absolutely nothing, and I'm going to love every second of it.

I would be enjoying it right now as we speak, but I had one more Song Girl meeting that I had to attend. I also had to return some of my books.

But as soon as my books are returned, I can officially start my summer of nothing.

I can't wait to spend my days binge watching random shit on Netflix. Maybe I will even start reading, who knows? This summer is filled with possibilities of absolutely nothing, and I'm here for it.

Making my way to the bookstore, I feel like I have a little pep in my step that sure as hell wasn't there at the beginning of the month.

I guess that's what happens when you finally leave a situation you want no part of.

The pep follows me all the way to the bookstore and as I hand off my textbooks to the employee handling returns.

That pep falters slightly when I walk out of the bookstore and see Lucas walking in my direction.

He's holding books in one hand and his daughter's hand in the other.

I never understood what women meant about ovaries exploding when they see a man with kids. Now I do.

Seeing Lucas with Mia in such a casual fashion pulls on my heartstrings and makes me want a part of it.

Too bad the guy is a two-timing bastard just like my ex-boyfriend.

Lucas looks up and catches my stare, making it almost impossible to run away.

So I square my shoulders and prepare for whatever he is going to throw my way.

"Savannah," he says as the distance between us gets shorter.

There's a small smile playing on his lips, but I ignore it.

"Lucas," I say to him, before looking down at his daughter.

Mia is hiding behind one of her dad's legs, but she still looks up and gives me a wave.

With a smile, I give her one back.

"How are you?" Lucas asks, grabbing my attention again.

How am I? I think that's the first time he has ever asked me that. We don't do small talk, why does he want to do it now?

"I'm fine. How was the rest of your Sunday? Did you and your family have a good time?" Did I mean for that to come out sounding bitter? No, but it's a reflection of what I'm feeling right now, and I told myself that I wasn't going to hold anything in anymore.

Lucas raises an eyebrow at me, and a smirk forms on his face. "It was good. Mia and I went home and watched a movie. Just the two of us." That smirk of his gets deeper. "You know since my mom was working a late shift, and Celeste went on a *date*. How was the rest of your Sunday?"

My eyes go wide as I take in everything he just said.

Did he say Celeste went on a date, right?

My ears have to be playing tricks on me. Unless... I heard correctly, and I just assumed wrong.

"Date?" I ask, feeling embarrassment creep up.

Lucas gives me a nod. "Yeah, some girl she met a little bit ago. She seemed excited. I can ask her how it went if you want."

I look at him, my mouth opening to say something but closing just as fast, not finding the words.

From the look on his face, he's telling me the truth. In a condescending way, but the truth, nonetheless.

Either way, I confirm it. "You and Celeste aren't together," I state.

The teasing from his face disappears, and he gives a small smile followed by a nod. "Haven't been for a while. She was just dropping off Mia and left soon after you did."

I let out a sigh. "And that's what you were going to tell me before I sped off."

He nods. "I was."

Great, now I feel bad for leaving and not hearing him out. Extra bad because I clumped him with the likes of Jason.

"We tend to do that a lot, you and me," I voice out loud.

"Do what?" he asks, giving me a knowing smile as if he knows exactly what I'm talking about.

He probably does.

"We both tend to see and hear things from the other, but we never get the full picture. So we automatically jump to conclusions and judge the other for things that they are not. Or place each other in a small bubble that we don't fit in."

He's silent for a second, probably thinking about how true my words are. As he thinks about it, I see him run a hand against Mia's curls, and when the little girl smiles up at her dad, my heart jumps a little.

This may be the second time I see him with her, but from what I've seen, Lucas is an awesome dad.

He's most definitely made to be a girl dad.

"Maybe we should work on our communications skills," Lucas suggests, an eyebrow raising in the process.

"And how would we do that?"

"Well, you can come to lunch with Mia and me, and

we can talk. Get to know each other a little bit more," he throws out as if we didn't spend the past semester hating each other.

"Um." I may be a little stunned and can't find words to say to him. "I can't."

"Why?"

Why indeed. I was literally thinking a little bit ago about how once I dropped off my books, I had nothing on my plate and was going to binge watch Netflix all summer.

But he doesn't know that, so I come up with a lie.

"I, um..." Think, Savannah, think of some excuse because you know for a fact you won't be able to handle the cuteness that is him and his daughter. If you see more of it, there will be a danger of you falling even harder. "I have to move out of my dorm."

That's not a total lie. I do have to move out, but moving day isn't for another two weeks. Even then, I won't be going far, just down the street into a new apartment.

"Don't you have until next month to move out?" he throws out, catching me in my lie. For someone who doesn't live on campus, he sure knows how to keep up with dates that shouldn't matter to him.

I know he doesn't live on campus because I've looked, okay? Every chance I got this semester, I looked for him and never once was I able to find him, anywhere near the dorms.

I let out a sigh. "Yeah."

"Then one lunch won't hurt you. Come to lunch with us, Savannah. Just one simple lunch."

It hasn't gone unnoticed that he hasn't called me

Corazón since the night of the party. I might miss it more than I should.

I look at him, and I'm about to tell him no again when Mia comes out from behind his legs and walks over to me.

She holds up her mermaid for me to take and when I do, she grabs my hand and starts to pull me. I look to Lucas for answers.

No way she knows her dad invited me to go to lunch with me.

"She's smarter than you think, and from the looks of it, she likes you, so she wants you to come."

"So you're going to use your cute as heck daughter to do your bidding for you?" I ask, raising an eyebrow at him. A smirk may be playing on my lips.

"Hey, whatever works to get us to have a real conversation." He gives me a shrug, not ashamed at all at using his kid to persuade me.

He must have coached her before, just in case they ran into me or something.

I look down at the little girl, and she gives me a toothy smile, pulling me some more.

No way I can say no to her.

Finally, I let out a sigh and look back up at Lucas. "Okay, I'll go to lunch with you two."

———

"PAPI, AGUA, PEASE," Mia says, looking up from her crayon masterpiece for a quick second to look over at Lucas and ask for more water in her cup.

Lucas reaches for the pitcher of water sitting at the other side of the table and fills up her cup.

I watch in amazement as Mia grabs her cup and takes a drink. No lid, no straw.

"How old is she?" I ask Lucas, taking a drink from my own cup.

After Lucas returned his books, we came to a farm-to-table restaurant close to campus. We've been here for a solid ten minutes, and all topics of conversation have been minimal.

"She's two, turns three in September," he says, looking at his daughter with a smile.

"How old are you?" I ask. Thinking about it, all I know about him is that he may be a business major, his name, and where he works. Everything else about him is up in the air.

"Twenty-two," he answers. So that means he was nineteen when Mia was born. He may have been in his late teens, but that was still young. "You?"

"Twenty."

Lucas nods. "So you just finished your second year here."

"Yeah, only two more years. You are almost done, right?" I ask. I've been curious from the beginning but haven't had the guts to ask.

A crayon slides out of Mia's hand, so I reach out for it and give it back to her.

"I just started actually. This was my first semester, so I will still be here while you're long gone," he says, looking over at Mia as if to silently say that he started late because he was taking care of her.

"Can I ask why you decided to get your bachelor's, or would that be too much?" I don't want to overstep, but I do want to get to know him better. I want to know him asd more than a guy who hates me occasionally.

"Not too much. We're getting to know each other so we don't jump to conclusions, remember?" he says with a smile that has my stomach jumping up and down. "I've always wanted to get my degree but given some of the shit I got into in high school, I didn't think it was possible. But things changed. Mia was born. So last year I finally decided to submit an application, and I was able to get in."

I try to control my face as he speaks, trying not to react, but from the look on his face, I'm not doing a good job at it.

"You can ask, you know. I can see that you want to," he says, lifting up his cup to take a drink of his soda.

This feels like a heavy conversation to have without food as a distraction.

Taking a drink of my water, I take a deep breath before I start talking.

"You don't have"—I look around the restaurant to see if anyone is near—"affiliations, do you?"

"Gang affiliations, you mean?" he asks, his tone neutral.

I nod. "I'm not typecasting you. It has nothing to do with the fact that your skin is darker than mine or because you have tattoos. You've just said a few things in the past, that raise questions," I say, but I quickly regret it, so I start rambling. "You don't have to answer. It's definitely not my place. I shouldn't have asked. I don't need to know."

I grab a crayon that's in front of Mia that she isn't using and start drawing on my napkin. Anything to distract me from tension brewing from my question.

"But it would be your place to ask, wouldn't it? Especially if we want to get to know each other and possibly spend more time together. Isn't that why you went to the garage, to talk about not forgetting our kiss at the party, to see where we could go? The way I see it, if we went further than this lunch, it would be your place to know what I did in my past."

I stop coloring against the napkin and take in his words.

He's right, I did go to the garage so we can talk about the kiss and the possibility of us seeing where we could go together. I didn't think he caught on to that, but he did.

And he wants to see where this could go, just as much as I do if he's willing to tell me about his past.

Placing the crayon down, I look up at him, and I find him already looking at me. His eyes show no sign of anger or indifference but understanding.

He's silently telling me that my question is okay and that he is willing to answer.

"Yes," I state. Yes to why I went to the garage and yes to this lunch going further.

He gives me a nod and collects himself for a long second before he talks again.

"Yeah, I have, or had, whichever you want to look at it, gang affiliations," he says before pausing and letting out a sigh. "This isn't the place to go into deep detail, but know that I was able to get out, or for the time being at least, and haven't done anything with those affiliations since Mia was born."

I take a hard swallow at his admission.

"What do you mean by you're out but 'for the time being?'" Is someone looking for him? Is he still in contact with people who might hurt him if he speaks to someone he shouldn't?

"Just because I say I'm out doesn't mean that someone is going to come looking for me saying otherwise. Some people say you can leave, but that life will always have a piece of you. I know guys that got out but when shit got tough, went back. You're never really out."

That is something I've always heard, especially growing up in Los Angeles, but I never met anyone who was in the middle of all of it. Until now.

"Are you scared?" I can't help but to ask. My eyes turn to look at Mia. She's in her own little world, not caring about anything us adults are saying.

Lucas shakes his head. "No, because I'm not doing anything that I shouldn't, and as long as I keep that up, there's nothing to fear."

I look at the man in front of me. He may be only twenty-two, but he's wiser than a lot of people his age would be, and I bet that has to do with all the things he has done in his life.

He's also doing a lot for his age. Working, going to school, providing for and raising his daughter. Most people would run away from that responsibility.

"The question is now, are *you* scared?"

It takes me a second to realize what he's asking.

Am I scared of him, or am I scared of being with him now that I know his history?

I don't have to think about it. I already know the answer.

"No. I'm not scared," I say, looking right into his brown eyes.

My response doesn't faze him. "Are you sure?"

"One hundred percent." There's no waver in my voice and when it comes to this man, there never will.

No matter how much he tells me otherwise.

"SO YOU AND Celeste really aren't together?" Savannah eyes me from under her lashes as she eats the last bit of her food.

After spilling my guts about being a reformed gang member, our food arrived and the conversation got a bit lighter.

First, we filled it with mundane things like how our classes went this semester to which ones we are taking in the fall. Then we moved on to why we chose to major in business. Me because I want to open a shop and her because her father chose it for her.

When she told me that, I realized why she was completely fine with Jason walking all over her. Because her dad does the same thing.

Anger flowed through me when I heard it, but I kept my face as neutral as possible. Given where we currently stand, I don't think my thoughts matter much.

Now we're back to the topic that started all of this. Me and Celeste.

I give her a nod. "We tried for years, but we weren't made for each other. Something that we didn't realize until Mia was born."

"But you guys are friends?" she asks, her voice going up a little bit.

"Yeah, it makes life easier that way. We've always been better friends to each other than anything else. It works for us."

"I like that. I like that you're working together instead of hating each other for not working out," Savannah tells me.

"There's no point in hating her. Hating her would make life challenging for all of us, including Mia."

"Mia is lucky to have you. Both of you."

I give her a smile as a thank you right before we both turn and look over at Mia.

My little girl is having the time of her life. Having finished her chicken nuggets, she's finishing up another drawing, all while her fingers are in and out of her ranch container. She doesn't care that she's in the middle of an adult conversation. As long as she has ranch, she's good.

She'll get tired soon though, so that means that my time with Savannah is coming to an end.

Savannah realizes it too, because she starts to bite at her bottom lip.

Not giving a shit, I reach across the table and place my thumb on her bottom lip, releasing it from its hold. Once it's free, I rub my thumb against the soft, plump lip.

Not even the small gasp that she releases has me pulling my hand back. My thumb glides along her lip, my eyes taking in every spec of blue that hers have to offer. Until I feel a slap against my arm. For a quick second, I forgot where we were and who we were with. If it wasn't for Mia's slap against my arm, I might have gotten carried away.

Both Savannah and I clear our throats and are embarrassed like we just got caught by someone's mom.

"I think it's maybe time we get out of here," Savannah suggests a smile playing at her face as she nods toward Mia, who looks like she's about to fall asleep in the highchair.

That's what earned me a slap.

Mia saw I was paying too much attention to Savannah and not to the fact that she wanted to take a nap.

I would have slapped me too.

I'm just surprised she didn't use her lungs to tell me she was tired. That's her usual notifying device instead of her words.

Also that fact that she didn't spend all lunch talking our ears off is also a surprise.

I pay the bill, Savannah fighting me the whole time, and once that is settled, my lunch date helps me gather all of my daughter's things while I grab Mia out of the highchair.

As soon as her head hits my shoulder, I hear a little snore. She must have been more tired than I thought.

The three of us make our way out of the restaurant and head to the parking lot.

After the bookstore, both Savannah and I drove here

since we didn't feel the need to walk back to campus when we were done. That might have been the better choice because, right now I don't feel like ending my time with her.

Shit.

One make-out session with this girl and I'm already willing to fall to my knees. I might need to get my head checked, because how can I go from hating everything that this girl is to wanting to see every inch of her body and worshipping it?

"I'm surprised that you have a sedan. Here I thought that you would be driving Mia around in a death trap." Savannah voices as I finish buckling Mia into her car seat.

"Death trap?" I ask when I stand at full height.

"Yeah, your motorcycle."

"One, it's not a death trap. People who don't know how to drive make it a death trap. Two, as soon as Mia is old enough, she will be riding with me. The only reason she's not right now is because she has her car seat." I argue.

Life would be a lot easier if I could just ride my bike everywhere. If I didn't have a car seat to worry about, I would.

"That's the only reason?" she asks, a smile taking over her face.

I can't help but smile back. "Yup, that's the only reason. If I could strap a car seat to it, I would."

She lets out a laugh, and I just watch her, taking everything about her in.

Ever since the Center, something shifted in us, in how we are around each other. I, for one, like it. From the very beginning I've said that Savannah was beautiful, but seeing her more carefree and less cold makes her beauty stand out even more.

The more glimpses of it I get, the more I want to see it in my everyday life.

Speaking of the Center, I have something for Savannah.

"Yup, only reason," I say, popping open the trunk and pulling out the brown bag I left there yesterday.

"I want to see Celeste bite your head off when she finds her daughter on that thing," she says through a laugh.

"Oh, *Corazón*, that's not going to happen because she won't know." I send a wink in her direction, letting her know that I'm kidding.

She lets out another laugh, but as soon as I come back to her and hold out the bag for her, she stops.

Her eyes travel to the bag and then to me with confusion all over her face.

"What's that?" she asks, not reaching for it.

"Mia and I took a little trip yesterday after I got off of work, and we found something that reminded me of you. So I bought it. Figured if I saw you next semester, I would give it to you," I say, handing the bag to her.

She takes it but is looking at the bag like it's going to explode.

"You bought me something?" she finally asks, looking up at me with a look in her eyes that I can't place.

All teasing gone from the conversation.

I nod. "I did."

"Why?"

"Because I wanted to," I state.

Savannah continues to look at me as if this is the first time someone has gotten her a gift or something, and she doesn't know what to do with it.

After a long minute or so, she finally takes the tissue out of the bag and takes out the contents of it.

The second she takes out the small little box, I hear her let out a small gasp.

She doesn't say anything, though, she just continues to look at the small box. The silence is only broken when she starts to wind up the lever and music starts to play.

Yesterday, Mia and I took a quick trip to the Getty Center to see if we could find a music box. Luck was apparently on our side, because the employee said that they had just put out a new display.

I was just going to grab the first box I saw and go, but Mia got curious and started playing with the sounds until she found one she liked.

Thankfully there were two exactly alike, so I got one for her and for Savannah.

I thought that Savannah would be all happy when she saw it, but from the looks of things, she's more sad than anything.

Maybe getting her a music box was a bad idea.

"I can take it back if you want," I offer, and rubbing at the knot that is forming in the back of my neck.

"What?" She looked up right away, like she heard me talking but didn't understand my words.

"I can take it back if you don't like it or want it, for that matter."

"No," she says, shaking her head, her eyes moving back to the music box.

"No, you don't want it, or no, you don't want me to take it back?"

Savannah completely ignores my question. "Why did you get me this?" she asks, almost in a whisper.

"I saw the way you looked when you weren't able to find one when we were there. I thought that it would be a good way to bridge this thing between us."

When she looks up at me again, I see that her eyes are starting to fill with tears.

Great, I made her cry by giving her a stupid music box.

"Are those bad tears?" I ask warily. I can barely handle seeing Mia cry. I don't know if I will be able to handle seeing Savannah like that.

She gives me a tight smile as if she is trying to control her emotion, but it's only for a second.

As I watch her, everything starts to get a little blurry.

One minute, I'm looking at a crying girl, and the next her arms are around my neck, and she is bringing my face down to hers, and her lips are being pressed against mine.

It takes a second to understand what is going on. I wasn't expecting to be kissing Savannah today, yet here I am, so the second I do, all caution is thrown to the wind, and I'm kissing her back just as fiercely as she's kissing me.

Our tongues are sliding against each other, and my hands are moving down her body to bring her close to me.

I think we both remember that we're in public and can't get carried away, because we pull away at the same time, both panting for air.

I don't take my hands off her, and she keeps her arms around my neck.

Our foreheads rest against each other, and looking into her icy blue eyes shouldn't have a calming effect on me, but they do.

"They were good tears." Savannah finally answers the question I asked before she attacked with her mouth.

"Good to know," I say, still not letting her go.

We stand in that position for a few minutes, just staring at each other and taking the moment in for what is.

Whatever has been going on between us has shifted, and we both feel it, we just don't know what to do about it.

The way I see it, I'm going to definitely lose that bet against Celeste and will be attending dance classes for a whole month.

"We went from hating each other to kissing," she whispers, and I feel her breath against my lips.

I brush a piece of hair out of her face and cup her cheek as I respond. "*Corazón*, my hate for you never ran deep. It was always superficial. I hated who you projected, and when you showed me who you could be, that hate started to disappear."

"I've been telling you who I was for weeks."

"I know, and I'm sorry I didn't believe you. But I think it was something I needed to see with my own eyes to believe it."

We go silent for a second, but eventually Savannah leans into my hand and lets out a sigh.

"Where do we go from here?" she asks.

"Wherever you want to go. You want to get to know

each other more and see where this could go, then we do that. You want to never see each other again, then we can do that too."

"And if I want to be friends?" Her question is almost a whisper.

I think about it. Can I be friends with her? I can try but honestly, that's not what I want.

"I know what it's like to have your mouth against mine, to feel your hands on my body even though there are clothes separating your skin from mine. It's embedded in my mind, and I don't know if I can be a friend knowing that."

It's the truth, there's no point in lying to her.

She starts to bite at her bottom lip, thinking about the options that I've presented her.

I extend my thumb to release her lip. "It's not that hard, *Corazón*. Whatever you want to, we will do it. You just got out of something, so I know it won't be a good thing to jump into something so fast. So think about it and whatever you decide, we will do."

Her eyes look to mine, and eventually she gives me a small nod. "Okay."

My hands finally drop, and before I take a step back, I place another kiss against her lips.

I couldn't help myself.

After finally exchanging numbers, Savannah waves goodbye and makes her way to her car.

I watch her the whole time, and I continue to watch her as she drives out of the parking lot.

Whatever is going on between us is in her hands now.

CHAPTER NINETEEN

SAVANNAH

I CONTINUE to chew the skin around my thumbnail, contemplating if I want to send the text that has been staring at me for the past ten minutes.

A text to Lucas.

I'm not usually one to overthink a text message. I just send whatever is on my mind right there and then and don't give it another thought. For some reason though, I'm hesitating on sliding my thumb over and sending the message.

The message that tells him that I want to get to know him more, that I do want to see where this thing between us could go.

It's all typed out and ready to go, but I can't seem to find the courage to actually send it.

It might have to do with the fact that this isn't a conversation that should happen over text, but if I can't muster the courage to text him, how will I find it in me to call him?

Why is this so hard?

Maybe Jason messed me up more than I thought, and now I don't even know how to date someone of the opposite sex.

Feeling frustrated, I delete the text message and type out another. This time, I don't even think about it and hit send.

A few seconds later, the phone starts to ring with an incoming call, but it's not Lucas like I thought it would be.

It's my dad.

Great.

I've been avoiding him since the party at Sigma Alpha. I knew that the second I walked out of that house, Jason would tell my dad that I left him again.

He's been calling me at least two times a day since then, and the only reason he's calling this much is probably because Jason hasn't stopped calling him. I blocked Jason two days after the party, and every time he comes knocking on my door, I pretend I'm not here. From the text my dad has sent me, Jason has been in contact with him and it's getting to him.

I let out a sigh and pressed the green answer button.

"Hi Dad," I say into the phone, cringing at what might come in my direction.

"Savannah, finally. Is there something wrong with your phone?"

I cringe even more at his question. "No, sir. My phone is working just fine."

"So you've been purposely ignoring all of my calls and messages?" he accuses.

I make a face even though he can't see. "No, I've just been a little busy and haven't been able to get back to you."

I know the second that I say the words that he can see right through my lies.

Oh well.

"Hmm," he says, not accepting my answer, but thankfully he drops me. "Is there a reason why Jason keeps hounding me and saying something about you leaving him? I thought we had an agreement."

"I did leave him, and that agreement sucked," I say to him.

"Savannah. That boy is madly in love with you. Why the hell would you leave him?"

I can't help but to roll my eyes at his comment. The only thing that Jason loved about me is my name and the fact that I have the father that I do.

"He loves the fact you're my dad," I spit out. "And if he loved me so damn much, he wouldn't have cheated on me all the times that he did."

"Savannah," my dad tries to argue.

"Would Mom be okay with you cheating with any woman that crossed your path? Would she be okay with finding you in bed with someone else and being in a fake relationship with you, all the while you are still screwing other people? Would she be okay with hearing you say that all she needs to do is open your legs and you will stop? Would Mom be okay with all of that?"

I didn't mean to let all of that slip out.

When Jason and I first broke up, I told my dad why I did it. I told him straight up that Jason had cheated and I wanted nothing to do with him. I guess Jason had told my dad the same thing, except that he learned his lesson and would never do it again.

My dad was pissed, just like any dad would be, but he took him for his word.

For almost a year, my dad continued to believe him, and now that I'm telling him the truth, I have no idea how he is going to react.

My dad goes silent, but then he eventually clears his throat. "No, she would not."

"Then you should be okay with me leaving Jason because that's what I've been going through. And I got tired, Dad. I got so tired of putting on a front and not recognizing anything about myself. I got tired of being told what to do, and hearing that it will all change if I open my legs. Please, Daddy. Understand that I do not want to be with Jason. Not now, not ever."

Tears to form in my eyes, and I try really hard to push them down and not cry, but I can't.

My dad can force me to get a degree in something that I don't want. He can force me to be with Jason once, but he won't force me again. I won't do it.

I don't give a shit that he's my dad and that they are so-called friends, I will not go back to being with Jason.

Eventually, my dad lets out a sigh. "The only reason I went along with making you stay with Jason was because I thought it was a good fit for you."

"Jason was never a good fit for me. He only cared about my last name and never me."

I almost let out that there's a guy who may want me for

me, who could possibly make me happy, but I keep it to myself.

"I'm really sorry, Savannah," he states.

I let out a sigh. "Apology accepted. If it helps, you can block Jason's number so he can't stop bugging you. No guarantees though on him showing up at the office."

My dad lets out a snort, one that is rare from him and answers me. "No, it's fine. Let that fucker call me. I'll set him in his place."

"Thank you, Daddy," I say and mean it.

For the next few minutes, my dad and I have the first normal conversation that we've had in a very long time.

There's no other mention of Jason, and we end up talking about taking a week this summer and traveling somewhere together, just the two of us.

Dad and I haven't been on a trip together since Mom died, so I think this trip would be good for the two of us.

Throughout the call, I want to tell him about Lucas, but since I don't know what we are just yet, I hold it in. I'll tell him if and when we become official or close to official.

Fifteen minutes later, we end the call, and I definitely feel better about my relationship with my dad than I did before answering the phone.

Hopefully, Jason stops trying to contact him. Now that my dad knows everything, he won't be getting the reception that he thinks he's going to get.

The conversation with him served as such a good distraction that I completely forgot about the text that I sent to Lucas until my phone rings again, and I see his name across the screen.

"Oh, crap," I whisper to myself.

This is it. This is the moment I've been waiting for.

After taking a deep breath, I answer the phone.

"Hello?" I say, closing my eyes as tightly as I can.

"Hey." Lucas's voice comes through the line, and a smile can't help to form on my face.

"Hi," I say back, finally opening my eyes and letting the smile spread even more even though he can't see.

"I just saw your message. You said to call you?" I hear him say through the noise of the garage in the background.

"Um, yeah. I can call you back if you're at work."

There's a slight pause, and then the background noise quiets down a bit. "It's fine. I'm just taking my break. What's up?"

I have to make this quick.

I take a deep breath before speaking again. "I know what I want to do," I say but then quickly add, "With us," to clarify.

"Okay?" he says, and a part of me wishes this was a FaceTime call so that I can see if he's smiling or not.

"I want option one, please," I say, my smile getting bigger.

"Which was?" he offers, and my smile starts to dwindle a bit. Did he forget?

"You don't remember?" I say, my voice sounding a lot smaller than it did a few seconds ago.

"Oh, I do, *Corazón*. I'm just waiting to see if you will say it."

I roll my eyes, but my smile returns. "I want to get to know each other for real and see where this goes."

There's silence from Lucas and it lasts so long that I pull the phone away from my ear to see if the call wasn't dropped.

"Hello?" I say, verifying.

"I'm here. I'm just thinking."

"Thinking about what?"

"On if we should have our first official date tonight or tomorrow. And where I should take you."

CHAPTER TWENTY

LUCAS

WHEN IT COMES TO DATES, I'm not one of those guys who lets the girls plan everything.

I actually take fucking initiative and make sure that whatever we do, the girl I'm with is going to have a good time. If she doesn't, then I give her as many outs as possible.

Sure, I've only dated a girl or two since Celeste and I ended things, but I still remember how to do things.

Which is why I'm pulling out all the stops with Savannah tonight.

This could be our first and only date, so I want it to, at least, be memorable for her.

In some aspects of life, I know how to be a gentleman.

I picked her up earlier at her dorm, which was filled with boxes ready for her move, and then took her to dinner at a pasta place that I found one of the few times I was on social media.

That was definitely a good choice, and we both left

there feeling a little too full with all that we ate. After that, we got into my car. I was going to bring my bike, but decided against it, since according to Savannah it's a death trap and all. So, in my sensible car, we drove down to the Santa Monica Pier and walked around a bit to let our food go down.

As we walked the pier, her hand was securely in mine, and it felt like we've been a couple and not on our first date.

All during dinner and the walk on the pier, we talked about everything that we could think of.

I found out that we both grew up in Los Angeles. It blew my mind a little that there were less than twenty miles between us, yet our paths didn't cross until college. But that's what happens when you live in a county that has over ten million people.

Savannah also tells me why she became a dancer, and when I told her about Celeste signing Mia up, she gets overly excited. She even offers to go with me when I take her.

I might have taken her up on it. Having her there would definitely make dealing with other parents less insufferable.

Tonight, I'm seeing a different side of Savannah, and I'm liking every moment of it. She's not the girl that I pegged her to be, and I'm glad that I was wrong.

After the pier, we got in the car again and drove to my favorite ice cream place. We each got two scoops, and then we drove to a spot that would give us a view of the city as it glows in the night.

"Okay, this ice cream is good, but I can't have anymore, I'm so full," Savannah groans in the passenger seat, throwing her head back in the process.

"I told you to get one scoop," I say to her as I bring up a spoonful of my horchata ice cream, a smile playing on my face.

"I know, but it looked too good to not get two. You eat it, I can't anymore." She extended her ice cream up to me and I chuckle but take her offering.

"So, do you bring all your dates here?" she asks after a few minutes as I finish up my own ice cream and start on hers.

I shake my head. "Nope. You would be the first."

And it's the truth. I usually just come up here to clear my head or to get some drawing done.

"I don't believe that. No way I'm the only one you've brought up here."

"Believe it," I tell her.

"Oh c'mon. You probably pull girls left and right. If you don't bring them here, where do you take them?" She asks enthusiastically.

I can help but let out a snort. "How many girls do you think I've been with?" I ask, completely avoiding her question.

Looking over at Savannah, I see that she has a smile on her face and gives me a shrug. "I don't know, like thirty maybe?"

"Thirty?"

She nods. "Yeah. You're a good-looking guy. Thirty seems plausible."

Finishing up the ice cream, I stack up the cup and turn my body fully to her. "You're not even close."

"Is it more?" she asks, her blue eyes going wide.

I shake my head. "No. It's less. Want me to tell you?" She gives a very assertive head nod. "I've been with a total of four women, and none of them have I brought up here. Not even Celeste."

Savannah's mouth drops open a little bit at my admission.

"Really?" I give her a nod yes.

"Yup." I tell her, throwing an arm around the back of her seat. "Should I ask how many guys you've been with?"

Savannah's eyes go wide again for a different reason. She didn't expect me to ask her that.

I assume she had a boyfriend or two before the dickwad came into the picture.

"Um, been with in what sense?" she asks, a small blush creeping up her cheeks.

"In whatever sense you are comfortable with me knowing." I'm not the type of guy who isn't going to be with a girl just because of her body count. That's a dick move.

"Well, I've had two boyfriends. One in high school that lasted about three months and well, you met Jason. So there's that," she says, giving me a small smile, and I nod, about to change the subject, when she starts up again. "As for having been with someone," she starts, hesitating a bit before starting back up again. "I haven't been with anyone in that way."

I lose all ability to speak.

Did she just say that she's a virgin?

She was with the douche canoe for a while. How is that possible?

When we were at the party, and I asked her if he had ever gotten on her knees for her and she told me no, I didn't think anything of it.

But damn, Jason is a bigger douchebag than I thought. Who sleeps with everyone but his girlfriend?

"You're..."

"A virgin. I'm sorry if that puts you off. I wanted to wait, and well, when I was ready, situations arose, and I pushed it off. I didn't want to give Jason a part of myself that I would never get back. Something I'm very happy about, actually."

Her voice is almost a whisper, but it still fills the whole car as if she were talking into a microphone.

A part of me is pissed that she was with someone who she hurt her so badly. The other part of me is fucking elated that she didn't give the fucker that piece of her. It would have been another trophy to add to his shelf.

Shifting, I take her face between my hands and lean in so that she could look right into my eyes and see that I mean every word that I'm about to say.

"It doesn't put me off. I would never be put off by something like that." I brush a few strands of hair behind her ear. "I'm happy actually, and not because you're a virgin and never been touched, and there's a possibility that I might be the first. I'm not happy for me." I take a deep breath, trying to convey everything with my eyes and my words. "I'm happy for *you*. You made a choice that was best for you, and it wasn't taken by a douchebag who didn't deserve it."

Savannah brings her hands up to mine and holds them in place.

"So you don't care?"

I shake my head. "No, I don't care. If we're going to do this, and you want to wait, then we will wait. I don't mind and sure as hell won't be looking anywhere else."

She gives me a smile. "There are no ifs. I want to do this if you do."

I don't hesitate to answer her. "I do."

Savannah closes the distance between us and places her lips against mine.

The kiss starts up slowly, but eventually it picks up. My hands move from her cheeks to her hair, giving her a hair pull followed by another.

She moans into my mouth and her tongue slides against mine, her own hands moving from my arms to my chest.

"We don't have to do anything right now," I say, as I pull my lips from her and start making my way down her neck.

"I know, but we could do other things that can be done," she pants out, throwing her head back, giving me more access to her neck.

"Oh yeah?" I kiss my way down to her chest. "What other things are you thinking?"

Savannah doesn't answer, instead she shoves me off her, causing me to land back in the driver's seat.

I'm about to ask what she's doing when she reaches

over the center console and crosses my lap until she reaches the lever to bring my seat back.

"What the—" I start the second that Savannah climbs over and straddles my lap.

"Much better," she says, a smile taking over her face, just before she leans forward and starts up the kissing again.

It's one thing to have her in my hands while she's sitting on a counter, it's another to have her body on top of mine and rubbing against me.

My hands are on her ass, and hers are making their way under my shirt.

A groan escapes me when her nails scrape against my skin. If it feels this good against my stomach, I can't help but imagine how good it would feel if they scraped along my cock.

As if I woke up the beast, my cock twitches at the thought, and of course because Savannah is on my lap, she no doubt feels it.

Savannah lets out a giggle that doesn't help the situation calm down, but she doesn't care. She just continues to kiss her way down my neck.

"Someone's getting excited," she says, poking her tongue out and licking me along the column of my neck.

I dig my fingers into her ass, pulling her closer to me. "What would you expect? You're grinding yourself against me, my body is going to react to it."

She hums against my neck. "Maybe we should make your body react even more."

"What the fuck does that even mean?" I ask, bringing

her face back to mine. I may have only kissed her a handful of times, but I think that I'm getting addicted to it.

"Scoot the seat back all the way," she says between kisses.

Without breaking our kiss, I do as she says. There are a few awkward movements but it gets done.

Not a whole lot of room that gets added, but it's enough to give us more room.

Savannah pulls away and then starts to slide her body down mine until she is settled between my legs, looking at me from under her lashes.

"What are you doing?" I ask her, grabbing her hand and trying to pull her back up.

"Making you react even more," she says, swatting my hand away and reaching for my belt.

"We don't have to do that. I just told you I would wait for you when you were ready. That doesn't mean let's do something right now." I brush her hair back and caress her cheek.

"I know. That's why I want to do this. As a thank you. For opening your eyes to me, for wanting to be with me, for wanting to wait until I'm ready." She unbuckles my belt and pops open the button of my pants, but before she can slide a hand in and take my cock out, I stop her.

Her eyes look up at me in surprise and maybe a small bit of hurt.

"You don't want me to suck you off?"

I let out a groan. That image is already in my head and I'm liking every second of it but given what she told me about Jason and her waiting, it feels a little wrong.

"Savannah, baby. Trust me, I want you to, but let's just go slow. We don't have to rush this. We have all the time in the fucking world to do whatever we want to do."

"Really?" she asks, as she wasn't expecting me to say that.

I nod. "Yeah, really. We're in the learning stages here. Let's learn about each other before we do anything."

The smile on her face is back and she climbs back up my body until she is able to rest her chin against my chest.

"I'd like that."

"Good." I lean forward and place a kiss against her nose.

We go back to making out and feeling each other up. Eventually after a few hours, and our lips are swollen and we are liable to cross all the line, so we decide to head home.

On the drive back to her apartment, with my hand in hers, Savannah's voice sounds through the music playing.

"Lucas?" she says as I pull away.

"Yeah?"

"Thank you for giving me the best first date ever."

I turn to look at her. The blue in her eyes shines in the moonlight, and I want this picture forever in my mind.

A few months ago, I didn't think I would be here, and no way did I think I would like it.

I'm happy to say that I was wrong.

"You're welcome," I say, bringing her hand up to my lips and placing a kiss against her knuckles.

I won't tell her, but I'm vowing to give her all the best times that I can.

CHAPTER TWENTY-ONE

SAVANNAH

"I CAN'T BELIEVE that you are going to make me do this," Lucas grumbles as he follows Mia down the path.

It was my turn to pick a date for us today and when I thought it up, I knew from the start that it was going to go in one of two directions.

Lucas would either be a good sport and not complain one bit, or he was going to call me crazy the second that he realized what we were doing.

Given the amount of time I've spent with him in the last three weeks and how much I have come to know about him, my money was definitely on the latter.

Now that we've started our little journey, I knew I was right. I should have bet myself coffee or something as a reward.

"C'mon, it will be fun. It's not that hot, and we're outside and Mia can run around," I offer, though I cringe a little at the last part.

When he told me he had Mia this week, I tried to think

of something that the three of us could do. I thought a hike to the Observatory would be a fun thing to do. Now that I think about it, it might not be the brightest idea, bringing a little girl where there are cliffs everywhere.

But there are kids running around, so hopefully she will be fine.

"I'm not a hiker," Lucas grumbles but still starts to walk toward the main path.

"Neither am I, but hey, it's less than a mile up. We can do a mile," I suggest, keeping an eye on Mia as she walks a little bit ahead of us.

My panic starts to rise, so I close the distance a bit and walk a foot behind her.

"Have you done this hike before?" Lucas asks, flipping his hat around so the bill covers his face.

I haven't told him, but the dude looks hot when he wears a baseball hat. Backward or forward, I love it.

I give him a shrug. "I've always just driven up and then walked down."

Lucas deadpans me. "There are hills, Savannah. Steep ass hills."

I try to think about the times that I've been here and have walked down. I don't remember it being that bad. I don't think I even sweated the last time I did the trek.

"You'll be fine, I promise. I have plenty of water," I say, offering a smile.

He just shakes his head but continues to walk. "I can't believe you convinced me to do this."

"I'm actually surprised I was able to convince you to do this too," I say, which earns me a laugh from him.

He may complain most of the time but because it was something I suggested, he will do it.

That's something I've learned since our first date. In the three weeks that we have spent getting to know each other and acting more and more like a couple, I've seen a different side of Lucas.

I found that he's compassionate and actually cares about how I feel and whether or not I'm comfortable with something. He listens to the things that I have to say. He doesn't pressure me to do something I don't want, and when I want to do something that's a little crazy, he goes along with it. Like today.

For a few minutes, we walk up the path hand in hand, stopping occasionally whenever Mia finds something interesting on the ground or on the rocks.

She's good about staying away from the ledge, so my panic levels stay at a steady rate.

Eventually though, we start hitting the inclines, and then I finally realize what Lucas was talking about.

Holy crap, these are steep. So steep that my legs are starting to burn, and my lungs feel like they aren't getting enough air, and that's coming from a dancer.

They definitely don't feel like this on the way down.

"You're feeling it, aren't you?" Lucas voices from next to me.

I try not to pant as I turn to look at him. "Nope. I'm not feeling anything."

The man has the audacity to laugh at my lie. "Sure, you're not."

We climb up a little more until we hit an even patch,

and I think we're done with the inclines, but then I look up. Everything from here on out is an incline.

Great.

Without a doubt, my face will be all red when we get to the top. That's not flattering at all. Whoever told me this was a good date idea should go eat dirt. Especially the person who said that this was only a twenty-minute hike. If you aren't an avid hiker, this shit sucks. No way is it twenty minutes.

Not wanting to have my legs fall off, I decide that we need a break before continuing.

"Let's take a break. Let Mia get some rest," I say, trying my hardest not to pant out the words.

Lucas raises an eyebrow at me before looking over at his daughter. Following his line of sight, I look over at the little girl and see her running up the next hill and then running back down to us. All the while, she smiles and laughs. She's having the time of her life, that one, and I'm over here contemplating everything I've ever done in the gym.

"How does she have so much energy?" I ask, feeling my chest burn just by watching her.

"She's two. She has all the energy in the world," Lucas answers, laughing a little. I just don't know if he's laughing at the fact that his daughter is running literal circles around us, or because I didn't know she was a ball of energy.

My guess is that it's the first one.

I shake my head, and take a drink of my water, loving

how the cold feels against my throat. I offer some to Lucas, and he's a little more than eager to take some.

Yeah, we are definitely not hikers.

"Mia, *¿quieres agua?*" Lucas calls out to Mia, who comes running to us.

Lucas bends down to give her water, and my heart can't help to flutter a little bit at the sight.

Not thinking about it, I take a picture of the two of them.

"I love the fact that you speak Spanish to her," I say, walking over to them and crouching down next to him, placing a hand on his back.

A groan escapes me when I do it, my legs begging for mercy.

"It's something me and Celeste agreed on when she was born. We saw it as being beneficial for her. She knows words in both languages but tends to talk a lot more in Spanish."

I've been listening to Mia talk since she got out of the car. She is definitely a chatterbox, and even though I can't understand every word she says, just hearing her little voice makes me so happy.

When we went out to lunch, she didn't say much so this was a nice change and I absolutely love it.

"Hearing the two of you talk to each other makes me want to learn more Spanish. Other than the basics, I know nothing."

Lucas looks over at me. A smile I can't really place is playing on his lips. "I can teach you, you know?"

The way he's smiling has me narrowing my eyes.

"Why do I have a feeling that if you do that, all I will know is the dirty words and cuss words?"

He shrugs. "It is the easiest thing to teach."

I playfully shove him. "I can meet your mom one day, and all I will be able to do is cuss her out."

"My mom knows English, but it would be fucking hilarious if you do that."

"Fucking," a little baby voice says, and we both turn to look at her. Mia repeats it again right before she takes another sip of water.

"Is she saying ducking or fucking?" I whisper to Lucas, not wanting Mia to hear me and have her say it again.

He lets out a sigh and pinches the bridge of his nose. "It was definitely fucking."

"Is that her first curse word?" I ask.

Lucas shakes his head. "She has a tendency to repeat certain words I say."

I hold back a laugh. "Isn't that Rule 101 when it comes to kids? You have to watch what you say around them?"

That gets him to look at me with narrowed eyes. "It's hard, okay?"

"Celeste isn't going to be very happy that you taught her daughter the F word."

He rolls his eyes at me, but he knows I'm right. I may not know Celeste all that well, since I've met her only once, but I know she may not like her daughter saying fucking.

I slap a kiss on Lucas's cheek and stand up, my legs asking for salvation in the process, and I take Mia's hand to continue our hike up this ridiculous hill.

Lucas ends up taking Mia's other hand, and the three of us walk together. We stop a few more times before we make it all the way up to the observatory.

Both Lucas and I are a sweaty mess, more so him since he carried Mia the last hundred feet or so.

Once up in the main area, Lucas hands me Mia while he goes to find a restroom and some more water since we finished what I had brought.

Mia and I find a spot to sit, my legs glad for the relief, and just chill as we wait for Lucas.

After a few minutes, I feel her go slack in my arms and hear a little snore coming from her mouth.

She must have tired herself out so much that she couldn't wait until she was in the car to fall asleep.

I bring her little body closer to mine and rest my cheek against her hair, wishing I could fall asleep with her.

As we sit here, a few people walk by, giving me a smile as they see me with the little girl. I give them a smile back.

After a few more minutes, Lucas finally comes back with water in his hands, his hat backward, and his shirt off and hanging from the pocket of his joggers.

Jesus.

This man is like a woman's wet dream and not just any woman. Mine.

He's toned all over, with arms and shoulders that look like they were built by manual labor and not in the gym. And the tattoos, god, the tattoos. If I thought the ones on his neck, arms, and hands were hot these are even hotter.

His torso isn't covered in them, but the one he does have, makes this guy even more mouthwatering.

And as he walks over to me, I'm not the only one that is taking notice. A few of the women who decided to take this hike on this fine Tuesday also take notice and watch him as he makes his way to Mia and me.

Lucas gives me a smile before he takes a seat next to me.

Not being able to help myself, I lean in and give him a chaste kiss on the lips.

Mostly because I wanted to, and partly because I was showing the women watching us that he is taken.

Is he taken?

In my head he is, but that is definitely something we need to talk about.

"What was that for?" he asks when I pull away, a sexy smile taking over his face.

"To thank you for going along with this hike, even though I know you hated every minute of it."

He cringes, but he quickly masks it by throwing an arm around my shoulders.

"I didn't *hate* it," he argues.

"You're such a liar, you grumbled the whole way up."

"Yeah, but that doesn't mean I hated it completely. Having you and Mia there made it worth it."

I lean in and give him another kiss.

In a very short time, Lucas has made me see what it feels like to have a caring boyfriend.

There I go again, putting a label on us. I should really get a handle on that.

"What just happened?" Lucas asks, bringing Mia and me closer to him.

"What do you mean?"

"Your face just changed. Like you were thinking about something that made you sad or something."

Might as well tell him.

"I was just thinking how I need to train my brain better. I keep thinking of you as a boyfriend or that we're officially together and have to remind myself that that isn't the case."

Lucas is silent for a few seconds before he answers. "Boyfriend, huh?"

"I'm not trying to rush us into anything, it's just the way my mind is working is all."

Lucas watches me for a brief second before he speaks. "We're already heading in that direction. Why not make it official sooner rather than later?"

"Really?" I ask a little too quickly.

He lets out a laugh that warms my whole body. "Yeah, really."

"I'm completely on board with that," I say, giving him a nod.

"Good, because I am too." He leans in, and this time he's the one giving me a kiss. All too quickly, he pulls away.

Mia lets out a loud snore, and I can't help but laugh at it.

"I think it's time for us to head down, so this little one can get a real nap."

Lucas nods in agreement and stands up before reaching for Mia.

"I can take her," I offer, not ready to hand her over just yet.

He looks at me for a long moment, studying me. Eventually he shakes his head and holds out a hand to help me get up.

"What?"

"Nothing," he says, shaking his head again, debating if he should tell me. Eventually he does. "It's just I wasn't expecting you to be accepting of her this quickly. Some people see a guy having a kid as a turnoff and want nothing to do with them. Yet, here you are, including her and holding her, and it's throwing me off."

He scratches his head, as if the subject is making him uncomfortable, but I know where he's coming from.

Some people would walk away from him the second they found out he had a kid.

I'm not that person. Yes, it shocked me, but Mia is a part of him, and I'm going to care for her just like I care for him.

And yes, I do care about him. That's something that has been growing for the last three weeks.

I smile up at him and try to give him all the reassurance he needs.

"Mia is a part of you, and I can tell you right now that, as long as you are a part of my life, she will be too. I'm not going to run away because you have her."

I lean in and seal my promise with a kiss, and he gives me a smile that can light up a whole room.

CHAPTER TWENTY-TWO

LUCAS

THE SECOND I step foot through the door of the dance studio, I suppress a groan.

It's week three of bringing Mia to dance class and every minute of it I have hated so far.

After making things official with Savannah, I officially lost the bet with Celeste, which I knew was going to happen.

I did have hope, though, that I would be able to hold out on making it official until July. I guess I was too weak for that.

Savannah and I may have been going slow with things, but something deep in me told me that I wasn't going to let this girl go anywhere. Like I knew from the very beginning that she was meant to be mine, and my mind, body, and soul had accepted it.

I texted Celeste to let her know that she had won the bet, and she didn't waste time in rubbing it in my face.

And she continued to rub it in my face when I stopped by her place the first of the month to grab Mia.

I ended up telling Savannah about the bet because she wondered why Celeste and I weren't taking turns with the dance class this month.

She laughed and when she stopped laughing, she stated that I hadn't even had sex with her yet, and I was already pussy whipped.

I didn't agree or disagree. I just slid my hand into her hair and kissed the ever-loving shit out of her. That stopped the teasing on Savannah's part.

Fuck, I shouldn't have thought about that. Now all I have swimming in my mind is Savannah with her top off and my mouth sucking on her nipples.

Definitely not something I should be thinking about as I walk into a room filled with kids. Or even with my daughter next to me.

I shake all thoughts of Savannah to the side and do what I came here to do, suffer through dance class.

Mia and I walk into the designated room, and as soon as I take off her sweater, she runs over to her teacher and says hi.

I've seen a lot of changes in Mia in the last few months. She's been a lot more vocal, a lot more social, and really embracing being around kids her own age.

She is blossoming and a part of me is excited, but another part is a little sad that my little girl is getting bigger. Pretty soon, she'll be embarrassed to be around me.

With Mia settled, I head over to where all the other

parents are sitting and take a seat in the farthest seat that I can find away from everyone else.

I'm here for my daughter, not to make friends with parents who think their kid is better than mine.

Thankfully class starts, and everyone starts to aww at all the little kids dancing around, I don't have to worry about anyone talking to me.

Fifteen minutes into the class, and I'm bored out of my mind. I should have brought my sketchbook or something to distract me a bit. I could use my phone, but I've come to learn that there is no service in this place, so that's a lost cause.

Somewhere between the kids jumping and twirling around, my eyes start to droop. The only reason I even open them back up again is because I feel movement next to me.

My time without interacting with other parents has ended. Perfect.

I turn slightly to the person next to me, and when I see them, my whole perspective of this class shifts.

Because Savannah is sitting next to me.

A smile can't help but spread across my face. "What are you doing here?"

She gives me a smile back and leans in to give me a quick kiss hello.

"I thought I would come and keep you company," she whispers to me.

I throw my arm across the back of her chair to feel some closeness to her. "How did you know where the class was?"

Did I tell her and don't remember? It could be a possibility, but I honestly don't have a single clue. Maybe I did, but I have no memory of it.

"Celeste told me," she says, looking out to where the kids are.

"Celeste?" When did she talk to her?

"Yeah, we exchanged numbers when we dropped Mia off at her place on Sunday. So I used it today and asked her for the address. I figure you would be bored, and I can keep you entertained."

I don't know what I find more mind-boggling. The fact that she came here because of me or that she's texting my ex.

Definitely the second one.

"You don't find that a little weird?" I ask, messaging a knot that is forming at the back of my neck.

Celeste and I are good and all, but she knows shit about me that will make Savannah run for the hills.

"What?" Savannah asks, looking back at me. "Texting Celeste? No, why would I?"

"I don't know. She's my ex, for one."

"And she's Mia's mom. If she's going to trust me with her daughter, then she has to have a way of getting in contact with me if anything comes up. You guys may need someone to pick up Mia when neither of you can and I can step in to help."

She does have a point.

It would be nice to have someone else we can call if Celeste and I are tied up and my mom is at work.

But I don't want Savannah to think that I'm with her

just because I want her help with my daughter, or because I think she needs a stepmom or something.

Don't get me wrong, I love the fact that she wants to do it and that she wants to be a part of Mia's life this way. But I don't want to make that the core of our relationship.

"You know you don't have to do that, right?" I say, bringing her closer to me and whispering in her ear, "You don't have to step in and help me take care of my kid. I don't want you to feel obligated."

She pushes me away just enough for me to look into her eyes. "I know, but I want to do it. You and Mia are a packaged deal. It's both of you or neither of you, and I'd rather get both. If I didn't, I wouldn't be here."

I look at her, really look at her. At her expression, into her eyes. I look at it all and all, I see is sincerity.

She means each and every one of her words.

I could kiss her right now, like mual her to the ground, rip at her clothes and kiss her, but given the setting, I can't.

So I settle for a smile and a squeeze of the shoulder. I'll show her how much her words mean to me later.

"Thank you."

"Anytime."

CHAPTER TWENTY-THREE

MIA'S DANCE class went for a little over an hour.

Being in there brought back a lot of memories, good memories. The whole time I watched her, and her class-mates dance around, I had a smile on my face just remembering how fun dancing was at that age.

That is, after telling Lucas that I didn't feel obligated to do anything. I wasn't lying either. I really did want to be there, and I really want to be able to help when it comes to Mia.

It takes a village to raise a kid, and I want to be a part of that village.

Lucas and I may have only come together a little bit ago, but I finally know what I want, and I want to be a part of this. A part of his life, a part of Mia's life. A part of it all.

After dance class, I go with Lucas to drop off Mia back at Celeste's and once that is all said and done, it's just Lucas and me.

We decided to grab some food from a restaurant that

has become our go-to and head back to my place for a night in.

These have started becoming some of my favorite nights with Lucas. Okay, any night involving Lucas has become my favorite but these especially. Mostly because it's just the two of us, and we don't have to be anyone but ourselves.

These nights also mean that Lucas's lips will be on my body somehow. We've hardly done anything in the sexual department other than making out or him taking my shirt off and having his way with my breasts.

That's as far as we've gone. Whenever I've landed on his lap and started grinding against him, he makes me stop. When I reach for his belt and try to unbuckle it, he tells me not yet.

Yes, I told him I wanted to wait and all, but the man is taking it too seriously. He hasn't even touched my pussy since the party, and a girl has needs that can only be fulfilled by her boyfriend and not her vibrator.

So tonight, I'm going to make it my mission to change that.

I don't need anything romantic or anything overly special like dinner and candles, I just need him.

Fingers crossed it goes my way.

So far, it's looking like it is.

Lucas and I eat our dinner, and after cleaning up, we head over to the couch and put in a movie.

Since it's my turn to pick what to watch, I pick something that I know has sex everywhere.

"You're serious?" Lucas asks as soon as he realizes what

I'm putting, looking at me with raised eyebrows from where he sits.

He has one arm along the back of the couch, and my legs are laying very comfortably on his lap.

"What?" I ask innocently, giving him a shrug. "It's one of my favorite movies."

He gives me a look like he doesn't believe me.

Okay, it's not one of my favorites, but I have to pull out all the stops if I want tonight to go like I hope.

So I blew him a kiss and pressed Play.

For the first thirty minutes of the movie, not much happens. There is no dirty talk, no foreplay, not even a small bit of flirting.

I honestly think the movie is going to put me to sleep, but then the scene quickly changes to something juicy.

Instantly, everything in me wakes up and I start to pay attention to the movie more than ever.

The couple starts kissing, and it quickly shifts to their clothes getting ripped off and hands and mouths all over.

I won't lie, it's hot, but I don't voice it. Instead, what I do is I push myself deeper into the couch and start rubbing my foot against Lucas's groin.

There is definitely something happening there, but I don't know if it's because of the movie or because of me.

I'm just going to say that it's me, so I continue to do the movement even though the scene ends.

From where I'm lying, I can hear Lucas's breathing is getting a little labored, telling me that what I'm doing is definitely affecting him.

And because he is being a good sport about us waiting,

he's not going to do anything about it. So, I have my work cut out for me.

We continue to watch the movie, and when the guy asks the girl what her dirtiest fantasy is, a light bulb lights up in my head, and I decide to change up the plan.

Sliding my legs off Lucas's lap, I sit up and move my body closer to his. The whole time he's watching me every single one of my movements, trying to figure out what I'm doing.

Ignoring his looks completely, I continue to shift toward him, until I'm straddling his lap.

I find comfort in the fact that he doesn't hesitate in touching me and his hands go to my ass right away.

"Hi," I say, giving him a smile, moving a few strands of hair out of his face.

He's let it grow out a bit in the last few weeks, and I love that I can run my fingers through it.

"Hi," he says, holding me in place.

"I don't feel like watching the movie," I say, with as much conviction that I can.

His eyes dance a bit. "Okay, what do you feel like doing?"

"I want you to tell me your dirtiest fantasy."

If Lucas were drinking something, he would for sure be spitting it out at my words. His eyes are wide as my question rings through the room.

"I-I..." He tries to speak and then stops, words failing him at the moment.

Seeing that he isn't going to answer, I tell him mine.

"Want to hear my dirtiest fantasy?"

It takes a second, but he eventually gives me a nod. I can see his throat bob up and down as he prepares for what I'm about to say.

"I have two," I say scooting farther up his lap all the while my hands slide through his hair. "The first one is a little tame compared to the second one in my opinion."

"What is it?" Lucas asks, finally able to speak.

With a smirk on my face, I bring his face closer to mine and slide my nose against his as I tell him one of the dreams, I've touched myself to on numerous occasions.

"In the first one, it would just be you and me. I'm in my cheer uniform, with nothing under my skirt. So you slide your hand along my pussy and play with me until I'm all but screaming your name out. Then you would turn me around and fuck me from behind. I would come so hard that I beg you for more until I milk you dry."

I feather a kiss against his lips, and I circle my hips but against him.

He lets out a groan so I know that my tactic is working.

I continue.

"The second one may still be tamed compared to other people's standards, but to me, it's one of the dirtiest things I can do, and I absolutely love it." Another kiss lands against his mouth.

"What is it?" he says, his voice getting deeper, and the sound of it is like a vibration that I feel all over my body.

"A threesome. One where I'm the center of attention. Maybe we can do that one day."

A growl-sounding noise leaves Lucas and I feel his fingers dig into my ass.

I continue to place feather-like kisses against his lip and then move down to his neck where I get more aggressive with my kisses.

"Is that a good growl or a bad one?" I ask, pressing my face into his skin, taking in his scent, and embedding it even more into my mind.

His fingers dig deeper, almost to the point of pain, but I don't care. It's a good pain, and it means I'm getting to him.

He uses the leverage he has on my ass to move me up and down, grinding my body against his. I feel his cock growing harder under me with each move.

Opening my mout,h and I create a seal against his collarbone and suck. He's left a mark or two on me, it's time to leave one on him.

"A bad one. I don't share, *Corazón.*"

"Not even if it was only one time, and I really wanted one?"

My sexual experiences may be almost non-existent, but that doesn't mean that I don't know what I want to try.

Threesomes have always sounded so much fun to me for some reason. And when I watched my first threesome porn video, it was so damn hot that it went to the top of the list of experiences I wanted to have.

Lucas growls again, and before I know it, he shifts us, and I go from being on his lap to my back with him hovering over me.

His brown eyes bore into mine. "I don't share."

My whole body lights up hearing those words.

"Maybe you will change your mind," I say, teasing.

Sure, a threesome is on my sexual bucket list, but I'm not going to force him to participate in one.

If he doesn't want to share, then I don't want to either.

"I highly doubt that," he says, pressing his body against mine.

I drop the whole threesome talk and go back to the original topic at hand. "Tell me a fantasy that you have."

"You don't want to hear it," he says, leaning down and pressing his face against my neck.

He circles his hips and I feel his lips hot against my skin.

"Try me."

I feel his hands travel down my body until they reach my legs. For a split second, I think that he's going to rub at me, but instead, he grabs at my thighs and brings my legs up to wrap around his waist.

"I've had this recurring dream ever since we got together." He licks the column of my neck and moves down to my chest.

"And what happens in this dream?" This man is only pressing his body along mine, grinding his hips against mine, and I'm already a panting mess. I wonder how I will be once I'm naked under him.

Lucas sucks on the skin exposed by my shirt, marking me like I marked him. "I was fucking you." His hips thrust at the words. "Hard and fast. You were begging me for more, telling me not to hold back." Another thrust. "All the while, the fuckwad ex-boyfriend of yours watched. That's what really got me going,"

"You won't have a threesome, but you would share me with Jason?"

"That wouldn't be sharing, *Corazón*. That would be me showing that fucker that you're better off with me. It would be me showing him that from the day I met you, you were mine and mine only."

I feel like I'm about to combust.

You were mine and mine only.

He may have hated me, but he still wanted me.

And I wanted him.

I want him right now with everything I am.

Grabbing Lucas by his hair, I bring his mouth back to mine. It's aggressive, it's hungry and it's everything that I can ever wish for.

"Show me. Show me that I was yours from day one."

CHAPTER TWENTY-FOUR

LUCAS

"SHOW ME. Show me that I was yours from day one," Savannah says, her voice sounding as sweet as sugar, and all I want to do is obey.

She's been testing me all night, and I'm about to reach my breaking point.

There's just so much a guy can handle. Hearing her talk about threesomes, how she wants me to fuck her, how she is grinding herself against me, it has all become a little too much.

"You said you wanted to wait," I say, pushing a few strands of her hair back so I can look into her icy blues.

It's been close to two months since we agreed that we would wait. That doesn't seem like enough time. I don't want to pressure her into anything she's not one hundred percent ready for.

"I did, but I don't want to wait anymore. I'm ready, Lucas. I want to have this, and I want to have this with you."

She looks so beautiful right now that no matter how much I try, I know that I won't be able to deny her.

Letting out a sigh, I let my forehead fall to hers. "I had a plan," I groan out.

"I'm sure you did," she says through a chuckle. "But I don't need the romantic dinner with candles and rose petals on the bed. I just want you."

Rose petals? This girl had way too much faith in me. Sure, I was going to take her to a nice restaurant and give her a night that she wasn't going to forget, but my plan didn't include rose petals on the bed.

They included the bouquet of a dozen roses I was going to get her.

Lifting my head, I look back down at her. "Are you sure?"

"One hundred percent. I'm ready." The smile she gives me makes my dick twitch.

I give her a smile in return. "Then what you want, you will get."

My lips land back on hers, and we spend the next minute or so exploring each other's mouths.

When I feel Savannah's hands travel down my body, I pull back and pull off my shirt.

Before the piece of fabric even hits the ground, her hands land on my chest, and she lets her nails scrape my skin all the way down to my waistband.

"I need you to tell me what to do. I want to get it right," she tells me, sitting up not taking her eyes off where her hands are on me.

The fact that she wants me to be the one that teaches

her something like this wakes up something animalistic in me.

"I will, but I need to do something first," I say, shifting to the edge of the couch.

I can see the question in her eyes, but I don't give her enough time to ask it because, within a second that the words leave my mouth, I'm undressing her.

Her jeans slide off, and then her shirt quickly follows.

Savannah sits in front of me in just a bra and panties, and my mouth waters.

There are still silent questions in her eyes, but the second that I unhook her bra and start dragging her panties down her legs, she realizes what my end goal is.

"Lucas," she says, closing her legs a bit once she's naked from the chest down, but I don't let her. I hold her legs open and when I get situated on my knees in front of her, I don't waste any time in getting what I want first.

A taste of her pussy.

"Oh my god," Savannah says, falling back onto the couch.

I open her legs as far as they can go and feast on her.

This may be the only time that I've tasted her, but fuck, if I wasn't addicted already.

I can taste her, I can smell her, I can feel her, and I don't want to come up for air.

Lifting my face, I bring up a hand and slide my fingers against her folds. She's slick, and it's all for me.

"Tell me, *Corazón.* Has anyone ever licked you? Has anyone made you come on their tongue?"

I've heard every word that she has said. I have heard

the double meanings that have slipped out. I know what the answer is, but I need confirmation.

"No, you are the first," she pants out as I slide a finger into her entrance.

I want to punch her bastard ex-boyfriend for not treating her right but also thank him for giving me this.

My mouth finds her clit as I move my finger in and out of her. I start off slow but quickly pick up the pace.

When I insert two fingers into her, I feel her tighten around me. Given the hold she has on my hair, I know that she's close to exploding.

As much as I want to hammer into her, I don't. She's not used to this, and even though she may tell me that she can handle it, I still take it easy on her.

I give her pussy slow and methodical strokes with my tongue and keep my fingers at a steady pace.

"Lucas, please. I feel it right there. I need to come," Savannah lets out, her body lifting off the couch, looking for more friction.

Humming against her, slide my free hand up to her stomach and hold her down while I give her what she wants. What she needs.

I work her until she can't take it anymore. I lick every surface of her pussy, and when I feel her tighten even more around my fingers, I replace them with my tongue.

It doesn't take her long after that for her to explode onto my tongue. I take my time cleaning her up, and when I finally pull away from her, she's a panting mess.

"Oh shit. That was intense." she says, a look of amazement on her face.

"It'll get even better," I promise as I place kisses on her inner thigh before making my way back up her body.

I make my way up until my lips reach hers, and I kiss her so that she could taste herself on my tongue.

A sweet hum fills the room.

"Now it's my turn," she states when I pull away.

"We don't need to do that."

"But I want to," she says, a sex filled smile on her lips.

"Okay." I give her one more kiss before taking a seat back on the couch and lean back, giving her access to everything she wants. "Have at it."

Her eyes dance as she comes to kneel in front of me.

The image of her on her knees in front of me, with her lips swollen and hair wild, is going to be engraved in my head for a long while. It will definitely be the image I use to get myself off when she's not with me.

I help her with the buckle of my belt and lift my hips so that she can pull my pants down just enough for her to free me.

Her tongue pokes out, and she licks her lips as she pulls me free of my boxer briefs and holds me in her hand.

"I'm not the only one that's turned on," she states, giving me soft strokes.

"No, you're not," I say, trying to silently tell my cock that it needs to calm down, or I will be coming with just a few soft touches.

Savannah continues to stroke me, and after a minute or two, she looks up at me, giving me a shy smile. "Tell me how to do it the way you like."

"Baby, you can continue to stroke me the way you're

doing, and I will like it," I tell her, grabbing her by the chin to look into her eyes.

"But I want you to feel the same way I felt. I want you screaming my name like I screamed yours."

My dick twitches in her hand at that statement. This girl is going to be the death of me.

Honestly, I'm all for it.

"Apply more pressure to your grip on me," I order, and with a smirk, she does what I say.

As she continues to stroke me, I tell her a few other things to do. Slide your thumb along the head, cup my balls and give them a squeeze. When I tell her to use her mouth, she does it with fervor.

Her tongue slides from base to head, and when she slides it along the slit and licks away at the precum, I start to see stars.

Those stars get more intense when she finally slides me into her mouth and sucks on me.

My hand lands in her hair and I guide her to work me how I like it.

"That's it, *Corazón*. Just like that." I say to her, the grip that I have on her hair tightening.

Savannah releases me from her mouth with a pop, and I watch as she slides her mouth back down to my base and begins to suck on the skin.

She makes her way up to the head, and as she goes, her sucking motions become more intense.

Without a doubt, I'm going to have hickeys all over my cock, and I don't give a shit. My girl put them there as if she was marking me as hers.

I am hers, and I have been for a while.

The head of my cock gets wrapped in Savannah's mouth once again, but this time she slides me all the way to the back of her throat.

"Fuck, baby. I love watching you take me like that," I tell her.

Savannah hums against me and I'm on the brink of sending off my release.

"Pull me out, Savannah. I'm going to come," I warn her and at the very last second, she pulls me out of her mouth, and I quickly grab my cock. Within seconds, I explode cords of cum onto her chest.

My grunts and pants fill the room, and for a second, all I see are black spots

"Fuck," I pant out, slowing down my strokes and getting a handle on my breathing.

"Hmm," Savannah hums, and I look over just in time to see her swipe some of my cum with her finger and lick it clean with her mouth. "I think that it's time to take this to my bed."

I snort. "Your chest is covered, and you already want more?"

Her head bobs enthusiastically, and I'm about to give her what she needs, but I realize what taking her to bed would mean.

"Are you sure? We don't have to do that tonight." I look down at her, placing a hand against her cheek.

"I'm sure. I'm one hundred percent sure." Savannah stands up from her position and holds out a hand for me to take. "Please, Lucas."

I hesitate, but only for a moment. I don't want to rush her, but here she is telling me that she's ready.

Who am I to deny her?

Ignoring her hand, I stand up and place a finger under her chin so I can look into her eyes as I talk.

"We will go slow, okay? I want this to be good for you in every way possible."

She leans up and places a kiss just under my jawline. "It will be good for me. Because I will be with you. I know you will take care of me."

I kiss her then. I kiss her, but it's not a kiss that we are used to giving each other. It's slow and simple and sweet and everything we need at the moment.

I'm the first one to pull away, and as soon as I do, I take her in my arms and walk us over to her bedroom.

Since I helped her move in, I'm familiar with where her bedroom is.

I carry her down the hallway, and when I reach the room, I lay her down in the middle of the bed and just look at her.

She still has my release all over her chest, so I quickly head to the bathroom to grab a wet washcloth to clean her off.

Once that is done, Savannah is sitting against the headboard with a condom in her hand and a smile on her face.

I kiss her as I take the foil-wrapped square from her and cover myself.

When I'm ready to go, I lay on my back and motion for her to climb on top of me.

The whole time she is looking at me with a scared expression and her bottom lip between her teeth.

"I got you. I'm right here with you," I say, taking her face and releasing her lip.

She gives me a nod but still doesn't look relaxed.

So I lean up and kiss her with all that I can. I kiss her as I move her body on top of mine, and I continue to kiss her as I position myself at her entrance.

"It's you and me, Savannah. Slide down on my cock and give yourself what you need. I got you, baby. There's nothing to be scared of."

She lets out a breath and sinks down, wrapping my cock in her warmth.

With that small movement, she gives me a piece of her and in return, I give her everything I have.

CHAPTER TWENTY-FIVE

SAVANNAH

"BUT IT'S GOOD," I argue, holding up the piece of food.

"That shit is raw." Lucas throws back, making a face in the process.

"It's sushi."

"Yeah, and it's fucking raw."

"You ate raw shrimp last week. How is this any different?"

"The difference is that shrimp was cooked."

"They were still gray."

"Yeah, because it was *aguachiles* and it stays that color. I'm telling you that the shrimp was cooked, and what you are trying to feed me is raw as hell."

I mean, he's technically not wrong. It is raw tuna. But I don't see how he can eat raw shrimp but not even want to try this. It's all part of the same ocean, and I will bet him anything that the tuna is way fresher than the shrimp.

But there is no winning here for me.

So I try a different route.

Dropping my shoulders, I give him a pout, and ask one more time. "Can you at least try it? Please?"

Lucas looks at me like he isn't impressed by my antics, but after a minute or two, he rolls his eyes and concedes.

"Fine." He lets out a huff, letting me know that he's annoyed by me, but he will still do as I ask of him because he wants me to be happy.

I let out a squeal and held out the piece of tuna for him.

He leans forward and wraps his mouth around my chopsticks, taking the piece with him.

I watch him as he eats the piece of fish, but his face isn't giving anything away on whether he likes it or hates it.

"Well?" I ask, a little too excited for this.

He gives me a shrug. "I prefer the shrimp."

A loud exasperated sigh leaves me. "At least you tried it."

Lucas lets out a laugh as he stands up from his seat and bends down to give me a kiss before reaching for my food container.

"Are you done?" he asks, and I give him a nod, feeling completely full.

With another kiss, he grabs the box and heads out of the garage to throw it away.

It's a random Thursday in August, and I thought I would surprise Lucas at work with some lunch. Since school is starting up again in a few weeks, I want to get as much time together before we get swamped with class-work, my Song Girl schedule, and life in general. So for the time being, I'm taking advantage.

This summer has been one of the best I've had since I was a little girl, and it's all thanks to Lucas.

When he wasn't working, and I wasn't participating in the handful of events I had for dance, we were together.

Our summer was filled with everything that you can think of, from taking Mia to the beach to going to baseball games when his cousin Jennifer was in town to heading to the Getty at least every other week. We also spent countless hours every single day getting to know each other both with our words and with our bodies.

It's the bodies part that has a blush creeping up my face thinking about it.

When it came to sex, I always thought it was just going to be this action that I did with the person I was with. That it would happen once or twice a week or something and I would not think about it much. That's not what it is at all. At least not with Lucas.

Sex with him is an experience that I never thought I needed in my life. It's hot and combustible but filled with care and love. Love, even though neither one of us has said those words to the other. We might not have said them yet, but we feel it. Well, at least I know I do.

That doesn't matter, though, Lucas takes care of me, and he shows me how to take care of him. Its so damn exciting being with him that, whenever it ends, I want more.

I don't think I can ever get enough of that man. No matter how many times he slides into me, makes me feel so damn full, and how he makes me explode, I will always want more.

Lucas walks back to where I am in the back of the garage where he has his station ready to start painting and gives me a smirk. Like he knows what I was just thinking about.

"What?" I ask, crossing my legs a bit as if he has x-ray vision and can see my panties are wet just from my thoughts.

"You have a cute little blush going on. Want to tell me what's swimming in that pretty little head of yours?"

One of his fingers comes to rest under my chin, and the way he's looking at me with those dark eyes of his, is making me squirm and readjust on the stool I'm sitting on.

"I have no idea what you're talking about," I throw out a little too quickly.

His smirk grows deeper. "Really?" He closes the small amount of space that is between us and cages me against the car. "So if I were to slide a hand up this skirt of yours, I wouldn't find you at least a little bit wet?"

I feel a good chunk of my face get hot.

How? How the hell did he know?

"Is sex all you think about?"

"Only when it comes to you. Now answer the question."

Before answering him, I look around the garage, making sure nobody is close enough to hear what we are talking about. Thankfully, we are in the clear.

"Fine. You would, because I was thinking about all the amazing sex we've been having."

"Amazing, huh?" he asks, that smirk of his turning into a full-on grin.

I roll my eyes. "Like you didn't know, with me screaming your name every time."

He lets out a chuckle and leans down to give me a kiss, but before his lips meet mine, someone is calling out his name.

"Lucas!" Flaco's voice rings out.

A sigh leaves Lucas as he drops his forehead against mine, composing himself. "*¿Mande?*"

"A *friend* is here to see you," Flaco says.

At the word friend, Lucas stands up at his full height, and when he turns to look over at Flaco, his whole body goes stiff.

The way his face goes from happy to looking like it was made out of stone has me following his line of sight.

By the entrance of the garage stands Flaco, who looks pissed off and as stiff as Lucas. I don't know if that's because he caught me and Lucas about to kiss in his garage, or if it has anything to do with the man standing behind him.

I can't see much of him, just his face and some of his upper torso, but given how both Lucas and Flaco are reacting, they don't want him here.

Eventually, Lucas sends a nod over to Flaco and the mystery guest.

"I'll be right there," he yells over to them before turning back to me. "I'm going to see what they want," he says, turning to walk away.

Before I can say anything, a phone starts to ring. Looking down, I see that it's Lucas's phone, with Celeste's name flashing on the screen.

"Your phone is ringing," I say, instead of asking him who the guy is.

"Answer it," he throws out before walking out of the garage with Flaco and the other guy.

That was definitely not weird at all.

Shifting, I grab Lucas's phone and answer the call before it goes to voice mail.

"Hey, Celeste," I say into the phone.

In the last few months, Celeste and I have become closer as friends.

So me answering Lucas's phone when she is calling is not weird. We've hung out a few times just the two of us, and whenever Lucas has Mia, I'm always sending her pictures.

Lucas thinks it's weird since she's his ex and every-thing, but she's also a part of his life in some capacity. I'm not going to treat her like a bitch just because they were together once. If they can be friends, I can be friends with her too.

"Hey, Savannah. Is Lucas around?"

"He was, but he went to talk to Flaco and some scary dude," I tell her.

"Scary dude?" she asks through a small laugh.

"Yeah, both Lucas and Flaco didn't look very happy to have him here."

Celeste is silent for a second before she says anything. "What did he look like?" she asks. Her tone is a lot more serious.

"Um, he was tall and bald. His head was covered in tattoos, and he had a goatee," I say, leaning over to see if I can see any of the men from one of the garage open doors.

Celeste is silent again but this time for a lot long enough that it has me checking to see if the call was dropped.

"Celeste? Are you there?"

She clears her throat before answering. "Yeah, I'm here."

Her voice has a shake to it.

"Do you know who the guy is?" I ask. My curiosity is getting the best of me, especially now that I've seen both Lucas and Flaco's reaction, and now with Celeste not being her bubbly self.

"What?" she says, as if I caught her off guard with my question. She quickly recovers. "I'm sure he's just a customer looking to get some work done."

Why does it sound like she's lying to me?

"Yeah, maybe," I say, letting it go. "So what's up? I can pass on a message to Lucas when he gets back."

She lets out a sigh like she's happy that I changed the subject. "I just called to set something up like a dinner or so that we can talk about Mia's birthday. It's coming up, and I don't want to leave everything to the last minute."

"Oh, okay. Yeah, I'll tell him. I can watch Mia so that you guys can get everything figured out."

Some people would be freaking out that their boyfriend's ex was planning a dinner for just the two of them, but I see that as a normal thing.

"Oh, I meant him, you, and me when I said 'we,'" she explains.

"Me? Shouldn't that be just the two of you?"

"No, why wouldn't we include you? You're a part of Mia's life. Besides, I would rather have your opinion on things than have Lucas agree to everything I offer. He can take the fun out of things."

"Oh, okay," I say, not sure how to take all of this. Celeste may not see it as a big deal, but I do. I've only been a part of Mia's life for a few months. That shouldn't give me party planning privileges, should it? According to Celeste, it does. "I'll tell him, and I can text you when we can do it."

"Cool," she tells me, and I can hear a smile in her voice. "I have to go, but text me, and we will set something up."

We say our byes, and the call ends, and I'm left feeling a little giddy inside at the fact that Celeste is including me in something like this.

The giddiness continues to flow through my body all the way until Lucas comes back to his station.

He doesn't look as rigid as he did when he left, but he still doesn't look happy.

"Who was on the phone?" he asks, not looking at me as he picks up his sketchbook. He's trying to distract me so that I wouldn't ask about who he just talked to.

"Celeste. She was calling because she wants us to get together and talk about Mia's birthday," I tell him.

I guess he doesn't find it odd when I say "us" because he just gives me a nod, still not looking at me.

"We can meet up this weekend if she wants."

"Great, I'll let her know."

He gives me another nod. I don't like it.

Instead of letting go, I persist. "Who was that guy who was with Flaco?"

It's not my business. When it comes to the garage, I have no right knowing anything that happens, but given Lucas's reaction, I feel like I need to.

"Just a guy who wants me to do a paint job for him." He says with a shrug, like it isn't a big deal.

"Just a guy? Then why did Flaco call him a friend?"

That's what finally has him looking up at me. From the way his face shifts, he had hoped I hadn't heard that.

Lucas looks at me, but I don't back down. I just cross my arms and wait for him to answer me.

When he sees that I'm not going to drop it, he lets out a sigh. "He was a friend from an old life."

"An old life?" I ask to clarify, putting the pieces together rather quickly about what he's talking about.

"Yeah, an old life."

"You mean he's—" I start to say softly but Lucas quickly stops me.

"Drop it, Savannah. What he is, or what he was doing has nothing to do with you. So fucking drop it," Lucas says firmly.

He hasn't talked to me in that way since we got together, and I hate hearing it.

That's not the only thing I hate.

"I hate it when you say my name like that," I say, the hold I have in my arms is a little tighter.

"Then don't give me a reason to say it."

A coldness washes through me. One I never want to feel again.

CHAPTER TWENTY-SIX

LUCAS

WHEN I SAW Hector standing behind Flaco, all the blood in my body went to my feet.

I hadn't seen him since I took my beating and walked away, so seeing him only a few feet away from me was like a mind-fuck game.

All I could think of were scenarios as to why he was there.

Was he there for something strictly car related?

Or was he there to convince me to go back to the life I left behind?

I honestly didn't want to find out. And the thing that was fucking with my mind even more was the fact that Savannah was there.

He saw me about to kiss her, and all I could think of was if he was there to get me back into that life, would he use Savannah against me? Would he go after her so I would be at his disposal?

Thankfully, Hector was only there for something car related.

He got his hands on a Mustang from the sixties and he wants me to customize the whole thing. When he offered to pay the garage twenty-five grand to do it, I asked him what the catch was. I, for sure, thought that was where he was going to ask me to go back to being a part of his 'family'.

According to him, though, there was no catch. He said he knew how much work it was going to take to get the job done, so he offered what he thought was appropriate.

After talking to Flaco about it, who, by the way, was not happy to see Hector either, we agreed to take the job.

This project not only would be good for the garage, it would help me get one step closer to my dream.

I definitely wasn't happy that I was getting to that step because of Hector, but it was what it was.

Hector told me that he would reach out about when to drop off the car and the design he's thinking about, and then he left.

When I walked back into the garage, I thought I was composed. I thought I was okay with just seeing Hector.

But the second that Savannah started asking questions and was about to say exactly who Hector was, I lost my cool.

I saw it in her face how much it had affected her, how mad she was that I was talking to her that way.

So when she left five minutes later, faking a headache, I didn't fight her on it. I didn't beg her to stay, and I didn't call out her name so she could listen to what I had to say.

I messed up, and I had to deal with the consequences.

And now a few days later, I'm still dealing with them.

Since the garage, I've talked to Savannah a total of three times. To some dudes, that number is a lot, but as someone who has spent the last three months talking to his girl at least two times a day, three times in the last four days is fucking worrisome.

Right now, we're currently in the car heading to Celeste's place to talk about Mia's birthday. One of the three times that we talked was so I could ask her if she still wanted to come.

She sent me a clipped yes, and when I responded with the time, I was picking her up, I got crickets.

I haven't had any words directed to me since she said hi and got into the car. Now, sitting in silence is making me crazy.

Letting out a sigh, I finally break the silence. "*Corazón*."

"Oh, now I'm *Corazón* and not Savannah," she huffs out, crossing her arms and looking out her window.

Jesus.

"You have every right to be angry at me. I shouldn't have talked to you like that. I'm sorry. Really fucking sorry," I say, and I reach over for her hand.

If I wasn't driving, I would make her look at me and see that I'm being absolutely sincere.

Savannah doesn't say anything, she just continues to look out the window like she didn't hear my words.

She's going to make this a challenge for me.

"Savannah," I say, really wishing I wasn't driving right now.

Finally, she turns. "Did you lie to me?" she asks, her voice shaking in the process.

"About what?" I answer quickly, trying to run through the whole conversation in my head.

"About that guy just wanting you to do a paint job. You said he was a friend from an old life. Was he really there for the paint job or to get you to go back to that old life?"

I shouldn't be surprised that she came to the same conclusion that I did.

She's smart on top of everything else. Of course, she put two and two together and also thought that Hector was there to get me back to wearing his colors.

And now that I know that she's probably been stewing about this for days about the possibility of me going back to life that I've given up, I feel even worse about the way I talked to her.

Thankfully, we get to Celeste's place, and I'm able to look at her as I answer her question.

"No, I didn't lie," I say, trying to show her as much sincerity as I can.

"Are you lying to me now?" Her voice is strong, and I fucking love that she's not sitting here and just taking my apology. She wants all the details and won't accept it until she knows the absolute truth.

"No, I am not lying to you right now."

"Are you thinking about going back to that life?" she asks, and, for a second, my whole body goes cold.

I wasn't expecting that question.

In the years since I left, I have never thought about going back to it. Savannah and I don't talk about that part of my past. She has never asked questions, and I have never provided her with any information other than it was who I once was, and now it was behind me.

Seeing Hector and my reaction might have really messed with her head.

I reach over to her, and when I cup her face, I can't help but let out a sigh of relief that she didn't pull away.

"No, I'm not thinking of going back," I tell her the truth. "I will never go back, not as long as I have my mom, Mia and you."

"But what if we break up?" she asks.

"That's not going to happen, but that's not what I mean. I mean in the way of death. As long as you three are alive and breathing, I won't turn back to that life."

I can see it in her eyes that she is trying to piece together the meaning behind my words.

She knows who I was as a teenager, she knows that my dad died, but she doesn't know how the two connect.

She doesn't know how my dad died or how that led me to get involved with the wrong people so that his killer wouldn't get away with it.

I should really tell her. I should tell her every single detail about who I was and how I got there, and I will. One day I will tell her everything.

Just not while we are in the car parked about to head in to meet with Celeste.

"There's more to the story." It's a statement, not a question.

I nod. "There is, and I promise I will tell you everything, but not while we're in the car. Soon, though, I will tell you soon. For right now though, can you please forgive me?"

She looks me in the eyes, and for a second or two, I think that she's going to say no. That thought only lasts a few seconds though, going away the second Savannah leans in and places a chaste kiss against my lips.

"Apology accepted," she says softly when she pulls away.

I let out a sigh and gave her another kiss. "Thank you, *Corazón*."

A small smile plays at her lips when I pull back from her. "We should get inside."

I give her a nod, and we both start making our way out of the car.

As we make our way up to the apartment, I feel like the wedge that was between me and Savannah these last few days has gotten smaller, but it isn't completely gone. And it probably won't be until I tell her my whole life story.

Maybe then the wedge will be gone completely.

CHAPTER TWENTY-SEVEN

LUCAS

"I KNEW PLANNING a kids party was going to be stressful, I just didn't think it would be this stressful," Savannah voices as she looks at the list that she made of things that we need to get for the birthday party.

For the past two hours, the three of us have been sitting around Celeste's kitchen table going through every detail that has to do with Mia's birthday. There was no way of getting out of it either, or even using the excuse that someone had to watch Mia since she was with Celeste's parents. They are both trying, she said, and I just rolled my eyes. Not because her parents were spending time with their granddaughter, but because they had to take her on the one night I needed her to escape.

If I did things my way, there wouldn't be any party planning. Mia would just be having a small cake with a few gifts while me, Celeste, Savannah, and my mom stood around her.

Of course, I got voted out by both Savannah and Celeste. Now, in a few weeks we are having a birthday party for a three-year-old who won't remember a single thing.

But try telling them that.

"Oh, you should have seen the planning that went into her first birthday. This is nothing," Celeste says as she comes back to her kitchen table with bottles of water.

I let out a groan at the mention of Mia's first birthday party.

Not only did Celeste and my mom treat that party like it was a wedding, wanting everything to be perfect. On top of that, there was also a lot of shit going on behind the scenes.

Celeste and I had broken up a few months before, and we hadn't gotten a handle on the whole co-parenting thing just yet. There were a lot of backhanded comments from both of us, a few nasty stares, and even some tears from both Celeste and Mia. And that was all before the party even started.

Savannah lets out a laugh at my groan. "Does Mia's first birthday bring bad memories for you?"

"A few," I say, placing a hand on her thigh.

"Well, I promise you that this birthday party will be a whole lot better." She leans over and slaps a kiss on my cheek.

"I'll take your word for it."

"Are you sure you are okay with the day, though, Savannah? I don't want you to miss it," Celeste throws out.

School is starting up again in a few weeks, and with school comes the start of football season.

Savannah has Song Girl events almost every single weekend, starting next weekend until February. Mia's birthday party happens to fall on a day with a home game.

Another reason why just having a cake would be better. If Savannah not only helps Celeste plan this thing, but also attends, she's going to be pulled thin.

"Oh, yeah. It's totally fine. It's a morning game, so I should be done by three. No big deal."

Celeste gives her a nod and a smile. "Well, hopefully it all works out, because I'm excited."

"I am too. Maybe we should take Mia shopping for a birthday outfit," Savannah suggests, the smile on her face spreading.

"Oh my god, we totally should! We can take Lucas's mom with us and Mia and we can turn it into a girls day," Celeste tosses in, looking like she's about to jump up and down out of excitement.

"Yes!"

The two girls start to plan out the whole thing, and I'm just left here scratching my head. When the fuck did they become friends?

Do I even want them to be friends?

"What the actual fuck is going on right now?" I say, my eyes moving from one to the other as they plan their day out.

"We're planning out a girls' day," Savannah says to me, raising an eyebrow at me like I wasn't just listening to their conversation.

I roll my eyes at her. "I know that, but why?"

"Because we want to?" Celeste throws out, like I'm missing the point.

"You guys don't find that weird?" I ask, scratching my head.

I can't be the only one who thinks this way. It's not sane for your baby momma and your girlfriend to be friends, is it?

They text each other; they're planning Mia's birthday together, and now they are planning on having a girls' day, with my mom? That shit is not normal.

"Why? Are you scared that we are going to swap stories about you?"

That wasn't even a thought, but maybe it should be. "No, I just think it's weird. This isn't not normal."

"It also isn't normal to be friends with your ex, yet you guys are," Savannah says, patting my thigh.

"You should be happy about me being friends with your girlfriend, because not only do I trust her with our daughter, but you also won't have to hear about my dating life anymore." Celeste says, giving me a shrug.

Thank god for that. I don't know if I could handle another conversation about her flavor of the week.

Celeste is enjoying single life, and I'm all for it, but damn. The father of her daughter can only hear so much. There's no need for me to know how much pussy and dick she pulls.

"Wait, you tell him about your dating life?" Savannah exclaims, a huge smile on her face, like this is the best news ever.

My ex-girlfriend gives her a nod like it was no big deal. "I had to tell someone, and he seemed like the logical choice."

"Does he cringe all the time?"

"Yup, just like he's doing now. And he gives shit dating advice." Celeste nods in my direction as if to prove a point.

I narrow my eyes at both of them, and they both start laughing like this is the funniest shit ever.

"Okay, I'm leaving," I say, making a move to stand up.

Savannah places a hand on my leg to stop me and tries to talk through her laugh. "Babe, don't leave. I promise we'll stop."

I sit back down as the girls try their hardest to calm down.

After their laughter dies down, they go back to talking about their girls' day before moving on to some mundane stuff like their favorite hair products and clothing store and which leggings they liked best.

If this is what my life has come to and it's going to be life from now on, I guess I have to find a way to deal with it.

When their conversation shifts to past relationships, my ears perk up. Not to eavesdrop, but to make sure they don't swap stories about me.

"He sounds like a dickwad and a half. I'm so happy you're not with him anymore," Celeste says after Savannah tells her about Jason the bastard.

Savannah gives her a smile before turning to me. "Yeah, I am too."

I give her a smile back before throwing an arm around

her shoulders and bringing her close enough to place a kiss against her temple.

"He wasn't your first, was he?" Celeste asks and she must see Savannah go stiff under my arm because she quickly retracts it. "Sorry. Don't answer that. It doesn't matter if he was. I shouldn't have asked that."

Celeste gets up from her seat and starts doing busy work in the kitchen.

Savannah looks over at her and then to me. Her eyes hold mine as she silently asks a question. She wants permission to share this part of her sexual experience with Celeste.

I give her a nod. She doesn't need my permission to talk about her body and her sex life with her friend. No matter how uncomfortable I may be with it.

"Actually," Savannah says, causing Celeste to stop what she's doing. "No, Jason wasn't my first."

Celeste turns, giving her a smile. "That's good. Guys like that tend to treat a girl's virginity like a prize that they like to brag about with their friends."

"Yeah." Savannah gives her a nod before turning to me. "I'm glad my first time was with someone that cared about me."

It doesn't take much for Celeste to put two and two together, and when she does, she lets out a loud aww.

"That's cute, and also a piece of information I didn't need to know," Celeste lets out.

Savannah lets out a chuckle. "I guess talking about my sex life is out of the question."

"Oh definitely." Celeste nods eagerly. "Unless you want to talk about your experiences before him, then I'm all for it."

Celeste excuses herself and heads out of the kitchen. When it's just the two of us, Savannah lets out a sigh, leaning more into my body.

"What's up?" I ask, bringing her closer.

"Nothing," she says a little too quickly.

I give her hair a little tug. "C'mon. Tell me."

She lets out another sigh, but this time, she takes a second to respond.

"Do you think that she will judge me if I tell her that, other than a few make-out sessions, I don't have any other experience before you?" She looks up at me and actually has some worry in her eyes.

I furrow my brows as I look down at her. "No, why would she judge for that?"

She gives me a shrug. "Because it's not normal for someone my age to not have those experiences. Hell, you two had a kid at my age."

"Everyone is different. Everyone goes through life differently. Just because you didn't lose your virginity at sixteen doesn't mean that you're weird or that you deserve judgment. It's your body, and it's your choice what to do with it. Nobody has a right to judge you for that."

She gives me a smile right before she leans up and places a kiss right under my jawline. "You're right. Thank you."

I give her a nod and give her a kiss back.

As my lips meet hers, my mind starts to work through a few things.

I have no plans to let Savannah go. She's mine until she tells me otherwise, or I take my last breath. Whatever comes first.

Until then, every single one of her experiences will be with me. That's something I'm completely fine with, I can live with my cock buried in her until the day I die. I've had my chances at experiences, I know what's out there, and I know that I won't have a hunger for anyone else like I do for Savannah.

I know for a fact that Savannah will be happy with every single experience that we go through together. But will she beat herself up for not doing more before we got together?

Possibly.

All of those thoughts go away when my tongue slides against her, and I swallow the small moan that she releases.

For a second, I forget where we are and where my mind was just at, and start to think of ways I can get my girl undressed and have her sit on my face.

That thought lasts all of two seconds, until a clearing of a throat sounds through the room and brings us back to the present.

Savannah jumps a little, pulling away from me and we both turn to look over at Celeste, who just walked back into the room.

"Damn. You two sure know how to get a girl going," she says, fanning herself. "Let's add 'not watching you guys fuck' to the list on top of 'not hearing about your sex life.' Unless I can join," Celeste jokes.

Savannah cringes in embarrassment and hides her face against my chest.

Celeste's laugh fills the room as I bring Savannah closer to me, placing a kiss against her hair.

"That's not embarrassing at all," Savannah murmurs against my chest.

She says it loud enough for Celeste to hear it, which just causes a huge smile to spread across her face. "It was hot, and you definitely should not feel embarrassed."

"But you guys were together once," Savannah whisper yells like that isn't something that we are both aware of.

"Savannah, honey," Celeste starts. "Trust me when I say this, I don't want your man. Haven't in a long ass time. So watching him make out with his girlfriend doesn't affect me. There's no anger, no jealousy, just pure happiness that he found the person who is perfect for him."

Wow.

Where was this speech a few months ago when I thought that she was going to ask me to give us another chance?

"Really?" Savannah asks.

Celeste gives her a nod. "Yes, really." She claps and heads over to the fridge. "Now, Mia is taken care of for the night, the party planning is done, who wants a drink?"

A bottle of tequila is pulled from the fridge, and the sight of it makes me cringe.

"I'm down," Savannah announces, and instantly, the two girls start making drinks.

Awesome.

What better way to spend the night than with my ex and my girlfriend, drinking.

Let's hope that I don't regret them being friends after this.

CHAPTER TWENTY-EIGHT

SAVANNAH

OKAY, so tequila might have been a really, really bad idea.

But that's for the Savannah of tomorrow to take care, because right now, I don't care. I'm having the time of my life and it's just me and Celeste dancing around her living room.

After Celeste brought out the tequila, we started making drinks, and music filled the apartment. Now we are about four drinks in, and the two of us don't want the night to end.

Lucas, on the other hand, is trying really hard to make us believe that he wants to be here. I can see right through it, but because I'm having a good time, he won't say anything.

He would rather sit here with an untouched beer in his hand, bored out of his mind, all so I could have a good time. He wants me to be happy, and he would do anything to achieve that, even if it meant he was going to be miserable.

Take the hike at the beginning of our relationship. He complained the whole time, but because I wanted to do it, he finished the hike.

That's one of the things I love about him.

Woah, love?

Did I just think about love?

I did, and as I move my body to the music, I know that I mean it with everything I have in me.

Wow, I love Lucas.

I definitely didn't think that would happen, but it has, and I couldn't be happier about it. I should really tell him, but maybe I should wait for a time when I don't have so much alcohol slushing through my body.

But just because I may be a little too drunk to say 'I love you', I'm not too drunk to make him dance with me.

"Come on, dance with me." I sway my way over to where Lucas sits on the couch.

His eyes move up my body as he takes a drink of his beer, taking every single inch of my body. A heat travels through my whole body when he looks at me in that way, and right now is no different.

I can feel a blush crawl up my face, and if we were alone, I would definitely be asking for more than a dance.

"I don't dance," Lucas states, putting his beer down, but staying seated.

"Everyone dances," I say, closing the distance between us, adding a little shimmy in the process.

From the corner of my eye, I see Celeste dancing, not paying any attention to us.

"I don't."

My bottom lip sticks out, and I give him the biggest puppy dog eyes that I can muster. "Pretty please. I will make it worth your while."

"Oh yeah? How are you going to do that?" he challenges me. He doesn't know what I'm capable of.

I give him a smirk and lean over him, just enough so that he can see under my shirt and take a peek at the bra that I'm wearing.

I may have been mad at him when I got into his car earlier, but I still dressed with him in mind.

And from the looks of things, he definitely notices.

"Remember that night a few weeks back when we were talking about our dirtiest fantasies?" I say against his ear.

He nods.

"I was thinking that maybe it was time to see one of mine through."

"Which one?" His voice has a rasp to it that makes my insides all warm and fuzzy.

I smile at the fact that I'm affecting him. "The one with my cheer uniform."

My teeth graze his ear while one of his hands lands on my hip, holding me in place.

"Tempting," He says, his fingers digging into my hip.

"So is that a yes?" I pull away, excited to feel his body sway against mine in a different way.

"That's a 'maybe later,'" he says, wrapping a hand around my waist and bringing me down to sit on him.

"You're no fun." I pout, crossing my arms for effect.

"Don't worry, *Corazón*. I will show you how much

fun I can be when we head back to your place." A kiss lands just under my ear, and I can't help but melt into his hold.

"That's a promise that I will hold you to," I tell him, turning to give him a kiss in return.

"Stop making out with your boyfriend and come dance with me," Celeste orders from the other side of the living room.

I don't even think about it twice before I'm pushing myself off Lucas and swaying over to Celeste.

We turn the music just a smidge louder, and we laugh as we grind against each other like I wanted to grind against Lucas.

"Where did you learn to dance like this? I love it!" I say, as I throw my arms around her shoulders.

"A lot of parties, and a whole lot of *quinceañeras* growing up. Oh, and a girl I used to date worked at a club, so she taught me a thing or two," she answers, swinging her hips against mine.

"Oh, she sounds like fun! What happened with her?" I usually try not to ask people about their previous relationships, but I'm blaming this time on the alcohol.

"She moved to Portland about two months after we met," she answers with a shrug.

"That sucks."

"Tell me about it. If she hadn't moved, I definitely could have seen us going somewhere." Her face shifts a little bit, but she quickly slaps a smile on her face as if nothing happened.

I don't have to ask to know that girl moving away really

affected Celeste and here I am asking about it. So I try to change the subject.

"Can I ask you a question?" I ask her as she twirls me around in her arms. We both laugh as she does it.

"Go for it."

"Is it different being with girls than it is with guys?"

She's not even the least bit surprised by my question. "Not really. I think it all depends on the individual. People have different needs, and those needs aren't gender specific. Both genders could be hard and easy."

"Are you looking for anything serious?" I ask.

"Nope, I'm in my 'no commitment, just sex' era, and I'm absolutely loving it." She smiles as she reaches for her drink and takes a swig before handing it to me.

The tequila burns but in a good way.

"I'm so jealous, I've never had one of those," I say as I move my hand to her hips and rock us back and forth to the beat.

"If you weren't with Lucas, I would have suggested you try it," she says, taking another drink.

"Even if I wasn't with him, I probably wouldn't have one. I can be completely confident on the outside but on the inside, I'm like a shy bunny."

"Have you explored any?" Celeste asks before pausing. "Wait before you answer that, let's get another drink."

She grabs my hand and drags me to the kitchen. To my surprise, Lucas is there grabbing another beer.

He gives me a smile, and I step into his arms as Celeste prepares two more margaritas.

A part of me is tempted to tell her to make mine with

no tequila, but then I decided against that. One more tequila filled margarita won't hurt.

"Okay, now you can answer," Celeste says as she hands me my drink.

I take a sip before I respond, shifting in Lucas's arms so my back is to his front. "Define explored?"

"Have you kissed a girl?" Celeste asks, not even thinking about the question.

A nervous laugh escapes my mouth, but I tell her the truth. "I have not."

"Do you want to?"

"Are you offering?" I ask.

It might be possible that the alcohol has gone to my head.

A smirk lands on Celeste's. "I mean if it's okay with your boyfriend, I would be up for it."

I'm about to ask if she's joking but by the look she is giving me, I can tell that she is one hundred percent serious.

Crap, maybe we did drink too much.

Shifting slightly, I look up at Lucas. Not to ask permission, but to see if he's as shocked by the direction that this is going as I am.

His face is completely unreadable as he looks from me to Celeste.

"Is that something you'd be okay with?" I ask, trying to get something out of him.

Finally, when he looks down at me, he gives me a small smile. "If that was something you wanted to experience, then yeah I would be okay with it." He leans down and buries his head in my neck, his hold on me tightening.

I don't deserve this man.

"But it would be cheating, wouldn't it?"

He places a kiss just under my ear. "Not if I'm giving you permission to do it, and I'm here with you."

"Are you sure?" I ask, not wanting to do something he's not one hundred percent comfortable with.

A small yelp escapes me when he nips at my skin. "If it's something you really want to do, then say yes, Savannah. I will be okay with it."

I really don't deserve him. He would really do anything to make happy, even this.

Still in Lucas's arms, I square my shoulders and look at the woman in front of me.

"Okay, let's do it."

She wastes no time closing the distance between us and pressing her lips against mine.

The kiss is soft at first, like what someone would experience during their first kiss. There is no rushing, no real urgency, just soft simple feather-like touches.

It quickly changes though when her tongue glides along my bottom lip asking for entry. I stiffen up at first, but then I feel Lucas's arms still around me, causing me to relax and let Celeste in.

All the soft and simple aspects of the kiss disappear, and the kiss becomes everything that it wasn't. And it isn't Celeste that is giving either, I'm matching every one of her motions the more the kiss moves along. There are so many sensations happening all at once. Celeste gliding against mine all while Lucas is behind me, his body against mine and his mouth still on my neck. It's becoming too much and I don't want it to stop.

Eventually it does, when Celeste pulls away, closing the kiss and leaving us both panting. Following her lead, Lucas finally comes up for air but doesn't let me go.

"How was that?" Celeste asks, a perfectly sculpted eyebrow raising in the process.

I take a second to collect myself. "It was good. Thank you."

"My pleasure. I'm not going to lie, it was hot. Especially knowing that Lucas was right behind you."

Oh, trust me, I know ,and I know it even more given what part of him is currently pressing into me. But no way in hell am I going to tell her that.

"It was definitely something," Lucas says, murmuring against my hair.

It's as if the kiss sobered all of us up, so we decided to start cleaning instead of continuing the dance party.

The night definitely turned out to be a lot different than I expected.

After everything is all cleaned up, Lucas ends up calling us an Uber, and after saying goodnight to Celeste, we're on our way to my apartment.

"Thank you for tonight," I say to him once we are back at my place, and in bed, waiting for sleep to take over.

"I didn't do anything." he murmurs.

"You let me have fun even though I know you wanted to go home. Plus, you let someone else kiss me. That right there is doing something," I say, pressing a kiss against his bare chest.

His arms tighten around me, and he brings me closer to his chest.

"It gave you something that you wanted. So I was happy to comply."

Throwing the blankets off my body, I shift so that I'm no longer lying on against him but straddling him.

"Not many guys would have done that."

He shrugs as much as he can laying down. "I'm not many guys."

"No, you're not," I say right before I lean forward and kiss him.

It's been days since we've been together, and his look from earlier, mixed with everything from the kiss with Celeste, is all finally catching up with me.

I grind my hips against his to let him know where my mind and body are at.

By the way his hands go from my thighs to traveling up my tank top, he gets the hint.

For the rest of the night, I make it worth his while, just like I promised him earlier.

CHAPTER TWENTY-NINE

LUCAS

"REYES!" Flaco yells through the garage, grabbing my attention.

I started working on Hector's custom job a few days ago, and so far I've restarted the back panel about six times so a distraction is welcome.

Wiping my hand clean, I walk over to the front of the garage to see what Flaco wants.

For a second, I think it might be Savannah coming to bring me lunch or something, but when I walk outside and see who it is, I'm disappointed.

Not only is disappointment running through me, but my jaw starts to tic as well.

Seems like the only viable reaction when Hector is concerned.

"Lucas," Hector greets me as if I were the guest of honor at a party or something.

"What's up, man?" I ask, walking over and shaking his hand.

I may be terrified of the shit that this man can do, and I don't want anything to do with him, but I'll still show him respect.

Respect goes a long way with Hector.

"I came to see the progress on the car," he says, giving me a smile that I can't read.

It's not uncommon for people to come in to see the progress that I've made. It's a big investment, and they want to make sure it's in the right hands.

I've just never had anyone come in this soon after starting the project or when I have next to nothing done. A part of me can't help but wonder if he's here for something else.

"Right," I let out, massaging at the knot forming in the back of my neck. I won't be able to get rid of him, so I might as well show him what I've done so far. "C'mon, let me show you what I got so far."

Hector follows me into the garage and over to my station.

I cringe a bit when he sees the car and finds it almost the exact same as when he dropped it off.

"I've been throwing some ideas around, but nothing has stuck. But you can look at a few things I've sketched out and see what you think." I hand over my sketchbook to Hector, but he looks it over with no interest whatsoever.

"I trust you, man. Do whatever you want to do," he says, handing the book over as he takes a seat on my stool.

He's not here to check on the car.

"No way you came over here to tell me to do what I

want with your car," I say to him, my voice becoming harder than it was earlier.

The change in my tone doesn't get past Hector either.

"You're smart, Lucas. I always liked that about you." A smirk takes over his face, and for the first time since I took on this project, I regret it.

"What are you really doing here, Hector?" My stance becomes more defensive. Arms crossed, hands forming fist, legs more than shoulder length apart.

"What? Can't a guy visit an old homie? Check in on how he's doing? Check on his family? Check to see if they are strapped for cash and see if maybe I can help?"

I knew it. I knew it from the fucking beginning that this was more than just a custom paint job.

Hector is after something, and the twenty grand was just the start of it.

"Me and my family are fine, and we're not strapped for cash. We're doing fine without any help," I say, feeling every muscle in my body going hard.

"You sure about that?" Hector asks, that smirk of his growing into a full-on grin. "Word on the street is that blonde chick you're with likes money. Not only that, that school of yours cost a pretty penny. No way you can afford that with what you make here."

Word on the street? What the fuck?

Hector has to have eyes on me and has for a while, because how else does he know that about Savannah? I sure as hell didn't tell him. Flaco can barely stand the sight of him, so I highly doubt that he would talk.

"And what? You can help me with all of that?"

Hector gives me a nod, that grin of his growing more sadistic. "I can," he says, not elaborating.

He's here for the long game and he's not going to say anything else until I pry it out of him.

This tactic used to work when I was younger to get me excited about something, but it's not working now.

"Look, I don't have time for this shit, so how about you tell me why you're here, and I can get back to work on your car."

I watch him stand from his seat and walk around my station, surveying every little thing in front of him.

"You happy working with Flaco?" he asks, toying with some of my tools.

"Yeah," I say, not even stopping to think about it.

Hector nods, still surveying everything. "Even if the pay is shit, and he will never hand the shop down to you?"

I roll my eyes. Working with Flaco has never been about the pay, and I never thought about him handing the business over to me.

Flaco gave me an opportunity when I needed it and has had my back ever since.

"Even then." I stand my ground.

"And what if a better offer came by?" Hector throws out, copying my stance, trying to intimidate me.

"What offer would that be?"

Just by his smile, I should know that it's bad. "The one where I offer you the opportunity to have your own shop now, and by the time you're Flaco's age, you can retire with actual money in your pockets."

"What the hell are you talking about?"

Hector has money. Everyone in a three-mile radius knows that. The fucker flaunts it every time he can. With cars, watches, and clothes. But the thing with Hector is, he may have money, but it's not like the type of money Savannah comes from.

His money is made from the streets. From the drugs he helps supply to the weapons that he sells. This *carnal* thinks he's the head of the Muertos cartel or something, but in reality he's nowhere near that level.

Hector is street level, and that's it.

"I was thinking of opening up a shop on my block, and I need someone to run it. Oil changes, custom jobs, everything. And you, *mi amigo,* are perfect for the job."

That's not what I thought he would say. In my head, Hector was going to tell me that he was going to buy out Flaco's shop and turn it into his own. Not open one that would be in direct competition with him.

Flaco's garage is one of millions here in LA, but it's one of few that offers custom work. There's a waitlist of car owners who want work done by him and up until recently, me.

If Hector opens one like he says, and I go with him, it would be stabbing Flaco in the back.

Yeah, I want my own shop, but I want to do it on my terms, with my money, how I want it. I don't want it handed to me by Hector.

And without a doubt, his shop will be in the middle of the life I left behind at nineteen. I will be back to looking over my shoulder and carrying my mom's rosary with me everywhere I go, hoping I make it home every night.

"Think about it, *carnal*. Your own shop and all the money in your pockets. What more could you ask for?" he says as if it were a trip to fucking Disneyland and not signing my life away.

"Shops don't make money right away," I say, instead of telling him fuck off with his offer.

"Mine would. You say yes, you're seeing twenty grand in your pocket every single week for the rest of your life."

It's going to be a short as hell life because no way in hell is that possible, especially with the side shit he does.

The only way he has that kind of cash is if he's involved with something and knowing him, he probably is. And if I say yes, so will I.

But even knowing that, I can't find the stupid words to tell Hector to take his offer and shove it up his ass.

Why?

Because the offer is too good to turn down, and he knows it.

The catch I was worried about when he first came to the shop just dropped, and I don't know if I can say no to it.

"You don't have to give me an answer right now, but think about it. Just don't tell anyone about it. You have my number. Let me know when you have an answer."

Without another word and a clap on my back, Hector makes his way out of the garage.

"Fuck," I say, under my breath, letting the sounds of the garage flood my mind.

Hearing tire wrenches is a lot better than thinking about what was just offered to me.

One-half of my brain is telling me that there isn't much to think about, that no matter what the offer is, I'm going to turn it down. Yeah, it's good money, but no way am I going back to that life.

The other half is telling me to take it. Take it and deal with the consequences later.

But saying no can also have consequences.

The second I say no, Hector can come after me.

It's a lose-lose situation, and I don't know which way to go.

CHAPTER THIRTY

SAVANNAH

I LOOK at the time on my phone and let out a sigh of relief that I'm able to get out of here with plenty of time to spare.

The game ran a little long, but thankfully, not as long as I thought it would. I'm still able to head to my apartment to change out of my uniform and grab a bag before heading to Lucas's house for Mia's party.

I was a little worried about time during the game but thankfully it all worked out.

"Hey, awesome job today," Jasmine, a senior Song Girls, tells me as she walks by. "You were hitting every single beat."

I can't help but smile at her compliment. "Thank you. Today did feel good, but it wasn't just me, it was all of us."

All of our performances were freaking amazing. Not a single thing went wrong. The crowd was loving every single second of it. I just wish that Lucas was here to see it.

That would have made it all that more special but of course, he couldn't come because of the party. But one day, he will be in the stands watching me.

She beams down at me. "It was, wasn't it?" I give her a nod and her smile grows even more. "Anyway, I also wanted to tell you that, not only were you great today, but that I really appreciate you stepping up this semester. I don't know what it is, but I've noticed a change with you, a good one and it really suits you. So whatever it is, keep it up."

That change she's noticing is the fact that I'm not acting like a huge bitch with a stick up her ass.

All last year, I was miserable because of the situation I was in with Jason. I hated him, and I hated myself, and I took that out on anyone. Nobody wanted to be around me or talk to me unless they were forced.

But ever since I left Jason for good and got together with Lucas, I feel like a changed person. A better person.

"I guess I should thank my boyfriend for that," I tell Jasmine with a laugh.

"Jason?" she asks, lifting her eyebrows at me.

I fake gag at his mention. "God, no. He and I have been done for a while. I'm with someone else. His name is Lucas."

"Ah, okay. I didn't know you were seeing anyone new. I must have missed that Instagram post or something."

I shake my head. "I haven't posted about it. I want to keep what's going on between me and him for myself."

Don't get me wrong, I've taken so many pictures of

him, of the two of us, of him and Mia, and I want to share them with the world, but I don't.

Not because Lucas doesn't let me, but because I have a feeling that Jason is watching my every move.

I haven't heard much from him since I told my dad the truth about what went on between us, but that doesn't mean he's still not around. Without a doubt, he's waiting in the shadows waiting to pop out and threaten me with something.

And given that he hates Lucas down to his core, who knows how he is going to react when he finds out we are together. It's better to keep what Lucas and I have to myself for now.

"Oh, I love that."

"I do too," I say, beaming. "I should get going though, he's waiting."

Jasmine gives me a nod and walks away, telling me that she will see me on Monday for practice.

For the first time in a long time, I feel good about the possibility of making friends who actually like me for me.

After switching my shoes, I stuff my poms into my bag and after waving bye to the girls and to my Coach, I make my way out.

Thank god, I walked to the stadium because there is no way I would be making it out of the parking lot in a timely manner.

Even though the game ended an hour ago, there are still a ton of people hanging around.

Even though this is my third year as a dancer, it still

blows my mind how many people, especially people who don't even go to this school, attend football games.

I dodge people left and right, smiling at a few people as I pass by, and I'm almost out of the middle of the crowd when I feel something behind pushing me down.

It takes me a second to realize that I'm falling to the ground, but thankfully, it's enough time for me to put my hands out to stop from crashing into the cement. My palms take most of the impact followed by my knees.

"Ow, fuck," I say under my breath, feeling a little disoriented.

"Are you okay?" a lady says from next to me, placing a hand on my arm to help me get up.

Once I'm on my feet ,and I try to take a deep breath to slow down my heart, I give her a nod.

"Yeah, I'm fine. Thank you." I give her a smile before taking a survey of my body.

Both my palms are scrapped, and so are my knees. No blood though so that's good, but for sure I will be feeling it later.

"Were you pushed, or did you trip?" she asks, looking around the ground to see if there is anything that might have gotten in my way.

I was definitely pushed, but I'm not going to tell her that.

"Oh, I must have tripped. I may be a dancer but I still have two left feet," I tell her, a nervous laugh escaping.

She gives me a look like she doesn't believe me, but she quickly changes her expression and gives me a small smile.

"Okay, well you should go and wash the dirt off before you get an infection or something."

"Yes, ma'am. Thank you."

The lady walks away, and when I lose her in the crowd, I look around to see if I can find the culprit somewhere close by.

I can't. Whoever it was must have walked away as soon as it happened. Someone must take pleasure in pushing people to the ground.

Grabbing my bag from the floor, I continue to make my way out of the crowd and toward my apartment.

Twenty minutes later, the fall is behind me, the only reminder being the small throbbing in my palms and my knees, and I'm on my way over to Lucas's house.

It's his week with Mia, so it seemed fitting to have the party there. From the pictures he sent me earlier, Mia looks really excited about today and so cute in the outfit that we bought her.

I'm so excited about getting to the party and seeing Mia that I don't realize that the same car has been behind me since I left my apartment until I'm almost at the house.

Maybe they are going in the same general direction. Los Angeles is known for its traffic, so they must be taking the same streets I am to avoid it. I'm just being paranoid.

That may be the case, but that doesn't stop me from making a left turn at random, hoping the car doesn't follow.

But it does. I watch in the rearview mirror as the car makes the same turn and follows me down the street.

What the hell is going on? First the random shove and now someone is following me?

No way in hell these two are connected. Right? Getting shoved doesn't correlate with someone following you as you drive.

Paranoid, I'm just being paranoid. There is no way that this car is following me. Why would anyone even want to follow me anyway? I have nothing to offer.

Taking a deep breath, I make another random turn. This time though, I'm able to lose the car at a red light.

I might have lost the car, but that doesn't calm me down. For the next mile or so, I check my mirrors often to make sure the car isn't behind me.

Thankfully, the car doesn't appear anymore and I'm able to make it to Lucas with my head somewhat intact.

These last forty minutes have been weird, that's for sure.

With Mia's gift in hand, I make my way inside the house. Music is playing, and there are kids laughing and right away, a smile spreads across my face.

The smile gets even bigger when I walk to the backyard and spot Lucas with Mia in his arms as they talk to his mom.

I walk over to them, and when Lucas spots me, he gives me a smile but then it quickly disappears.

"Why are you limping?" he asks when I lean up and place a kiss on Mia's cheek and then his.

"Hi to you too," I say, giving him a smile before turning to say hi to his mom and then looking over at Mia. "How's the birthday girl?"

Mia gives me a smile.

"She's good. Now tell me why you're limping," Lucas orders as Mia wiggles out of his hold and goes to play with a few kids.

"*Deja la muchacha ser*," Lucas's mom, Sandra, tells him before she leaves the two of us.

Lucas just narrows his eyes at his mom as she walks away, before tuning the narrowing eyes at me.

And here I thought he wasn't going to notice.

I give him a shrug. "I fell earlier."

"You fell?" he asks, worry instantly filling his voice. "During the game?"

"Nope, the game went great. This was after. I tripped and scraped my knees," I say, not bringing up the fact that I was pushed.

If he's this worried about me limping, I can't imagine how he would act if I told him I shoved. Let alone that someone might have been following me on my way here.

"Are you okay?" he says, inspecting me up and down.

I throw my arms around his neck and lean up and place a chaste kiss on his lips. "I'm fine. Just a little sore."

"Hmm," Lucas says, not wanting to accept my answer.

I decided to change the subject. "C'mon, come with me to get food. I'm starving."

Thankfully the distraction works, and he follows me to the food table, dropping the subject altogether.

My limping or my fall doesn't get brought up again for the rest of the party. Instead, all the attention is on Mia and celebrating her birthday.

Most of my time is spent either with Lucas, making

sure that he is interacting with the other parents from Mia's dance class or with Celeste making sure that everything is in order.

It's been a month since the night we shared our kiss. At first, I thought that it was going to be awkward, that not only would that night ruin my blooming friendship with her, but also the relationship between her and Lucas.

While it was awkward at first, we were able to work past it.

We talked about it, and we all agreed that it was just a kiss, and it didn't mean anything. We also agreed that there wouldn't be a repeat.

Now a month later, it's as if what happened between the three of us is a distant memory. Which I'm happy for.

Well, Lucas was acting weird a few days after that night, and when I asked him about it, he said it had nothing to do with my kiss with Celeste and that it was school-related.

Other than that, it was an awesome night. I will forever be grateful that they gave that to me.

Right now though, I'm extremely content with having my boyfriend's arm around my shoulder and his little girl sleeping in my lap.

"Thank you," Lucas says, as he gazes up at the smog-filled Los Angeles sky.

The party ended about an hour ago, and after cleaning up, Lucas and I stayed in the backyard to watch Mia play with her new toys. She fell asleep ten minutes ago.

"Who are you thanking?" I ask, leaning my head back against his arm.

"You," he says, not taking his eyes off the sky.

"And what do you have to thank me for?" I ask, my voice almost in a whisper.

"For being here." He finally looks over at me. "For accepting her." He nods toward Mia, whose curls are splayed out on my lap. "And being kind and loving to her. She loves you, you know."

I look down at the little girl in question and smile. "And I love her."

If Lucas and Mia hadn't come into my life when they did, I don't know who I would be right now. It may have only been a few months, but they have already changed the trajectory of where I want my life to go.

"Hopefully, she's not the only one that you feel that way about."

His words have me looking up at him, and I find him giving me the most intense stare. The way his eyes look right now remind me of when I first saw him at the beginning of the year.

They are staring into my soul. Seeing right through me.

And I'm still a sucker for his brown eyes.

"She's not," I say, cupping his cheek. "I love her daddy too."

"The rich blonde girl was never supposed to fall for the brown boy from the bad side of town," he says, leaning into my touch.

"Well too bad, it happened. I love you Lucas Reyes, with every single thing that I have."

He closes the distance between us and places a

feather-like kiss against my lips. It might have been quick and soft, but I know what he was trying to say.

"I love you too, *Corazón*. More than I can express."

Never did I expect to hear those words from Lucas, and now that he is saying them, I want to hear them for the rest of my life.

CHAPTER THIRTY-ONE

LUCAS

I WATCH as my phone vibrates on the kitchen counter with Hector's name flashing on the screen.

He's been calling off and on since he paid me a visit at the garage a few weeks ago. He wants a response, and I have yet to give him one. I know where I stand with it, but for some reason, I can't find it in me to say that to him. I honestly don't know what's holding me back

I flip the phone over, ignoring the call and go back to pouring the cups of coffee.

"*Buenos dias*, I wasn't expecting you to be up this early," my mom says, coming into the kitchen in her scrubs.

It's the day after Mia's party and even though she went to bed late last night, she looks as fresh as ever, ready for work.

"I couldn't go back to sleep," I say to her, sliding over a mug.

"*Gracias,*" she says, taking it and taking a drink. "*Tienes algo en la mente?*"

I shake my head. "Nope, nothing on my mind."

"Your face is telling me otherwise," she says, raising an eyebrow at me as she takes another sip of her coffee.

I hate that I can't hide anything from my mom.

"Just stressing about a paint job I need to finish at the shop," I tell her, which is not a total lie.

My mom seems to relax a bit. "I thought you were going to tell me that Savannah was pregnant."

"What? No. Why would you think that?"

I know I have a history with getting my girlfriend pregnant, but damn, my mom should give some credit. I know how to be responsible.

"I've seen you two together. It's not a far-fetched idea. Especially since you already have Mia."

"Savannah isn't pregnant."

At least, I hope she's not. I've worn a condom every single time we've had sex and she's on birth control, so we should be good.

"Good." she says, finishing up her coffee. "Don't get me wrong. *Si quiero más nietos,* but not anytime soon."

"Good to know, Mom." I'll add 'don't give Mom more grandchildren in the near future' to the list of things to do.

"Alright, *mijo.* Thank you for the coffee. I'm off to work. Make good choices." In other words, don't get my girlfriend pregnant.

With a kiss on the cheek, my mom is off.

Grabbing the two mugs of coffee, I head back to my room, stopping along the way to see that Mia is still asleep.

Once in my room, I try to make as little noise as possible, trying not to wake up Savannah, but the second I sit on the edge of the bed she stirs and her blue eyes glow in the morning sun.

"Good morning," she says, her voice groggy.

"Morning." I put the coffees down on the nightstand and lean over and give her a kiss.

There is something about seeing this woman in my bed and wearing my clothes that does things to me. It doesn't happen often enough, so when it happens, I take advantage of it.

Forgetting about the coffee altogether, I roll my body over to lay on top of hers, all while not breaking our kiss.

If there weren't any blankets between us, I would have her naked and moaning under me in two seconds, but of course, luck isn't in my favor right now.

"Mia could wake up any minute." Savannah pants out as my lips travel down her neck.

My lips stop right away.

She's right. Of course she's right. Mia might be knocked out, but who knows when her little eyes are going to pop open and she will come running in here.

Better not to traumatize the kid.

With a sigh, I slide off of Savannah and reach for a coffee mug to hand to her.

"Thank you," she says, sitting up and taking the mug from me.

Her hair is a mess on the top of her head, and my shirt that she is wearing, rides up just enough to tease me.

I bring up the blankets a bit so I don't get tempted even

more, because trust me, I'm tempted. I'm about to drag Savannah into the shower and have my way with her so that Mia won't walk in on us.

"Did your mom go to work?" Savannah asks, leaning her shoulder against the headboard to look over at me.

I nod. "Yeah. Oh, by the way, she thought I was going to tell her you were pregnant."

Coffee lands on my face.

Note to self, do not tell Savannah anything while she is drinking a hot liquid.

"She thought what?" she exclaims, wiping at her mouth with my shirt. "Why would she think that?"

I grab a towel from the hamper to wipe my face. "She asked me what I had on my mind, and when I told her, she said she was expecting a pregnancy announcement."

"What did you tell her?" Savannah asks, her eyes wide and looking like they are going to pop out of her head.

"That she has nothing to worry about," I say, reaching over and wiping some of the coffee that dripped down her chin. "At least not for right now."

I don't know why I said the last part, but I did and now I can't take it back.

Savannah's eyes get even wider, if that is even possible. She looks like I shocked her beyond repair.

I take the coffee mug out of her hands in fear that she's going to dump in on my head or something.

"You want to have kids with me?" she says after about a minute of her opening and shutting her mouth.

"Maybe not while the two of us are still in school, but yeah." I tilt her chin up, so I can look into her eyes. "I would like to give Mia a sibling or two. Maybe one with your eyes."

"Really?" she asks, the word barely a whisper.

"Really. Did you think I was lying last night when I said that I loved you more than I could express?"

She gives me a shake of her head. "No, I believed every single word. I just didn't expect to be talking about kids this quickly. Like, it seems fast but at the same time, it doesn't."

I know what she means.

Savannah and I have only been together since May. With it now being September, it's a short time, but it feels so much longer than that.

"I'm with you on that," I say, scratching my head.

"I love that we've gone from hating each other's guts to talking about making babies together."

"I didn't see us going in any other direction."

We end up finishing up our coffee and turning on a movie on the TV. We have no plans today, besides dropping off Mia at Celeste, but that's not until later.

Even with a cup of coffee in my system, my eyes start to droop as the movie plays on, and it doesn't help that Savannah is rubbing rhythmic circles along my bare chest.

I'm on the edge of falling asleep when I hear Savannah say something.

"What?" I ask, not hearing her the first time.

"I was just asking what this tattoo means," she says, drawing a circle around the tattoo that I have on the left side of my chest.

I don't need to look down to see what tattoo she is talking about.

The date and time stamp of my father's death.

A part of me is surprised that she hasn't asked about it sooner. It's not like this is the first time she has seen me shirtless.

The second I tell her what it is, the closer she is to asking questions.

But this is what I've been waiting for, isn't it? Since the night at Celeste? To find a way to tell her everything. This is my way, my opening.

"It's the time stamp of my father's death," I say, looking up at the ceiling.

"Why not just the date?" she asks softly, her voice filled with curiosity but also caution.

"Because I wanted to remember the time I decided to become the person that I never thought I would be."

Savannah pushes herself up from where she lays next to me and looks down at me.

"Will you tell me?" she asks, her nervousness peeping out.

I look at the girl who owns a part of my heart that I didn't think was going to ever see the light of day. Finding someone like Savannah was never in the cards for me. I wasn't meant to find a happily ever after like this. I had Mia, I had my mom, and that's all that I needed.

But now she's here with me, she has a part of me in her hands, and she deserves to know the whole story.

So I tell her.

I tell her everything. Absolutely everything. From the

gunshots that changed my and my mom's lives forever, to me seeking out help to find my father's killer, to the beating I took when I wanted to leave.

I don't hold anything back. Every single detail of what I went through, and what I did in those six years of my life are laid out between us.

Every. Single. Thing.

"That's what you meant about not going back to that life as long as the three of us were alive," Savannah whispers a whole five minutes after I finished speaking.

"Yeah." I say, but it doesn't feel like enough.

Savannah doesn't say anything else, she just sits in front of me crossed-legged and her hands slack on her lap. I can't even get a good read on her face, she's just stoic, digesting everything that I told her.

Eventually I break the silence.

"I guess your douchebag ex-boyfriend was right when he called me a lowlife," I say, leaning my head back against my headboard.

My eyes close, and the only thing noise that flows through the room is the blankets shifting, telling me that Savannah is moving.

She's probably getting up to leave and never come back.

I don't open my eyes to check, so when I feel her climb on my lap and straddle me and place her hands on either side of my face, it takes me by surprise.

My eyes pop open, and I'm met with her bright blues staring back at me.

"You're not a lowlife," She whispers.

"But I am."

"No, you're not. Yes, you made some bad choices, but you also made choices to do better. For both you and your daughter. You. Are. Not. A. Lowlife."

When I don't answer her, she leans in and places a kiss against my lips.

"So you're not running away?" I ask against her mouth, my hands sliding along her body.

"I didn't run away when you first told me about your affiliations, and I'm definitely not running now. Thank you for telling me everything."

I place a kiss against the tip of her nose. "You had a right to know."

"And it's something that I appreciate."

She leans in, but right before her lips land on mine, she stops when we hear small footsteps, sounding in the hallway.

Mia's awake.

"*Papi?*" Her little voice fills the space, and I can't help but love the smile that spreads across Savannah's face when she hears it.

"In here, Mia," I say to her.

Within seconds the little girl with wild hair comes into the room, rubbing the sleep away from her eyes.

When she looks up and sees that Savannah is here, all the sleep is gone and she starts jumping up and down in excitement.

"'Vannah!" Mia yells out, running in our direction.

Savannah jumps off me and opens her arms for my daughter. "Mia Mia."

I wasn't lying when I told Savannah last night that Mia loves her.

I see it in the way she asks about her when Savannah isn't with us. I see it in how she talks about Savannah and how she asks about her when she's not with us.

Anybody could see that Savannah feels the same way about her.

And I fucking love it.

After finishing up the movie with Mia, we all have breakfast and get her ready to drop her off at Celeste's.

The day passes by quickly, and before I know it, Mia is with her mom, and Savannah is back at her apartment because she has an early class tomorrow.

There's schoolwork waiting for me, but instead of getting it done, I stare at my phone.

I had turned it off earlier after getting a second call from Hector. If he's calling me more than once a day, that means that he needs an answer sooner than later.

If his offer had come when I was sixteen, I would have accepted it as soon as it left his mouth. I wouldn't have thought of any of the consequences that would come in my direction.

Now though, the consequences are the only thing I can think of and who they affect. Not only do I have to factor my mom and daughter into this, I also have to think about Savannah. More so now because conversations about the future are happening, and I promised her that that life was something that I was never going to go back to.

If I accept Hector's offer, I'll be back in that life that I fought so hard to get out of. I will be in the damn middle with no way out. Back to a life where I'll be looking over my shoulder every second. I will be not only putting my life at risk, but also my family's.

That right there should be reason enough to say no.

But...

Running that shop will be a fucking dream come true.

Then there's the money.

What Hector is offering can set me up for a long time. It can pay for school, pay for everything that Mia needs for years, give me and Savannah a possibility of a future where we don't worry about money, and set my mom up for retirement.

That money can give us everything we need.

When it came to this offer, Hector knew what he was doing. He knew what I needed to hear and how to get me to second guess everything.

But, is the money and fulfilling a far-off dream enough to convince me to go back to that life?

I don't even know anymore.

Hector must have sensed that I was thinking about all of this, because as soon as my phone is powered on, it starts to ring. And his name is staring back at me, taunting me.

Against my better judgment, I answer the call.

"Hey, man."

"Have you decided yet?" he says instead of a greeting. His voice is hard and a little unnerving.

It takes me a split second to answer, and even I'm surprised by my response. "Yeah. I have an answer for you."

"*Bien*, let's meet up, and we can go over everything."

A part of me is telling me that I'm going to need more than the rosary tattooed on my neck to help me through this meetup.

CHAPTER THIRTY-TWO

SAVANNAH

SOMETHING IS UP WITH LUCAS.

He seems agitated in a way. Moodier in a way, if guys can be moodier.

I don't know what it is, but as soon as I saw him right before our one and only class together, I noticed it.

The smile he gave me was tight, and the kiss seemed hungrier than a kiss hello should be. That is what told me that something was up. As our lips danced together, it felt like Lucas was trying to tell me something that actual words couldn't.

I just don't know what that something was.

The way that Lucas is acting stayed with me throughout the whole class. Now that class is over, I'm fighting with myself about whether I should ask him what's going or not

"I seriously hate that class," I grumble as Lucas and I walk out of the classroom together, trying to distract myself from what's going on with him.

"Then drop it," he responds, taking my hand in his and guiding me through the building.

"I can't. I need the class to graduate." If I didn't, I would have never signed up for it and would have added another art elective.

"You don't if you change your major," he says as we walk out into the dark afternoon.

This isn't the first time that the subject of me changing majors has come up.

Lucas knows that I hate it and would rather major in art history, or at the very least something art related. So every time that the conversation comes up, he suggests I make the change, and every time I tell him that I can't.

My relationship with my dad is a lot better now than it was a few months ago. Telling him about what I was going through with Jason really helped with that. We talk a lot more often and make it a mission to spend more time together. He's even met Lucas and thinks that he is a better fit for me than Jason was.

And while everything is going great between us, one thing that hasn't budged with my dad is my major and him wanting me to follow in his footsteps.

He is still very adamant about it, and I've honestly given up on fighting him on it.

I love the arts, I do, but I do see his point when he says a business degree can go a long way.

"I know, but I've already put in too much work to change it now," I say to him. "I don't feel like starting over in a new major."

"Maybe you can take up a minor or something," he provides.

"Maybe," I say with a shrug.

I've thought about it, but with my Song Girl schedule and wanting to spend time with Lucas, taking a few more classes seems like an added stress that I don't want to deal with.

"I just want you to be happy," Lucas says, his grip on my hand tightening.

"Don't worry, I am," I say, speaking more about my relationship with him and where I am in my life than my potential business degree.

"That's all that matters then," he brings my hand up to his mouth and places a kiss against my knuckles.

"The way I see it, a business degree has its benefits. If I get my degree, I can help you with opening up a shop one day. You can take care of all the car stuff, and I can take care of all the administrative stuff."

Lucas goes stiff at the mention of that possibility. His jaw even starts to tic.

That's weird.

He has always gotten excited whenever one of us mentioned the possibility of him opening up his car garage one day.

This reaction is definitely not one I'm used to.

Is this connected to what I noticed this morning?

I won't know unless I ask.

"Okay, what's up with you?" I ask, pulling the both of us to a stop.

"Nothing," he says a little too quickly, which just raises more questions.

"Really? Because you've been acting weird all morning."

I can see by the look on his face that he didn't think I would notice. He thought that I would go about my day and not notice something being off with him.

Well ,that thought came to bite him in the ass because I notice everything when it comes to this man.

"It's nothing that you have to worry about," he states, pinching the bridge of his nose.

So there is something.

"Well, I am worried. So maybe if you tell me what is going on, I can help," I offer.

If things were reversed, he would do the same thing.

"You can't," Lucas says, his voice rising a bit. He lets go of my hand to run a hand through his hair.

"You don't know that. Just tell me what's going on," I urge, taking his hand again.

For the first time, Lucas steps out of my touch. I don't know what hurts more, him not telling him what is going on with him or him rejecting my touch.

"Savannah, just drop it please," he says, his voice coming out loud and angry.

His eyes are filled with fury, but it doesn't stay there long.

Within seconds, the anger is gone, and he's reaching out for me again, but now it's time for me to reject his touch.

"I'm sorry," he says, letting out a sigh. "You're right, I

have been acting weird. There were just a few things going on at the garage that were getting in my head, but they are handled now. It really isn't anything to worry about."

I see the truth in his eyes, and I want to believe what he's telling me, but if things were handled he wouldn't be annoyed and his body wouldn't be filled with tension.

"Are you sure?" I ask him, not backing down easily.

"Yeah, baby. I'm sure. I'm sorry that I worried you." He breaks the distance between us and places a kiss on my lips.

I want to believe him, I really do. But something is telling me that whatever he's going through is bigger than what he wants to say.

"You can talk to me, you know? About anything," I say, when he rests his forehead against mine.

"I know. I didn't, because I didn't think you wanted to hear about boring garage stuff."

"Anything that involves you, I want to hear." I want to hear everything. The good, the bad, the stuff with Mia, the things at the garage, every aspect of his life, I want to know. If he needs me to listen or just to be there for him, I will. No matter what.

"The same goes for me," he says, giving me another kiss.

"What the fuck is this shit?" A voice sounds through my ears right before Lucas's lips meet mine.

I jump at the sound of the voice, recognizing it instantly.

When Lucas and I pull apart, I'm met with the murderous stare of Jason.

A chill runs through my body but not in a good way.

I haven't seen Jason in months, not since the frat party. He's tried to get a hold of me, calling me from a different number that isn't blocked, messaging me on social media, and even showing up at my apartment every now and then according to my neighbor. How he got a hold of my new address is beyond me.

When school started back up, I thought that I was going to have a hard time avoiding him. In my head, he was going to be in every class, in every corner, and he would hound me every chance he got.

The fact that this is the first time I'm coming face to face with him is more surprising than him knowing where I live.

Right away, my back goes ramrod straight ,and the bitch that has been dormant all these months comes out.

"It's me kissing my boyfriend.," I say to him, meeting his stare straight on.

Jason lets out a growl, turning his glare over to Lucas. "I knew you wanted my girl, Reyes. What did you do, huh? Were you whispering shit into her ear when I wasn't looking so she would turn on me?"

Lucas doesn't hesitate to get into Jason's face. "I didn't have to whisper anything in her ear. She figured it out all on her own that you're a douchebag who doesn't know a good thing when he sees it."

Hands land against Lucas's chest, and he gets shoved back. Right away, all the hairs on the back of my neck stand up, and fear starts to creep up my body.

"If anyone is a douchebag, it's you," Jason says, shoving Lucas again.

Lucas lets out a chuckle that tells me he's not going to take any of Jason's shit. "Oh yeah? Why is that? Because she's with a real man who treats her right?"

Jason's face looks like he's about to explode and possibly start swinging.

"Lucas," I start to say, trying to warn him.

But he ignores me.

"I fucking treated her right. It's her fucking fault that I went looking elsewhere. If she would have opened those pretty legs of hers, things would have been different, and she fucking knows it," Jason spits out.

That little speech is the turning point. One second Lucas is calm and collected, and the next his fists are swinging.

A scream escapes me as soon as Lucas's fist lands against Jason's face.

The punch, though, wasn't enough to bring him down.

"Lucas, stop!" I yell toward them, but it's like they're in their own world.

"You fucker. You're going to pay for that." Jason swings his arm back, but Lucas is able to dodge the hit.

"I beat your ass once before, *pendejo*. I can do it again, and this time your frat buddies aren't here to stop me. Keep fucking trying me," Lucas taunts.

Jason is able to land one punch against Lucas and it's hard enough to bring him to the ground.

Another scream leaves me as I fall to my knees and take Lucas's face between my hands. Blood is spewing from his mouth, and as much as I try to make him look at me, he doesn't. His stare stays on Jason.

If I wasn't in the way, Lucas would have probably jumped up already and beat him to a bloody plump.

"Lucas. Look at me. He's not worth it. He's just trying to get under your skin. Let's walk away right now and forget about him." I start to wipe at the blood that is coming from his lip.

"Move, Savannah," he says through his teeth.

"No." I shake my head, tears threatening to form in my eyes.

"Savannah, I'm going to beat the ever-loving shit of this fucker. So move before you get hurt," Lucas growls out, grabbing me by the wrist and pulling me away.

"No, I'm not going anywhere." I argue, pushing him down when he tries to stand up.

"You should really listen to the man, Savannah and move. There's no need for a pretty girl like you to be in the middle of all of this. You should run along, and see if any of his buddies will come by and help him out. You know since he has friends in high places. He might need it," Jason chimes in.

I turn to face him, growling out words. "What the hell are you talking about?"

Jason looks down at me with a look that could only be worn by a villain in a comic book movie.

"He didn't tell you?" he asks, a smirk forms in his face.

"Didn't tell me what?" I ask, looking from him to Lucas, who looks like he's ready to push me to the side and beat Jason to the ground.

"I thought you said you were a real man, Reyes. Real men don't keep secrets from their women." Jason lets out, just as Lucas stands back up.

"Secrets? What is he talking about Lucas?" I say, standing up, pulling at Lucas's arm so that he could look at me.

"Nothing. He's just talking out of his ass." Lucas responds, ready to punch Jason again.

Much like earlier, I don't believe him.

CHAPTER THIRTY-THREE

LUCAS

THREE DAYS AGO

It's been a week since Hector called for my response.

You would think that me telling him my decision was important enough that he would want to meet right away. I would have too. Because the faster all the pieces start coming together the better.

But no. Instead of making me meet him that very night, he had me wait until a week later to have our talk.

My guess is someone was on his ass, and he needed to lay low for a bit before working on anything else.

That might explain why he had me meet him at a seedy looking restaurant in North Hollywood in the middle of the day. He wanted to keep a low profile.

Walking in, I look around the place until I find Hector in the back corner of the restaurant, trying his hardest to blend in.

If there is one thing that Hector doesn't do, that's blend in. The dude is huge and is covered in more tattoos than I am. There is no way to miss him.

I walk over to him and the whole time, my stomach is churning.

Once I tell him my decision, this meeting can go a number of ways, and I have all my fingers crossed that it goes in a direction that is favorable to me.

"Hey, man," I say as I approach his table, not daring to take a seat before he tells me to.

"Lucas, llegaste a mero tiempo." You got here right on time. "I ordered us some food and it's almost ready," he responds, waving for me to take a seat in front of him.

"Thank you," I tell him, rubbing at the rosary as I sit.

"Claro. Now, let's talk about my offer."

"You don't want to wait for the food?" I ask. This conversation might go a lot smoother if I had food as a distraction.

"Nah, food just gets in the way," he says, before leaning back in his seat and meeting my stare head on. "What did you decide?"

It's now or never.

After taking a deep breath, I tell him, "I appreciated it, man, I do, but I'm going to have to say no. I can't run your shop."

The second the words leave my mouth, I instantly go on high alert. Anything could happen right now, and I need to be ready.

Hector is silent for about two minutes, his expression not giving away anything.

"Did Flaco get to you?" is his first question.

I shake my head. "Flaco had nothing to do with my decision."

And it's the truth. My loyalty to Flaco and the shop were low on the list when it came down to making a choice.

"Then why turn it down?" he asks like he doesn't already know.

I decide to tell him the truth. "That life isn't for me anymore, man. Your offer is too good to turn down, but I have to. It's what's best for me and my family. You and the rest of my guys have my respect and loyalty, but I can't go back to that. I walked away already. I don't belong there anymore."

After all of that, I thought that Hector was going to be pissed. I thought he was going to go off the rails and start threatening me until I said yes.

But he stayed silent and accepted my response for what it was.

He told me that he respected my choice and that there wasn't much more he could do or say to convince me to take it.

I felt like I found breath after that, but it only lasted a little while. When I walked out of the restaurant after finishing up the meal with Hector, an uneasiness came over me. Like I was being watched.

I looked around the whole damn block to find its source, but I came out empty.

It wasn't until I was climbing onto my bike that I noticed a car across the street. Dark as hell windows and matte black exterior. It's supposed to blend in, but to *someone that works on cars, it stands out in every possible way.*

To the normal eye, it was a regular car, but to someone that is used to looking over their shoulder, I knew someone was inside, watching my every move.

The question is why?

————

THERE'S no way in hell that this fuckturd knows that I met with Hector. Even if he was the one in the car, he had no way of knowing if I even talked to someone while I was in the restaurant.

He has to be talking out of his ass, there's no other explanation for it.

"What is he talking about, Lucas?" Savannah asks again, this time the question coming through gritted teeth.

I want to answer her, I do, but I have no idea what to tell her.

She knows someone from my old life came to visit me, and since I told her my life story, she knows exactly who he is, but that's about it. I told her that he wanted me to do a custom job for him, but I didn't tell her that I took on the project. She doesn't know about the offer or the fact that I've seen and talked to him since the day he stopped by the garage.

I've kept it all from her. I kept her in the dark because I knew that the second I told her, she would either start to ask too many questions and worry or possibly walk away from me if she knew that I was considering going back to a life I promised her I left behind.

I did it to protect her and to protect what we had, and now it's come back to bite me in the ass.

"Nothing," I say, hoping that she drops it. I'll tell her everything but not while her bastard ex is within a hearing radius.

"There you go lying again. Tell her," Jason says. "Tell her who you were having lunch with three days ago. Tell her who you made a deal with. Tell her all about Hector."

This confirms that he knows that I had lunch with Hector but has no fucking clue what we even talked about.

Either way, I lose it.

I grab Jason by his shirt, lifting him a few inches off the ground so that I can look right into his eyes. "You following me, Wright? Because no way in hell you know any of that."

The fucker had the audacity to shrug. "Maybe I am," he taunts, spitting in my face. "Anything to get my girl back."

"Get it through that hollow skull of yours. Savannah is never going back to you. She's mine," I say through gritted teeth.

Having enough of this asshole, I let him go with a little more force than necessary, and he fell to the ground with a thud.

It doesn't faze him though. No the asshole just laughs as if getting shoved to the ground is the funniest thing in the world.

"You sure about that?" he says, giving me a smirk.

"Because from what I'm seeing, *your* girl is seconds away from walking away." He throws a nod in Savannah's direction.

I follow his line of sight, and the second I see the expression on Savannah's face, I know I messed up big time.

Savannah is taking all my attention now, what with the angry expression on her face, and I don't notice Jason get up from the ground and come over and give me one last punch to the face.

"I'm not done with you, Reyes," he spits out when I fall to my knees, my hand cradling my jaw. "You'll pay for everything that you've done to me, everything that you've taken away. I would watch your back if I was you."

I didn't take him seriously when I met the bastard, I'm not going to take them seriously now. Jason Wright is all talk and no fucking action. The only reason he's fought me these last two times is because there have been people around who he wants to impress.

Savannah and his frat buddies.

When there's no one around, he's going to crumble like the pussy that he is.

For right now though, I ignore his threats and decide to move my attention over to what actually matters.

Savannah and the fact that she's walking away.

Getting up from the ground, I throw one last look at Jason before following behind my girlfriend. I can feel blood coming out of my mouth and my nose, but I don't care. Right now, she's more important than my injuries.

"Savannah, wait," I call after her but she doesn't turn or stop. "Savannah."

She stops walking but she doesn't turn.

When I place a hand on her shoulder, she tenses up.

This is what I get for keeping things from her.

"What are you keeping from me?" she says in a soft voice that is filled with hurt. Not only do I hear the hurt in her voice, but I also see it in the way she stands.

It's now or never.

I let out a sigh, trying to find my bearings. "Do you remember that 'old friend' who came by the shop when you were there and wanted me to do a custom job for him?" I decided it's best to tell her everything.

She gives me a nod ,but she doesn't say a word.

"I ended up taking the job."

That's what finally makes her turn around. Her eyes are wide, and her face looks a little pale. I know exactly what she's thinking.

"Why would you do that?" she asks, her voice shaking in the process.

"It was a job."

"Yes, but I saw you that day, Lucas. That guy being there made you angry. You said you left that life behind and willingly put yourself back in his line of sight. Why would you take that job?"

"Because the money was good, Savannah. If I didn't take the job, I would be struggling to pay for school right now."

We've talked about money before. I know her financial situation and she knows mine. But we come from different tax brackets, and if it wasn't for jobs like Hector's I wouldn't be going to a school like USC.

"Other jobs might have come by, better-paying ones. You could apply for more scholarships. Hell, we could have asked my dad to help you."

I let out a snort. "Yeah, because that's what I need. My girlfriend's daddy paying for my education."

The second her face turns cold I know I have said the wrong thing.

"That's not what I meant, and you know it," she says through her teeth. "But it's interesting, don't you think? You'll take money from an old friend, but you won't accept help from someone like my dad. Kind of a double standard don't you think?"

"Hector is paying me for a job, not because I'm his daughter's boyfriend who needs a handout." Now, I'm the one getting angry. If we continue down this path, we're not going to get anywhere.

"And is the paint job all that it is? Or is there more?" Savannah asks, folding her arms across her chest. She's going into a defensive mood, and I don't blame her.

My eyes fall closed, and a sigh leaves me as I prepare to answer her question. "He came by the shop a few weeks ago and offered me a job at his garage. Told me that I would be running it and would get a hefty pay every week."

I open my eyes again to find her fuming.

Her bottom lip is in between her teeth but not in a nervous way. She is biting down on it like she's holding in all the words she wants to throw in my direction.

"When was this?" she asks, a little too calmly.

"A few days after the night at Celeste's."

"So when I asked you what was wrong, you lied to me and gave me a bullshit answer. But in reality, you were stewing over a job offer that was given to you by an 'old friend' who you used to run the streets with?"

If she wasn't so pissed off at me, I would marvel at how damn smart this girl is.

"Yes," I answer.

She nods. "Did you consider it?"

"Yes."

Tears start to form in her eyes. "You considered it. You considered going to work with a guy who was at the center of the life that you left. You considered stepping back into that world, even though you said you never would as long as me, your mom, and Mia were breathing."

I bring up a hand up to her cheek, but she takes a step back. "I turned it down. I told him no."

"But you considered it, Lucas. You thought about accepting the offer and going back to that. Yes, you said no, but you still thought about it. Why would you do that?"

"Because that's who I am, Savannah. I'm a gang banger, a *cholo*. Just because I change the way I dress and hang out with different people, doesn't mean I'm not a different person. Being with you doesn't change me. I considered it because it's who I am, no matter how many years I've been out. In the back of my mind, I knew that that life would come back and knock at my door. Did I think it would be just a few years after? No. But it happened, babe, and for weeks, I considered going back to it. Because I thought it would be the best decision for me and Mia and for us. If you can't accept that then maybe, we should just end this thing between us."

Tears run down her face, and I try my hardest to not reach out and wipe them away.

"You don't mean that," She whispers.

"Maybe I do. I'm just a lowlife who has no business being with a pretty rich girl like you."

Savannah wipes away at her tears with a frustrated hand. "You're just saying shit to make me walk."

I give her a shrug. "Maybe I am. You're already pissed off at me, what more is it going to take?"

"I'm pissed at you because you lied to me and because you considered breaking a promise that you said time and time again that you would never break. That doesn't warrant walking away from each other."

She's right.

But I don't respond. I just stand there looking down at her with a look of indifference. The same way she looked at me when we met.

When she realizes that I'm not going to say anything, she gives me a shake of her head and walks away.

The best thing that has ever happened to me is walking away from me, and I'm letting it happen.

CHAPTER THIRTY-FOUR

SAVANNAH

I STORM into my apartment and slam my door behind me before running straight to my room.

Tears have been running down my face since I turned my back on Lucas, but the second that my face hits my comforter, the sob that I've been holding in escapes.

We've fought before, but not like this. Not in a way that seems so damn final.

It hurts so damn much.

How can he consider going back to that life? I saw the pain in his face and heard it in his voice when he was telling me about what happened to his dad and how he ended up in that life.

In those short minutes, I saw the lost thirteen-year-old boy who was scared that he wasn't going to make it home one night.

All I wanted to do was go back in time and protect him from that. I wanted to change history so that he wouldn't have to be thrown into a man's world that he didn't belong in.

And he doesn't belong in it now, no matter how much he says that he does.

It may be who he is, but that doesn't mean he is where he belongs.

And I'm to spend the rest of my life showing him.

I'm not walking away, and I'm not letting him walk away either. This is just a little fluke that we will get past.

It's just going to take some time. Things between us aren't going to be fixed today or tomorrow, but they will get fixed.

For right now, I'm just going to let the tears flow.

CHAPTER THIRTY-FIVE

LUCAS

WATCHING Savannah storm off was fucking painful. Every part of me was begging to go after her, to apologize for everything that I said, and tell her I didn't mean a single word.

But I didn't.

We're not over, but we were both pissed off and needed to calm down a bit.

Yet now, two days later, I haven't heard a single thing from Savannah. No texts, no calls. Nothing. This fight definitely isn't like our last one. At least with that one communication was minimal but still existed.

One bright side in all of this is that we have our one class together today, so I'm going to be able to see her, but who knows if she will let me talk to her and really apologize for everything that I did and said.

If she doesn't, I'm not against getting on my knees and begging for forgiveness.

Before I do that though, I need to do something.

Meet up with Hector and a few of his guys.

I shouldn't be doing this because it's just another lie that I have to keep from Savannah, but it's something that needs to happen.

Especially with all the shit that Jason told me.

I need to know if my old friends are working with him, or if he's digging somewhere he shouldn't.

The only way to find that out is heading to a place that I thought was behind me.

My bike roars through the streets, and the noise calms me a bit as I make my way over to Hector's warehouse.

The roar of the engine announces my arrival at the warehouse and causes a few of the guys who are inside to trickle out and greet me.

"Damn," Isaiah, one of the guys that joined Hector's family a few months after I did, says as I kill the engine and take off my helmet. "Didn't think that I would be seeing that bike back here anytime soon."

We meet halfway and give each other a pound shake. It's been a while since I've seen him, and while we may not run in the same circle anymore, it's still nice to see a friend.

"Yeah, neither did I," I say to him when we release each other.

"How are you doing, man? How's Mia and your mom?"

"Good, they're good. Mia is getting pretty big," I tell him.

"That's good," he says, nodding for me to follow him inside. "You guys take her trick-or-treating?"

I nod, scratching my head. "Yeah, she's finally at that age where I can't get out of Halloween."

Halloween was two weeks ago. Celeste, Savannah, and I took Mia to get some candy close to my mom's house. The little girl looked adorable. What wasn't adorable was the fact that the two women made me dress up as well, and it wasn't a subtle costume. I was legit in a dog onesie with ears and a tail. It was embarrassing as hell.

But honestly, if it made Savannah talk to me, I would do it again.

"I know the feeling, I had to take my little sister and it was bad," Isaiah offers as we walk through the main door of the warehouse.

There's music playing in the background and people are talking all around us, but it seems like the second we walk in everything goes silent.

All eyes are on me, telling me that Isaiah is not the only one surprised to see me here. This is what I expected.

"Lucas." A booming voice sounds out, and I turn in its direction.

Hector is standing in the back corner of the room, his eyes on me.

I didn't tell him I was coming today, so me being here is a surprise for him too.

"Hector." I nod in his direction.

"To what do we owe this visit?" he asks, trying to keep himself composed. He probably thinks that I'm here to see if his offer is still on the table.

"I wanted to ask you about something," I say, mostly to him but also to whoever might be listening in the room.

"What's up?" I get a nod to continue.

"Do you know a guy named Jason Wright?"

———

"BLACK ON BLACK?" Isaiah asks from where he sits next to the boss.

After I told them why I was here, a few of us came to a room that Hector uses as a room to talk.

I told them about Jason and him knowing that I had met up with Hector and how he thought I had made a deal with him.

I also told them that I had my suspicions that maybe he had followed me there.

Turns out, Hector and the guys didn't even know that Jason existed. They have no idea how he would know that there was a deal going on between me and Hector.

That right there raised so many red flags.

If he didn't get the information from my old friends, then from who?

The only two people who knew about that lunch and what was talked about during it were Hector and me.

I keep running through everything, and the only thing that I can think of is that I'm being lied to and Hector has been speaking with someone that he shouldn't be.

"Black on black sedan," I say, nodding to Isaiah. "Dark tint, black rims, and matte black body. I wasn't able to see the make or model."

He gives me a nod. "I think I've seen it around, but I never really paid attention to it. I'll keep an eye out for it."

A few other guys say that they will do the same.

"Is he dangerous?" I get asked.

I think about it. "I doubt it. He's unhinged that's for sure, but if he is really following me, and knows shit that he shouldn't, I wouldn't put anything past him."

Everyone nods, taking note.

"We'll keep an eye out, *hermano*," Hector offers.

"Thank you, I appreciate it."

With that, all the guys disperse, and I's just me and Hector left in the room.

"And here I thought that you were here because you wanted back in." He voices when I stand up from my chair.

"Sorry to disappoint," I tell him.

"It's all good. I know this life can take a toll. I sometimes think about leaving myself." That takes me by surprise.

"Why don't you?" This man has run the street for as long as I can remember.

"A guy like me can't walk away. He will always be involved and will always have the police knocking at their door. The way I see it, the only way out would be in a wooden box because jail isn't going to do anything."

Damn, I never heard him talk like this.

A part of me feels bad because while I was able to leave, he never will. His name will always be involved in this, and there will never be a way out.

That's what happens when you're the boss.

He will be known as the ringleader until the day he takes his last breath.

I give him a slap on the back because I have no idea what to say to the man.

He gives me a nod ,and we both walk out of the room.

I say goodbye to the guys, all of them telling me that they will keep me posted if they hear of Jason lurking around or see the black sedan.

I appreciate them, but I sure as hell hope that I didn't open up any doors by coming here.

 Heading back outside, I see that the sky has gotten darker and from the look of the clouds, it's about to start to rain.

Fucking perfect.

Getting on my bike, I take out my phone and check the time. The meeting with the guys went a lot longer than I thought it would, and now looking at the time, I see that not only am I late for my afternoon class but going to completely miss it.

The very same class that I share with Savannah. And there was going to be a fucking test today that I just remembered about.

Fuck, I really didn't plan this whole thing out very well.

The day keeps getting better when my phone dies.

Just great. Fucking great.

Grunting, I turn on my bike and head home. There's no point in going to class now, I'll just email the professor and ask if I can make up the test tomorrow. I decide that I might as well spend the rest of my evening figuring out a way to grovel to Savannah so that she can forgive me.

If she's willing to forgive me, that is.

CHAPTER THIRTY-SIX

SAVANNAH

I LOOK at the time on my phone and let out a sigh. Class starts in three minutes, and Lucas still isn't here. In the time that we've shared a class, he has never missed a class. Especially one where there's a test involved.

Hell, he's the reason that I'm early to all of my classes now.

So him not being here right before the doors close, is a little alarming.

We haven't talked since our fight, and a part of me was a little relieved that I was going to see him today because it would have given us a chance to talk.

But, I guess I was the only one who thought that way, because the seconds continue to tick by, and Lucas is still a no-show.

Yes, we're mad at each other, but not showing up to class isn't like him.

So either he's mad beyond belief and can't even face me, or something is wrong.

I'm about to send him a quick text message, but as I'm typing out the message, our professor announces to put away all electronics.

The message I'm typing out is a jumbled-up mess, so instead of hitting send on it, I just decided to let it be.

Maybe he's on his way and just running late.

The professor starts to pass out the test, and the whole time I'm watching the door, waiting for Lucas to walk through it.

There's no Lucas when I get handed my test, and there's no Lucas five minutes later.

It's fine, he's fine. He's not here because he didn't want to see me. Knowing him, he probably planned this and emailed the professor to schedule a retake. That seems like a logical thing Lucas would do.

I start the test, and I start answering the questions, but I still can't stop looking over at the door and wondering where Lucas is.

Even when I tell myself to concentrate, I can't. Lucas is at the center of my mind, and I'm starting to freak out a bit.

Somehow, I'm able to collect myself a bit and actually pay attention to the questions in front of me, but Lucas is never far from my mind.

An hour and twenty minutes later, the last question is answered, and I'm turning in my test.

It will probably be my worst score yet, but I don't care. The only thing that is on my mind is getting out of here and going to go look for Lucas.

I take out my phone, and the first thing I do, is dial his number.

It rings and rings, but he doesn't answer, and the call goes straight to voice mail.

He never not answers my calls unless he's busy, or Mia is taking up his attention.

Mia is with Celeste this week, so it can't be her.

Maybe he went to the garage to work for a little bit?

Without even thinking, I dial the shop number and hope he is there so that I can, at the very least, control my breathing.

"Thank you for calling Flaco's Auto Body and Customs, this is Adrian."

"Hi, Adrian, it's Savannah. Lucas's girlfriend. Is he there today? He's not answering his phone."

"Hey, Savannah. Nah, he's not here today." Adrian answers, and right away my heart starts to beat rapidly.

"Oh okay. Maybe his phone is dead or something. Thank you," I say before ending the call.

He didn't come to class, and he's not at work.

Maybe I'm overthinking everything, and he is not ready to talk to me yet.

That has to be it, right?

Maybe, but something in me is telling me that it's more than that.

Not wanting to leave anything to doubt, I start running across the campus toward my apartment to get my car.

I'm out of breath by the time I have my keys in and start making my way to where my car is parked.

It started raining halfway through the jog. The water starts to come down harder the second I get into the car and start driving.

As soon as I'm on the road, I start thinking that I should call Sandra or even Celeste to see if they have heard from Lucas, but I don't want to worry them if it turns out to be nothing.

Which it probably is, and I'm just being paranoid.

I'm seriously acting like a clingy girlfriend, but I don't care. I'm going to continue to act this way until I can get a hold of Lucas.

The city streets are slick from the rain.

I should be more cautious as I make my way through the different neighborhoods, especially since it seems that people forget how to drive when a little bit of water starts to hit the asphalt.

But I don't, because something deep in me is telling me that something is wrong. Seriously wrong.

Because this isn't like Lucas.

I should have forgotten all about the test and walked out of there as soon as my mind told me something was off.

Now, as I drive over to his house and my fourth call to him goes unanswered, I know that I'm right.

Right away, my mind goes to the worst-case scenario.

Is it him?

Is it his mom?

What if it's Celeste?

Or worse yet, Mia?

Scenario after scenario pops into my head, causing me to push down on the gas pedal some more and take the last exit that I need way above the speed limit.

My knuckles are white as I grip the steering wheel. Maybe it's as a precaution because of the rain, maybe it's from the nerves because I don't know what's going to greet me once I reach my destination.

Car horns sound out as I pass by, but I don't care.

I need to know that everything is okay.

Making the last turn onto his street, I relax as I drive closer to the house.

Why?

Because not only do I see his car and bike in the driveway, but I see him getting off his bike and heading to the front door.

His figure is small given my distance, but I know it's him.

I can literally point him out from a mile away.

He's here.

Oh thank God.

There's nothing wrong, and he most likely didn't answer his phone and didn't go to class because he doesn't want to talk or see me.

That's fair, but he can't ignore me any longer.

I ease my foot off the gas and continue to make my way down the street toward him. When I'm a few houses down, I decided to honk my horn to let him know that I'm here and he can't keep ignoring me.

I'm about to sound the horn when the sight in front of me stops me.

There's a car at the end of the street that is driving in my direction a lot faster than is legal in a neighborhood like this.

Just like I was driving to get here, but whereas I've

slowed down, the car doesn't look like it has any plans to stop.

From the looks of things it's coming right at me.

Instead of hitting the horn to notify Lucas, I do it to call attention to the car, but it doesn't do anything.

The horn sounds out, but the car continues to move down the long road lined with houses.

Not wanting to get hit, I pull to the side, and keep an eye on the moving vehicle.

Lucas must have heard my horn go off or seen the car coming down the street because I saw him turn to see what all the commotion was about.

The car keeps driving, coming closer to the Reyes' house and to where I am. For a split second, I think the car is going to crash into one of the many parked cars that line the street, but it doesn't.

The car continues down the street and it only slows down when it's in front of the Reyes' house.

I see everything before I hear it. From where I'm parked, I see the window go down, and I see the black object being pointed out. I see it all, but then I hear it.

The tires screeched and then three loud bangs.

Bang.

Bang.

Bang.

It takes me a second to register what I just heard, and when it hits me when I see Lucas fall to the ground. A scream leaves my mouth.

No.

No, please, no!

I'm about to jump out of the car and hurry to Lucas, but right before I open the door, the other vehicle passes by so fast that I jump back into the car in fear that they will see me.

As the car passes by, I'm able to get a good look, but that doesn't matter.

Lucas matters.

I jump out of the car and run across the street. Sobs leave me as I make my way to Lucas, and when I make it to the front of the house, a blood-curdling scream leaves my body.

"Lucas!" I run over to him, my whole body shaking.

"Please no. Please no. Please no." I fall to my knees next to him, trying to survey him as best as I can through my tears.

His eyes are open, and he looks like he is trying really hard to take in a deep breath.

"It's okay. You're okay. Stay with me, okay? Please stay with me!" I say, bringing his head to rest on my lap.

I reach for my pocket for my phone but it's not there. I remember that it's still in the car. Knowing that Lucas keeps his phone in his front pocket, I reach for it, letting out a sigh of relief when the device is in my hands. When I take it out and turn it over in my hand, I see that it's dead. That's why he didn't answer any of my calls.

And now I have no way to call for help.

So I start to scream. "Someone help me! Please help me!"

Another sob leaves me, and desperation takes over.

"Please help me!" I yell again, hoping someone will hear me and call an ambulance.

I look down at Lucas. His brown eyes are open and looking up at me, begging me to do something.

"Everything is going to be okay. Help is coming. Just stay with me. Stay with me. Please don't leave me. Don't leave me, Lucas."

"*Co-corazón,*" he pants out, his eyes closing.

"I'm right here. I'm not leaving you," I say, leaning forward and placing a kiss against his lips.

"Please, someone help me!"

CHAPTER THIRTY-SEVEN

LUCAS

CAR HORNS.

Tires screeching.

Gunshots.

Screaming.

Sirens.

All of those sounds are currently on replay in my head.

For a split second, I was back to being thirteen years old and hearing those same sounds on the day that my dad was shot. I thought it was my mind playing tricks on me. I thought I might have been dreaming. It was nine years to the day, it seemed plausible.

But then it all came rushing back in. That's when my mind finally connected that I wasn't reliving my dad's shooting, I was living my own.

My dad wasn't the one lying on the bed hooked up to machines, waiting for a miracle to happen. He wasn't the one that my mom was sitting next to, while she prayed that he'd make it out alive.

It was me. I was the one lying in a damn hospital bed. I was the one hooked up to machines. I was the one who had my mom was sitting next to me as she prayed that I would make it out of here.

History is repeating itself.

The only difference it that the fucker who shot me, had shitty aim, and didn't hit any major arteries.

It's been three days since the shooting according to the date on the whiteboard.

I don't remember much about the shooting itself. I remember everything right before it. Getting on my bike and leaving the warehouse, to getting pummeled by with the rain as I rode home. I remember pulling up to the driveway and walking up to the door, but after that is when everything starts getting blurry and all I remember are the noises.

A few things have come through in the days since, though. One of them being Savannah running toward me right after it happened and her holding me as we waited for the ambulance to come.

Her cries and her screams will be embedded in my head until the end of time.

But it's because of her, I'm alive.

If she hadn't shown up when she did, I would have bled out before my mom got home.

I look over at where she is curled up in the recliner in the corner as she sleeps. We were in the middle of a fight and in spite of all that, she still saved me.

Four bullets went through my body, and thankfully, all four made their way out.

One bullet hit my shoulder. Another hit my liver, then my thigh, and the last one hit my right lung.

The doctors were worried about the one that went through my lung, but they were able to repair it, and now they are just keeping a close eye on everything to make sure they didn't miss anything.

I just want to go home.

I miss my daughter, the food sucks, and the bed is hard as fuck. And being in a hospital brings back unnecessary memories that I don't want to deal with.

Savannah stirs in the recliner, stretching as she wakes up from her nap.

Her sleep-filled eyes meet mine and she gives me a small smile before getting up and walking over to me.

"Hi," she says, taking a survey of my body.

"Hi," I respond, my throat still having some rasp to it from when they stuck a tube in there for my surgery.

"How are you feeling?" she asks a little tentatively.

This is how she's been since I woke up a few days ago. Tentative, guarded, and as if she doesn't want to touch me for fear that she is going to hurt me. I fucking hate it.

"I want to get out of here," I grumble, trying to adjust myself as much as I can. A bullet to my shoulder and thigh doesn't help much with that.

"I heard the nurses talking earlier ,and I think they said that you might be able to go home tomorrow. So that's something to look forward to."

"I fucking hope so," I say, ready to get out of this place.

Savannah gives me a nod and starts biting at her lower lip.

I hate this.

Reaching out, I take the hand closest to me in mind and give it a squeeze. "How are *you*?"

"I'm fine," she says a little too quickly.

She's been here every day since the shooting, but the conversations have been minimal. Mostly having to do with how I'm feeling.

"*Corazón*," I start, holding her hand even tighter.

Somehow, that's the breaking point because the second that the nickname leaves my mouth, tears start to form in her eyes, and they start to fall instantly.

I pull her hand for her to come closer to me, and she falls to my chest, carefully avoiding my injuries.

"It's okay, baby," I say against her hair and she sobs into my chest.

"I thought I lost you. There was so much blood." She sobs, her tears seeping through the thin hospital gown.

"But you didn't. I'm here with you." I place a kiss against her temple, taking in her scent of lavender.

"Only because you wouldn't answer your phone, and I was worried about you. If I hadn't gone to the house, I can't imagine what would have happened."

Those were my same thoughts too.

"It doesn't matter now. I'm here," I say against her hair.

Savannah sobs into my hospital gown for a few more minutes, and hearing her like this brings my own set of tears.

Eventually she is able to calm down enough to stop the

sobs, but when she pulls away from me, I still see the tears in her eyes.

She reaches out to wipe at my tears before she wipes away on her own.

"I'm sorry," she whispers as she wipes at her cheeks.

"You have nothing to be sorry for," I tell her.

"Yeah, I do. If you weren't trying to avoid me, you wouldn't have missed class and you wouldn't be here. I shouldn't have walked away the other day."

She's putting all the blame on herself when I was the one that was in the wrong here.

"You walked away because of my words and my actions, not because of something you did. And I wasn't avoiding you, Savannah. I had every intention of going to class, but I got caught up in something, and by the time I was done with it, it was too late. I'm the one who should be sorry."

A small smile plays on her lips.

"We can both be sorry," she tells me right before she leans down and places a soft kiss on my mouth.

A knock on the door has her pulling away and causing us both to look over at who's about to walk in.

I was expecting a nurse, but two guys in suits ended up walking in.

Cops.

I've been waiting for this.

"Mr. Reyes?" one of them asks.

"Yes," I say, giving him a nod.

"I'm Detective Wilson," the first guy says introducing himself. "And this is my partner Detective Taylor. We're with the Los Angeles Police Department Gang and Narcotics division, and we were wondering if we can ask you any questions."

Of course, they are.

It doesn't go over my head that the LAPD has decided to treat this as a gang related act instead of just a regular attempted homicide case.

I'm not the only one that realizes it either.

"Wait, Gang and Narcotics? No offense, but why is your division taking care of this?" Savannah asks, her voice a whole lot stronger than it was a minute ago.

Detective Taylor answers. "Given Mr. Reyes's past, we are treating this as gang related."

"His past? But he has never been arrested for gang related activity. He hasn't been arrested, period."

"That is true, miss. But just because he hasn't been arrested, doesn't mean that his associations with certain individuals aren't known," Detective Wilson states.

"That's bullshit," Savannah says through her teeth.

"Savannah." I try to calm her down a bit, reaching for her hand.

"No," she says, shaking her head, not taking her eyes off the detective. "This isn't even gang related, so it shouldn't even be treated as such."

"Miss, unless we have clear evidence that it's not, there's not much that we can do in that regard. It was a drive-by shooting that involved an individual with known gang affiliations. We have to hit this from all sides."

"His affiliations have nothing to do with this is what I'm trying to tell you," Savannah tells them frustratingly. "I was there. I saw the driver, and I am one hundred percent sure that the person who shot Lucas is not associated with any gangs."

She saw the driver?

I thought that she had gotten there right after the shooting. Never did it cross my mind that she was there for the whole thing and actually knows who might have done it.

"You saw the driver?" Detective Wilson asks, taking a notebook out of his pocket.

"Yes," Savannah answers with a curt nod.

"Are you able to describe him?"

"I can do you one better. I know exactly who it was," she says.

That has all three of us looking over to her.

"Who was it?" I ask, ready to go after whoever it might be.

Savannah looks down at me with fresh tears in her eyes, as if she's trying to decide if she should give these detectives this information. I give her an encouraging nod, and after a long minute, she lets out a sigh and tells us who is responsible for putting me in here.

"Jason Wright."

CHAPTER THIRTY-EIGHT

TO SAY that the blood drained from my whole body when I saw who was behind the wheel of the car is an understatement.

It was quick, but even through the dark tint and the speed at which they were going, I was able to catch a small glimpse of the driver.

At first, I didn't know what to do with the information, so I put it in the back of my mind. Getting to Lucas and getting him help was more important than anything else.

Once we got to the hospital and they told us that Lucas was going to make it, I decided that I was going to tell the first police officer who came by what I knew.

I just didn't think that it would take three days.

The first set of officers came by while Lucas was in surgery, but I had gone to the house and my apartment to get things for both his mom and myself, so I didn't get the chance to talk to them.

My only opportunity came when Detectives Wilson and Taylor walked through the door.

I didn't think that they were going to believe me since they were so adamant that the shooting was gang related or at least had gang ties.

I thought for sure I would have to force someone to listen to me.

But they took in every word.

They asked every single question known to man, and I answered.

Descriptions, time, the direction that the car was coming from, was there anyone else on the street, the type of car.

The type of car and its description was the tipping point.

Turns out Lucas had seen a similar car a few days earlier and felt like he was being watched.

Not only had Lucas seen it, but it was also the same car that had followed me the day of Mia's party. I just didn't put two and two together until I saw it again. Knowing what I know now, Jason was probably also the one that pushed me to the ground. If he wasn't him, he most likely told one of his frat buddies to do it.

That little tidbit set Lucas off the rails. He was more than pissed that I didn't tell him that I was followed. So much so that a nurse came in to check on him because his blood pressure was rising, which wasn't good when he had a hole in his lung.

After Lucas was settled a bit, the detectives asked us if we were connected to Jason in any way.

When I told them that he was my ex-boyfriend, a new round of questions started.

They wanted to know everything. So I told them. Everything from the day that Lucas walked into our first class together to the fight that had happened two days before. I told the two detectives about the way Jason saw Lucas and how he always threatened him.

Apparently, that was enough information for the detectives. They told us that they were going to take everything and look deeper into things and once they had more information, they would reach out.

When they left, I let out a sigh of relief.

I really hoped that Jason goes down for this. If Jason had better aim, we would be planning Lucas's funeral instead of taking him home.

My hatred for him has grown beyond measure, and I want to see him suffer beyond belief.

I can't believe that there was a point in my life when I thought I was in love with him.

I honestly hope I never see the bastard again, but given that this ordeal isn't over yet, I will see Jason again. And that day can't come and go fast enough.

Today, though, I won't think about Jason. Today, the only thing that will be on my mind is Lucas and making sure he makes it home okay.

One of my top priorities today is making sure he sees Mia.

Given everything that was going on, Celeste and Lucas agreed to keep Mia away from the hospital. She may only be three, but her little brain is like a sponge, and seeing her dad like this could be a memory that stays with her forever. So, it was decided that she wouldn't see him until he was home. Though, Celeste has been checking in every chance she gets.

But he's going home today, and I know he really wants to see her, so I'm doing everything in my power to make it happen.

I already talked to Sandra, and she thinks it's a good idea. Now I just have to ask Celeste.

"You don't think it will be too much?" she asks during our call. "I don't want to stress him out."

"A few hours should be fine. He really wants to see her," I say to her. They were supposed to make their weekly switch today but given the circumstances, Mia is staying with her mom a little longer.

"Okay, text me when you guys are home and he's settled."

"Thank you, Celeste," I say, grateful for her.

"Of course. I'm really glad he has you in his life. He needed someone like you," she tells me and coming from her, it means a lot.

"Thank you," I say, a smile spreading across my face.

We end the call and I head over to Lucas's room where he is with his mom.

He's all set and ready to go, and once he has his discharge papers in hand and his medication in hand, we are on the way home.

The Reyes' house had been a crime scene for the last couple of days, but thankfully they were able to clean everything up before Lucas was released. Thank God too, because no way did I want Lucas to experience that.

When we get to the house, Sandra and I help Lucas out of the car and into the house. He's able to walk somewhat, but because the bullet ripped through the muscle in his thigh, his motions are very limited.

But he does it without complaints.

As soon as he is settled in his room, I shoot off a text to Celeste.

"Are you okay? Do you need another pillow? Another blanket? How about something to eat? Maybe I should put on a movie." I fuss over him, making sure that there's nothing that makes him uncomfortable.

"Baby, I'm fine," he insists, grabbing my hand as I move to fluff the pillow under his leg some more.

"You were shot," I argue

"And I'm fine."

"You have four holes in your body. You're not fine." I look around the room for the TV control.

"Savannah, stop," he urges softly, pulling at my hand some more. "You're going to drive yourself crazy worrying about little things."

"I just want you to be comfortable," I tell him finally taking a seat at the edge of the bed. "You are here because of me."

"We already talked about this. This isn't your fault."

"But it is. If I hadn't listened to my dad and had broken up with Jason back when I wanted to, none of this would have happened. He wouldn't have cared if you paid me any attention, and he sure as hell wouldn't have done this.

This is my fault. He was a thorn in your side because of me."

I don't know when I started crying, but I didn't and I don't realize I am until Lucas reaches over his one good arm and wipes the tears away.

He cups my cheek, and I lean into his touch. "This isn't on you. You didn't know he was capable of this. *I* didn't know he was capable of this. Every time he threatened me, I thought he was all words and no action. So trust me, I'm as surprised as you are, but it's not your fault. It's all his."

"How can you be so rational about this?" I say, wiping at my nose.

"Because there's nothing I can do about it now. I got shot, but I'm still here. My mom doesn't have to go through another painful December burying someone that she loves. Mia doesn't have to go through life without a father, and you still have someone to grow old with. That's all that matters to me right now."

He brushes a few strands of my hair away, and he gives me a smile.

My heart flutters seeing it.

There was a period a few days ago where I thought I was never going to get that chance to see that smile again. But here, it is aimed at me and I couldn't be more grateful to see it.

"You want to grow old with me?"

That smile of his grows. "I thought that was clear when I told you that you and I were never breaking up."

"Maybe I needed to be reminded," I tell him, turning my face to place a kiss against his palm.

"I love you, Savannah, and you will never get rid of me. And I will remind you every single day."

Now it's my turn to give him a smile. "I love you too."

The chiming of the doorbell sounds through the house and right away I jump up.

Lucas gives me a weird look, but I ignore it and head out to open the door.

Thankfully, Sandra is one step ahead of me and has already invited Celeste and Mia in.

Celeste gives me a smile while Mia fights to get out of her arms.

The little girl goes to hug her grandma before coming over to me and doing the same.

"Where *Papi*?" she asks, looking around the room.

"He's in his room. You want to go see him?" I ask her and she gives me an enthusiastic nod. "Okay, let's go," I say, offering my hand to her.

She takes it without question.

"Remember, Mia. *Papi* is hurt, so we have to be careful, okay?"

"Okay." Mia nods at her mom.

Mia and I walk down to the room, and when we walk in and Lucas sees her, tears form in his eyes.

I can only guess what must have gone through his mind when the bullets hit him.

He probably thought that he would never see his little girl again, and now that he's in the clear and she's here in front of him, it's hitting him hard.

"Hi, Mia Mia."

Mia lets go of my hand and goes to her dad, climbing on the bed carefully before going over and giving him a hug as gently as possible.

Whatever Celeste told her worked because Mia is treating Lucas with so much care, you would think she was well beyond her age of three.

Watching them brings tears to my eyes.

And when Lucas looks over at me and mouths a thank you, a sob threatens to escape.

As I watch them, my hatred for Jason grows even more, because he wanted to take this away from Lucas. From Mia.

I understand hating someone, but that hate should never go as far as wanting to kill them and actually taking a try at it.

Jason's day will come, though, and when it does, his fraternity president title won't save him.

I'll see to it.

CHAPTER THIRTY-NINE

LUCAS

MY BODY FEELS like it's been through the fucking wringer.

I guess that's what happens when four bullets rip through you and destroy you from the inside out.

If there was a way to speed up the recovery period, I would take it in a heartbeat.

Even three weeks later, my body is still in constant pain. But I will take the pain over being in a wooden box six feet under.

With a groan, I swing my leg over the edge of the bed and try my hardest to get up without waking up Savannah or Mia in the process.

Savannah has slept here every single night since I got home, not leaving unless it's to go to her apartment for clothes or to the store. I told her that she didn't need to fuss over me, that I was fine, time and time again, but she kept shooting me down.

Eventually, I just accepted it. It does help that she's here, especially with Mia, and having her here twenty-four-seven has been something that I didn't think I needed, but I do.

She's been my fucking salvation through all of this, and I don't know how I will ever repay her.

Once I stand up from the bed, I look over to see that both my girls are still sound asleep with their arms wrapped around each other.

Letting them be, I walk out of the room and head to the kitchen in search of some coffee.

It's not even six in the morning, but the pain going through my body right now isn't going to let me go back to sleep. So, coffee it is.

Stepping foot into the kitchen, I see that I'm not the only Reyes up at this hour.

Her eyes meet mine right away and she gives me a smile. "I didn't wake you, did I?" she ask, putting her mug down on the table.

I shake my head. "No, the pain did."

"Have you taken your medication?" she asks, concern coating her face.

I take a seat at the table to ease some of the pain in my leg. "Not how I'm supposed to."

"Y *por qué no?*" I can hear a slight tinge of anger in her voice.

"I don't want to depend on them. The pain will go away eventually, I just have to be patient with it."

"Lucas." The long sigh she releases tells me that she doesn't agree with my methods.

"It's fine, Mom. I can handle it," I say, placing a hand over hers.

She gives me a nod and a small smile, and thankfully she changes the subject. "I didn't see Mia in her bed."

"Yeah, she came into the room around two." It's not the first time that Mia has come to sleep in my room since the shooting.

She may be three, but she knows that something is wrong with me. So for the past three weeks, all she has wanted to do is be near me.

On my first night back home, she cried when Celeste told her it was time to leave. She was clawing at my shirt as her mom took her from my arms, and I heard her cries all the way out the door.

It hurt me seeing her like that.

So now on the days that I have her, she's never far away from me.

It's as if she knew there was a possibility that she was going to lose me.

"*Ella sabe que la necesitas ahorita,*" she knows that you need her right now, my mom states.

"Yeah, she does," I say with a nod. "What are you doing up?"

My mom took a leave of absence from work when the shooting happened. She's not going back for another week. She should be sleeping in.

"*Pensando,*" she tells me, giving me a small smile.

"What are you thinking about?"

"Moving," she says, taking me by surprise.

"What?" I ask, stunned.

For years, I tried to convince my mom to move away from here. To move out of LA and if she wouldn't leave the city, then at the very least go to a different neighborhood.

I first brought it up when I was seventeen. I was in too deep in that life, and the only way out that I saw was moving away. For months, I begged my mom to move, but she wouldn't budge. The subject was brought up again when Mia was born. In my head, if we moved, I wouldn't have the temptation to go back to that life. But again, she told me no.

She wanted me safe; I know that. But living here meant she would still be close to my dad in some way. If we moved away, she wouldn't have that.

Now she's willing to leave?

"Too many bad things have happened here. It's time for a change," she voices, looking around the kitchen.

My parents moved here before I was born. There are a lot of memories here.

"You're serious?"

She nods. "I am."

"Why now?"

The kitchen gets one final look before her eyes land on me. "I don't want to keep being reminded of how I lost my husband or how I almost lost my son. You may not see it, but every time I pass the garage, I see a blood stain. It may be faded or cleaned up, but it's there. I see it every single day. And I hate it. I don't want to see it anymore." Tears form in her eyes, and her voice shakes as she speaks.

I extend my hand and place it over hers. "Where would we go?"

Her hand slides from under mine, and she reaches for something in her robe pocket. A piece of paper appears, and she starts to unfold it. From the looks of things, she has unfolded it and refolded it a few hundred times.

"There's this house in about twenty minutes from here," she says, unfolding the paper and showing me what it is. It's a house listing. "It has two houses on the property. The main house and then a studio. It doesn't need any upgrades, and there's a big backyard for Mia to play in. You can live in the main house, and I will take the studio."

My mom sounds so excited as she goes over every detail that the house has to offer. A smile even spreads across her the more she talks about it.

The house is perfect but looking at the price, getting it is unrealistic.

"It is a great house, but I don't think we can afford it," I tell her, hating that I'm bursting her bubble.

"Of course we can," she says, looking at me like I'm crazy.

"Mom, I have to pay for school, plus with the hospital bills that are about to arrive, we won't have anything left over to even look at this house." I want to give this to her, I do, but financially it's impossible.

"The hospital bills are taken care of," she states.

"No, they're not."

"Yes, they are," she urges.

"How are they taken care of? We didn't magically become millionaires overnight."

Mom looks at me for a second, and after a minute or so, a look of realization crosses her face. "*No te dijo.*"

"Who didn't tell me what?" I ask.

A sigh leaves her mouth, and her shoulders slouch a bit. "Savannah's dad paid for the hospital bills. She told him what happened, and when you were in surgery, he stopped by and paid for everything. Both Savannah and I tried to stop him, but he insisted. You matter to his daughter, he said, so you matter to him too."

I don't know how to feel about that. I'm not used to people giving me something like this without anything in return. Yeah, I've done jobs that were worth a couple thousand of dollars, but that was work, and this isn't. This is a personal thing that my girlfriend's dad shouldn't be paying for. I should be left with the burden. I should be left to take care of the bill, not him.

My pride says that I should be mad at this, but everything else is telling me to accept it. To thank him the next time I see him and vow to pay him back every penny.

Option two seems like the most logical thing to do.

"No. She didn't tell me that."

"Don't be mad at her."

I shake my head. "I'm not. I just wasn't expecting it."

"None of us were." My mom squeezes my hand in reassurance.

After a minute of digesting the news, I give my mom a smile. "You really think that we can get this house?" I ask, nodding toward the piece of paper in front of us.

"I do."

"What do we do with this one?" I look around the place.

I was born here. Mia was born here. This is the only

place that I've ever called home. I don't know how I feel about just giving it up.

"We rent it. As much as I want to move, I don't want to get rid of it."

It's like she's reading my mind. "Neither do I."

A bright smile takes over her face, and she looks so damn excited about what this discussion might bring.

"*Bueno*, we can talk more about it later. Go see if you can get a few more hours of rest," she says, standing up from her chair, coming over to me and placing a kiss on my head. "*Duerme, mi niño.*"

After she leaves the room, I spend a few more minutes by myself in the silent kitchen and let everything that I was just told settle in.

My mom wants to move.

Savannah's dad paid my hospital bills.

It's a lot, and for the first time in a long time, it feels like I have someone watching over me.

A few years back, I felt like the God that I was finally able to believe in for a short while after my dad died, had disappeared. He was there with me every night, making sure I came home, but apart from that, it felt like he left me to my own devices.

And now as I sit here, I'm able to feel him again.

If you had asked me at the age of eighteen if I thought I would be here, I would have said no. Because at eighteen, I thought I was never going to live past nineteen.

But I did.

I'm here. I'm alive. I'm breathing, and I have my whole life ahead of me.

A life with my beautiful daughter and a woman who loves me for who I am, no matter who I once was.

It's not a life that I thought that I would have, but I wouldn't trade it for anything.

To whoever is watching over me, I will be forever in your debt.

Feeling good about everything, I push myself up from the seat, ignoring the pain, and head back to the room.

Savannah and Mia are still sleeping, both of them wrapped around each other's arms.

I climb back into the bed slowly, and for a few minutes, I just watch them.

These two are my whole life. I have no idea how I got so damn lucky. I don't deserve it.

I reach for my phone to take a picture of the two of them when I notice a text that came in while I was talking to my mom.

It's from Detective Wilson.

Only three words fill the screen...

We got him.

CHAPTER FORTY

SAVANNAH

I LOOK at the painting in front of me like it's the very first time I'm seeing it.

I take in every single detail and let my mind create a story of what might be happening. Of what the artist might have been thinking when they put the brush to the canvas.

The picture is of a woman surrounded by children. All of their faces look stoic, but one of the kids has a small smile playing on her lips.

She's the rambunctious one. The one who always gives her mom a hard time. The one who is always loud and likes to treat the backyard like it's a whole new world every time she steps on the grass.

She's the silly one who tries time and time again to make her siblings laugh.

To an outsider, she may be the wild child, the one who always misbehaves, but their assumption of her couldn't be further from the truth.

The little girl may act like she's only about having fun,

but deep down inside of her, there's a protector.

When her siblings get picked on, she's the one who stands up for them. When her mother needs help around the house, she's the first one to volunteer. When someone is sick, she's the one who is helping them get better.

The little girl puts everyone first before herself. So having fun is her way of escaping that.

"That's a hell of a description," a male voice says from next to me, causing me to jump.

Looks like I was talking under my breath again.

Turning, I find a guy who looks like he just stepped out of a movie standing next to me.

I instantly feel embarrassed that he heard me talking to myself, and it doesn't help when a small blush creeps up my cheeks, so I quickly apologize. "Sorry."

"Oh, don't worry about it. I liked it. It made me look at the piece a little differently," he says, throwing a smile in my direction.

It's a nice smile, don't get me wrong, but it doesn't do anything for me.

"Well, art can be subjective," I answer, looking around the room for my saving grace. Apparently, it hasn't arrived just yet, but according to the texts I was getting about five minutes ago, it's on its way.

"That it can," the guy says, his eyes traveling down my body, which just makes me want to roll my eyes. "I'm Jon, by the way," he says, holding out a hand for me to shake.

Great, a J name. I can't seem to escape them, can I? If I'm being honest here, they still make me want to puke.

Not wanting to be rude, I take his outstretched hand in

mine and give it a shake. "Savannah."

"It's nice to meet you, Savannah." Jon shakes my hand a little longer than necessary. Right about now would be a good time for that saving grace to come along. Just saying. "Care to tell me the story behind another painting?" He nods toward the next exhibit.

Jon is cute and all, but he's definitely not my type.

"Actually—" I start, but I'm quickly interrupted.

"She can't," the voice that I've been waiting for says from behind me.

He's here.

Turning, I'm met with a set of brown eyes that make me melt to the ground.

"Hi," I greet Lucas, a smirk threatening to come out.

"Hi," he greets back before looking back to my new friend. "Who are you?" he asks, a little bite to his tone.

The bite is mostly for Jon's sake and not mine. That doesn't stop me from finding it hot and wanting to hear it while we're in bed and he's having his way with me.

"This is Jon. Jon, this is my boyfriend Lucas," I say, introducing them.

"Boyfriend?" Jon asks, a scoff coming out in the process, like he can't believe that someone like me is with someone like Lucas.

"Yup, boyfriend," I say proudly. "Today is our one-year anniversary, actually," I tell him as I wrap my arms around Lucas's waist and bring myself closer to him.

Okay, it's not our official anniversary, that one isn't until the summer, but it is the one-year anniversary from when we came into each other's lives. That one may not count, but I'm using anything as an excuse to celebrate my relationship with this man. After everything we've been through these last few months, a little celebration is needed.

This time last year, I was sitting in a business class I didn't want to be in, and Lucas was the nameless classmate who turned my insides upside down.

"Wow. Congratulations," Jon says, his face revealing that he might be a bit uncomfortable. "I'll leave you to continue about your day, then. Sorry I interrupted," he excuses himself and walks away.

"Think I scared him away?" Lucas asks jokingly, tightening his hold on my body.

"Probably," I say, turning my body so that I'm able to wrap my arms around his neck. "Not a lot of people understand your charm."

"My charm, huh? I didn't know I had any," he says, his face becoming playful.

"Oh, you definitely do. How do you think I went from hating you to wanting to jump your bones every five minutes?" I say, running my hands through his hair.

I love it when he has it grown out like this. It gives me free rein to run my fingers through his silky strands anytime I want.

"I mean, you can jump my bones right now if you'd like," he says right before he quickly leans in and places a kiss against my lips.

A small giggle escapes me before I push him away and take his hand. "Want to finish the rest of the exhibits before we get out of here and go do that?"

"Lead the way."

For the next two hours, Lucas lets me drag him through the Getty Center as if it were our first time here. He listens to every story that I have to say and is patient when the stories in my mind take a little longer to come out.

This is something that we have done a number of times in the short period that we've been together, but it's still one of my favorite things to do. Every time we do this, I'm always taken back the first time we were here and how that one night changed so much for us.

That was when we first saw each other as something other than the pictures we had in our heads. There was no hostility, no hatred, just two individuals who would learn to grow with one another and become more than they thought possible.

I didn't think that a simple trip to one of my favorite places would change me or my life so much, but it did.

And it was all for the better.

Since that trip, I've become a person who I no longer hate but love unconditionally. I became a person who I'm proud of and it's all thanks to the man next to me.

In a short amount of time, he has shown me so much of what life has to offer. He's shown me what it's like to fall deep in love with someone and how not to take a single second we have together for granted.

That last part, though, is something that I've only come to learn in the last few weeks.

It's been two months since the shooting, and in those two months a lot has happened.

Lucas is almost completely healed. The exit wounds that the bullets left behind are closed completely, and he's close to having full mobility back in his shoulder and leg.

There's still the occasional pain, but according to him it isn't anything he can't handle. I think he's lying but I haven't called him on it yet.

That's not the only major breakthrough that we've had since the shooting.

Three weeks after Lucas was able to go home from the hospital, he got a text message that I honestly thought would never come.

It was a message from Detective Wilson, and all he told Lucas was that they had him.

The "him" in this case was Jason, and after three long weeks, he was finally arrested for attempted murder.

According to the police, all the information that we gave them about Jason was a major help. Since they had a suspect, they were able to take a deeper look into him. The police were able to find not only the car and the weapon abandoned in a junkyard.

Jason was smart enough to get rid of both of objects that typed him to the crime but not smart enough to wear gloves. His fingerprints were all over the place, and after some testing, they were able to connect the gun that was under his name to the bullets that went through Lucas.

That was the tipping point.

When police showed up at his doorstep, Jason acted like he didn't know anything. According to Detective Wilson, it didn't take long for him to confess and tell them exactly why he went after Lucas the way he did.

He wanted me back, and he needed a way to take Lucas out of the picture. The detectives told us that Jason decided to do a drive-by because he thought that the cops would automatically assume it was gang related. He thought that if the cops made that assumption, then they wouldn't go looking in his direction. Especially since things like this tend to go unsolved more often than not.

He thought wrong, though.

Jason wasn't counting on me being there and throwing his whole plan down the drain. He wasn't planning on anyone seeing him do it and pinning him to the crime. I guess he didn't learn that life works in mysterious ways.

Jason was arrested soon after the text message came in and is currently in county jail awaiting trial.

The detectives and the District Attorney's office think that Jason will be going away for a long time. Hopefully they're right, because that's the only thing that he deserves.

For now, though, we're going to try and move forward and not let this hold us back. We are going to concentrate on things that actually matter.

Us, Mia, and our future lives together.

Because there is a future for me and Lucas and nobody is going to take that away from us. We may be young, we may be the total opposite and we may have started out with hate running through our bodies, but we both know what we want, and that's each other.

When we finish going through the exhibitions, Luca guides me to the gift shop, just like he started to do months ago.

The store is filled with the same thing time and time

again but whenever we come here, we always try to walk out with one thing.

A music box.

It's become a little tradition of ours. Every time we would come during the summer, we would stop by and buy one, writing the date on the bottom.

And when we started bringing Mia with us, we would get her one too.

Today, there are two left, and it only seems fitting to take them both.

One for me and one for Mia.

A smile doesn't leave my face as Lucas pays or as we get on the tram to head to the parking garage.

The smile stays in place even when Lucas hands me a helmet and makes me get on his deathtrap of a bike.

"Admit it." He says, as I get on, wrapping my arms around his waist. "You have a thing for the bike."

The bike rolls to life and I tight my grip.

"I have a thing to the driver of the bike. There's a difference." I yell through the noise.

He lets out a laugh, turning slight to look at me. "You know, I have this fantasy, one that includes this bike, a cheer uniform and you bouncing up and down my cock. Think we would make that fantasy come alive?"

His eyes burn into mine, and I can't help but to let a blush creep up my cheeks and coat my whole body.

"Get us home and we'll see what we can do."

I don't have to tell him twice.

———

AS MUCH AS we wanted to make Lucas's fantasy come alive, we were in too much in a hurry to rid each other of our clothes to remember about having sex on the bike.

The second we were in my apartment, Lucas was on his knees in front of me, pushing me against the door, and feasting on me.

I felt his tongue, his fingers, his mouth everywhere. I was so wired up that it didn't take long for me to start trembling and say his name as if it were my own prayer.

That was only the start of it, and eventually we made our way to my bed, and I rode his cock as I would if we were on the bike. The only thing missing was mu cheer skirt.

It was fucking explosive and even though I saw black spots and was sated after I came, I wanted more.

When Lucas is involved, I always want more.

So, so much more.

For right now, though, I'm completely content with cuddling and having his arms around me.

"What does it mean?" I ask Lucas as I lay against his bare chest and draw gentle circles around the fresh tattoo that is adorning his skin.

Apparently, while I was at the Getty waiting for him, he was off getting a new tattoo.

This was news to me. He didn't tell me he had plans on getting another one, so when I first saw it tonight after ripping his shirt off, I was presently surprised.

At first, I thought it was the scar from his surgery to repair his lung had opened up because there was a bandage around it, but as it turns out, it was a new tattoo.

Salutis Meae.

It's a simple design, just the two words that I have no idea what they mean. It's the placement of it that has me wondering about the significance of it. The tattoo is right above the scar on his chest.

He had to put it there for a reason.

"It's Latin for my salvation, but it has more meaning than that," he states, brushing at my hair.

"Like what?" I ask, placing a gentle kiss just below it, not touching it.

"Well for one, the two words start with letters that have a significance to me. S and M. Savannah and Mia."

Oh my god.

Lucas shifts so that I'm no longer laying across his chest but, on my side, looking right into his eyes.

"I wanted it close to my heart and since I have my dad's tattoo on the other side, and it seemed fitting to put just above my new scar that could have taken my life.

Tears spring to my eyes and when one of the escapes, Lucas reaches over and wipes it away.

"After the shooting, you and Mia became my salvation. You two gave me the will to continue on and move in a way that I'm able to move past what happen. If you weren't there for me, if you weren't at my side through all that, I wouldn't have thought twice about going back. You and Mia held me down and I will forever be indebted to you. You, *Corazón*, are my salvation and I thank God every fucking day, that he brought you to me."

His words open up the faucet and tears come pouring out so fast that Lucas has to give up wiping them away.

Instead, he starts to kiss them away.

"You're not supposed to curse right after you say God."

"You're also not supposed to have sex before marriage." He says, against my cheeks.

I let out a small giggle and push away from him slightly so that I can see his eyes again.

"You really think of me as your salvation?" I ask, a sob threatening to come out.

He cradles my face and brings his lips to mine. "I do."

"You're mine too." I say, and I mean it.

Lucas coming into my life has saved me in a way that I never knew could happen. I was in unhappy situation, and I didn't give two shits what people thought of me. But he came into my life and changed everything. He made happy. He made me love life again. He let me love his daughter. He gave so much that I will be forever eternally grateful for him.

"I love you, *Corazón*."

"And I love you."

His lips land on mine and he shows me he loves me in ways that words can't.

And I do the same.

It's funny how you can go from hating someone to loving them, but that's the best type of love that there is.

THE END

playlist

R U MINE? - ARTIC MONKEYS
LIKE I WOULD - ZAYN
WRONG - ZAYN
HURTS LIKE HELL - FLEURIE
TODO CAMBIÓ - CAMILA
I'M YOURS - ISABEL LAROSA
STREET - DOJA CAT
LES - CHILDISH GAMBINO
PINK + WHITE - FRANK OCEAN
PRIDE - KENDRICK LAMAR

Check out these song and more on the Salutis Meae official playlist!

Powerful Deception

Fake Love

Salutis Meae

ABOUT THE AUTHOR

Jocelyne Soto is an independent author living in California. She loves reading romance and discovering new authors. She comes from a big Mexican family, and with it comes a love for all things family and food.

Jocelyne has a love for her mom's coffee and writing. In her free time, you can find her reading a romance novel on her kindle while writing heartwarming and chaotic romance stories in between. From sport romance to dark romance, there is no limit as to the type of stories that will come to Jocelyne's mind.

Check out her website for ways to connect with Jocelyne!
www.jocelynesoto.com

bookbub.com/authors/jocelyne-soto

goodreads.com/jocelynesotobooks

instagram.com/authorjocelynesoto

tiktok.com/@authorjocelynesoto

facebook.com/authorjocelynesoto

x.com/authorjocelynes

pinterest.com/authorjocelynesoto

threads.net/@authorjocelynesoto

JOIN MY READER GROUP

Join my ever-growing Facebook Group. You get first looks, sneak peeks and giveaways!

NEWSLETTER

Sign up for my Newsletter!
You will get notified when there are new
releases to look out for, giveaways and more!